SINS OF HER PAST

LILY DANES

A LOST COAST HARBOR NOVEL

Dark & Stormy Books

Cover Designed by Najla Qamber Designs
www.najlaqamberdesigns.com

ISBN 978-1- 944506-09-4

To the everyday superheroes

Sometimes, getting through
each day is enough.

CHAPTER ONE

For the first time in months, Bree Rogers took a deep breath.

Silence. Glorious silence. No screaming jackhammers. No pounding from eight in the morning till five in the afternoon.

She was a night owl, so at least it had been quiet while she worked—and bone-jarringly loud when she tried to sleep. It didn't matter how many earplugs or white noise generators she used. The minute the machines began screaming, she was wide awake and cursing like a sailor on leave. A pissed-off sailor with poor impulse control.

But now it was over. Yesterday, a parade of eighteen-wheelers headed out of town. Bree lay in bed, snuggled deep in her duvet, and savored the moment.

The shrill ring of her cell filled the room. Bree groaned and rolled over. She must have accidentally switched it off vibrate.

She fumbled for the phone. Maddie's face appeared on the screen. She was one of a handful of people who had this number—and one of the few calls Bree would answer.

"What?" she mumbled.

"I'm bored," Maddie announced.

Yawning, Bree sat up and swung her legs to the floor. "How awful. Should we establish a charity?"

"You mock my pain."

"Yep. You have a super-hot boyfriend who lives to see you naked. If you're bored, you're not trying hard enough." Bree climbed out of bed and headed directly for the kitchen—and the coffee maker.

"Gabe's at work, and the nursery is closed today for some irrigation repairs. So, boredom."

"You really need a hobby." Bree kept her tone wry, but she could only think how grateful she was Maddie had waited to start the repairs. The nursery had been one of Bree's safe harbors during the construction at the old Stanwick Ranch. For several months, she'd shown up with her laptop, said her internet connection was on the fritz, and got to work. She knew Maddie would understand if Bree simply said the construction disturbed her, but even that felt revealing too much. It was a weakness, and Bree worked hard to conceal any weakness.

It was ludicrous, saying she was without internet. Bree would give up a kidney before she'd live somewhere with a faulty connection. Her home was in the middle of the woods, but that was no excuse to use anything less than a T3 line. Before she signed the lease on her cabin, she made a deal with Coastal Telecom to upgrade their security system in return for the best connection the market could provide.

She could make those kind of demands. She was the best internet security consultant on the West Coast. If she'd asked for a pony and ten thousand M&M's sorted by color, they would have asked if the pony should match the candy.

Bree stood in front of the coffee maker, waiting for her first hit of sweet, sweet caffeine. She put the phone on speaker and grabbed a Pop-Tart. "How am I supposed to help with your boredom?" she said through a mouth of chemical pastry goodness.

"Have lunch with me at Donnelly's."

Bree stood on tiptoe to reach the medication bottles on the top shelf. She washed the pills down with a swig of coffee. "I need to work. I'm behind." Really behind, thanks to those bastards up the road. "Call Erin."

"She's out of town," her friend pouted. "Some work conference. After that, she's sneaking away with Will for a romantic getaway. You're all I've got. Help me out."

Bree tried not to laugh. After years of working her tail off to earn a promotion she didn't even want, Maddie was having a hard time adjusting to a calmer life. She was a much happier person, but downtime was still a foreign concept.

"Sorry, Mads. I have plans today."

Maddie grumbled, but eventually her friend gave up. The advantage of having the kind of job no one understood was people didn't bother to ask questions about your work.

And she would work…later. First, someone needed to pay for disrupting her life all summer.

Her electronic searches for the new owner had proven fruitless, but the completed building should have some clues. Whoever it was, they deserved regular phone calls from their credit card company confirming they were, in fact, trying to buy dildos from a different European country every day.

She dressed in a pair of faded jeans and an oversized sweater, then ran her fingers through her hair and checked her reflection. She'd fallen asleep without washing her face, so her eyeliner was extra smudged. Whatever. No one would see her.

Bree threw her laptop into her messenger bag, then checked the inside pocket for the bottle that went everywhere with her. Her supply was running low. Three months of hammering and pounding and buzzing hadn't done her brain any favors.

It pissed her off. Not only had the construction delayed work on Wanderlust, but it made things a lot harder inside her head. She was trying to take fewer pills, not more.

Once Wanderlust was up and running, she could quit the security work and have more time for lunch with friends. Maybe she could manage a bit of travel. Have a date.

Bree rolled her eyes at herself. *Aren't you the optimist.* One step at a time.

Before leaving, she did a quick mental review. The stove was off, and the coffee maker and toaster were unplugged. She'd checked the lock on the back door. It was safe to leave. Bree drew in a calming breath and stepped outside.

It took a few tries for her beat-up old truck to start, a process that involved a complicated ritual of chants and outright pleading. She grinned when it revved to life. It didn't matter that the red beast was an enormous junker. It was *her* junker, and they'd pry the keys from her cold, dead fingers.

She blew on her hands to warm them. Throughout the rest of California, late September meant warm, sunny weather, but Lost Coast Harbor used its own calendar. The days were cool and drizzly, and fog surrounded her house most mornings.

Her cabin didn't so much have a driveway as a winding dirt road that eventually led to a paved one, and that road took a circuitous route to what had once been the Stanwick Ranch.

The property was huge. The new owners could have built on any of the three hundred acres and come nowhere near her house. Maddie's nursery was basically on the property, and her friend hadn't been disturbed in the slightest.

Bree made the final turn, and the new building came into sight.

Check that. Buildings. Plural. The largest was in the middle. It was three stories tall and about two hundred feet long, and it was flanked by a couple of two-story buildings on either side. Five buildings total, plus a covered parking lot.

Based on the metal and glass the eighteen-wheelers hauled to the site, Bree had expected to find some modern monstrosity in the huge clearing. What she found was indeed modern, but there was nothing monstrous about it. With sloped roofs supported by wooden posts, the structures evoked famous national park lodges. The traditional shape was a marked contrast to the glass walls, which reflected the surrounding redwoods. The result was a collection of ghost buildings, a hint of something man-made within the natural world. It was stunning.

There was no sign of life, and no name on the building. Undeterred, Bree drove toward the parking lot. All she needed was a license plate number and a few questionably legal minutes with the DMV database.

A luxury car sat in the first reserved spot. Bree's heart lurched at the sight of the black Aston Martin.

No. Hell no. It wasn't possible.

There was more than one black Aston Martin in California. Maybe it wasn't the same one she'd seen in half a dozen magazine profiles, several of which featured Marcus Keller leaning against the sleek sports car like he was auditioning for the next James Bond film.

Bree drove close enough to read the letters.

HOURS01.

She struggled to take a full breath. That car could only belong to one person.

With numb fingers, she hit the callback button on her phone. "Mads?" Her voice sounded flat. "You still up for lunch? There's something I need to tell you."

Her ex was back in town.

"It's not too late to change your mind," Tommy said. "There's affordable land in Oregon. Lawrence, Kansas, has a booming tech scene these days."

Marcus's best friend and vice president peered through the passenger-side window as they drove around the Lost Coast Harbor town square. Tommy squinted like he'd never seen it before, though they'd both grown up there.

It hadn't changed much in the years they'd been away, either. The square was filled with everything a small town might need. A church, a courthouse, a market, and a healthy mix of businesses lined the one-way streets that surrounded the park in the center of town.

"Come on. It's good to be home." A grin split his face, the

one he'd been struggling to hold in since they passed the old wooden sign welcoming them to town.

Tommy shuddered. "Right. Because when I went to a music festival in the summer or ate at one of the dozens of restaurants in walking distance of my apartment, I was secretly thinking how nice it would be to return to a town so cut off from the rest of the state they literally named this part of California the Lost Coast."

Marcus laughed, though he knew Tommy meant every word. His friend wasn't wrong, either. It wasn't safe to build on the jagged cliffs that stood between their small town and the vast Pacific Ocean, so the freeways that connected the rest of the state hadn't made it to Lost Coast Harbor. The only way in was a narrow two-lane road, and few outsiders had reason to make the trip.

After years in the Silicon Valley spotlight, that isolation sounded like heaven. For Tommy, who loved city life so much he'd chosen to commute from San Francisco to their Mountain View offices, Marcus might as well have asked him to move to one of the damper levels of hell.

"Look at the bright side. After years of Bay Area traffic, rush hour now means you get stuck behind a slow truck for five minutes."

"Because no one's in a hurry to get anywhere," Tommy retorted.

"You can see the stars at night."

"When it's not rainy or foggy, so...two months a year?"

"It's friendly. Everyone in town knows us."

"Including the assholes who bullied us in high school, who we'll now run into every day." Tommy was attempting to sound more wry than annoyed, but he wasn't pulling it off.

Marcus had to concede the last point. Tommy was older than he was, so they hadn't been close in high school, even though their fathers were friends—or they had been, before the accident. But Marcus and Tommy had both been skinny computer nerds with zero interest in sports, trucks, or beer. They might as well have painted bull's-eyes on themselves their freshman years.

But Tommy was forgetting one critical detail. "You mean those bullies who now work at the local hardware store? The one we could buy with our millions and millions of dollars?"

That drew a reluctant smile from his friend. "Come on, boss. It's your company. I only have a couple mil. Not a single private island to my name."

"Wait until after the IPO. You can buy the damn high school and raze it to the ground, if that's what you want."

Tommy didn't look convinced. "Remind me why you think this was a good idea?"

"We can afford the land here. I want a campus, not an office building. It was here or Bakersfield."

Tommy winced. Bakersfield was flat, hot farming land in Southern California—an even worse option for his friend's San Francisco-loving heart.

"And I want to be near my dad. I'm going to convince him to work for me in the new lab."

His friend tensed. "Why am I just hearing about this now? He doesn't have any experience."

"You know he worked for Hastings Fishing for thirty years."

"Yeah, so did my dad, and I wouldn't trust him to be a

janitor." Tommy scrubbed his face. "That's why you built the imaging lab, isn't it?"

The question sounded rhetorical, so Marcus didn't answer. "Plus, there's no way in hell we could make this move after the IPO. The future board would pitch a fit."

"They'd be right to. You're moving a tech company to the middle of nowhere. You're isolating us, in a field that requires connections. Meetings. Schmoozing."

"All things I hate."

"That doesn't mean I'm wrong."

They'd been having the same argument for nine months, starting around the time Marcus began researching property in Lost Coast. He'd hoped by now Tommy would have resigned himself to his fate. If anything, he'd only grown more agitated.

Marcus couldn't blame him. Tommy wasn't close to his father, and he preferred sushi and concrete to diners and dirt trails. He had little reason to return to Lost Coast Harbor. Marcus, on the other hand, felt like he was suffocating in Silicon Valley. He spent more time in soul-sucking meetings or on interminable conference calls than he did on the programming work he loved.

It had all been worth it, though, because it got him here. One month away from the company's IPO. A company he created in his dorm room, that went on to become one of the decade's great success stories. This moment was the culmination of years of hard work, and he needed to be in Lost Coast Harbor when his fortune quadrupled overnight. He wanted to share that achievement with his father.

And if a certain heartless woman from his past happened

to notice his success…well, it would take a stronger heart than his not to feel smug when Bree Rogers finally realized what she'd given up. It was petty and a little pathetic, but that didn't mean he wouldn't enjoy it.

"I still say Kansas," Tommy said, oblivious to the direction Marcus's thoughts had taken. "People are supposed to be down to earth there, right? No one would care there was a celebrity in their midst. That's what you're really trying to get away from, isn't it?"

Marcus gritted his teeth. It wasn't the main reason, but it was a big, shiny bonus.

"It must be tough." Tommy oozed false sympathy. "Being number one in annual 'most eligible bachelor' articles. Trying to decide whether to date the lingerie model or the swimsuit model."

Tommy wouldn't believe how much Marcus hated that part of the job. When he created the Hours app, it didn't occur to him that he'd become the story. He thought he was developing a way for people to meet based on shared interests. It was just a bit of fun between homework assignments.

Then it took off, and it kept taking off, until Hours was the most popular dating app in the country. Unlike other sites that allowed anyone to join and made no attempt to stem the flow of unsolicited dick pics, Hours vetted all its members. Once approved, they submitted a questionnaire about their interests—for instance, kayaking, Ethiopian food, or poetry reading—and their free time. They deposited enough money to pay for their first date, and they waited.

Soon, they'd receive a text informing them to appear at the harbor, or a restaurant, or a bookstore, within the next ninety minutes. Marcus deliberately kept the window of time short to prevent the clients from stressing out or making too much of an effort. The couple met in public, and the first date lasted sixty minutes. Enough time to establish interest, not so long that they were desperate for an escape route in the event of a poor match. Afterwards, they informed the site if they wanted to share contact information.

Hours provided curated blind dates, and people loved it. No one had to worry about asking someone out or handling the inevitable end-of-night awkwardness. Sixty minutes and done.

It wasn't limited to dating. Some people used it for friendship when they moved to a new town, or because they wanted to see *Wicked* and none of their friends liked musical theater. And every last one of them paid for the service. Rae made sure of it. Hours's head of tech constantly reprogrammed the app to generate more income.

Marcus didn't try to find his own match through the app, but he found money. Buckets and buckets of it.

"I get on those eligible-bachelor lists because I'm fucking rich," he told Tommy. "Some women like that sort of thing."

"Riiiight. It's just the money. I'm not saying you're good-looking or anything, but if you got a six-pack in me, I'd think about it."

Marcus snorted. "Whatever. Those women wouldn't have looked twice at me in high school. I'm not interested."

"Of course. That's why you bought the Aston Martin. Because woman hate sports cars that remind them of British spies."

Marcus shifted in the seat of the Mercedes SUV. He wanted to settle slowly back into town, and the Aston Martin might as well be a big flashing light for all the attention it would draw.

"I like fast cars," he protested.

Tommy smirked, then glanced out the window. "Why are we driving in circles?"

"There's no parking," Marcus muttered, though he'd just passed an empty spot. This was the homecoming he'd longed for, and he didn't want to rush it. Already, he'd spotted several familiar faces. His old P.E. teacher, aka The Sadist, walked down Court Street with a grocery bag in both hands. Niall Donnelly popped out of his brother's bookstore, his red hair and height making him easy to spot. Mrs. Wandsworth wandered into the diner, aka the town's unofficial gossip center. God, he'd missed this.

And there was his former classmate Maddie Palmer, strolling into Donnelly's Pub. Maddie Palmer, who happened to be Bree's best friend.

A van outside The Sweet Spot bakery pulled out, and Marcus swung into the vacated spot. "Let's get a drink."

CHAPTER TWO

Maddie slid into the booth across from Bree. "So you changed your mind *and* you're drinking beer. Spill."

Bree sipped her ale. "Beer is acceptable at noon. If I ordered the kamikaze I really wanted, people might think I have problems."

Maddie scanned the menu, though they both had it memorized. Donnelly's offered basic, high-quality pub fare, and it hadn't removed or added a single item since it opened. "Since when do you care what people say about you?" she asked.

Since there was a risk of being the next topic of town gossip. Bree hopped out of the booth. "I think we need mozzarella sticks. This is definitely a deep-fried-cheese kind of conversation." She hurried to the bar before Maddie could protest.

God, it shouldn't be this hard to talk about. She didn't need to tell the full story. All she had to do was admit she did something stupid when she was eighteen. Maddie might even laugh.

The bar wasn't crowded, but several locals were there for a relaxed lunch. A few had staked out a spot at the bar, and she wondered how early they'd started.

Gavin threw a rag over his shoulder and made his way to her. "Hey, Bree. What food item with no nutritional value would you like today?"

As much as she longed to get out of town, there were benefits to living where everyone knew you. She placed her order, then returned to Maddie with confident strides. Best to get this over with. Bree slid into the vinyl booth and braced her palms on the table. "You remember Marcus Keller, right?"

Maddie blinked. "Do I remember the man who crushed on you all through high school? The one you complained about at least once a week?"

"Well, he was annoying." Bree took a long sip of beer.

"Why was that?" Maddie widened her eyes, too innocent.

"Because he was the only person in that damn school nearly as smart as I am."

Marcus might have been smarter, though she'd never admit it aloud. He'd made her work for every hundredth of a point of her GPA. They switched places for the valedictorian spot so many times she lost count. The MIT scholarship set up by an alumni could only go to one of them—and they'd both been determined it would be them. Marcus might have had a crush on her, but that hadn't meant he'd give up a six-figure scholarship without a fight.

Bree grinned, because that's what Maddie would expect. "Of course, I'm considerably less annoyed now, since I won."

That sounded like something she'd say.

"The loss doesn't seem to have adversely affected his life," Maddie noted. "Did you see him on the cover of *Newsweek* last year?"

"Yeah, I spotted it at the market." Then she'd bought a copy and read the article. Twice. "Anyway, do you remember the our graduation trip?"

Maddie winced. "I remember a lot of cheap beer and strawberry Boone's Farm."

"That was the first night, yeah. While you were having a sing-along with two cheerleaders you despised when you were sober, I hung out with Marcus."

Her friend's gleeful smile said she thought "hung out with" was a euphemism.

She had no idea. Bree prepared to drop the bombshell.

The front door opened, Marcus Keller entered, and the words died in Bree's throat.

Marcus didn't walk into the bar. He strode in like it was his name on the sign. The minute he appeared, the entire room felt smaller. Some idiotic part of her brain recited the principle of the conservation of mass as she tried to understand how he could occupy more space than his physical body allowed. He exuded power, an aura that extended several feet beyond his body.

Eighteen-year-old Marcus hadn't defied the laws of physics. It was hard to believe it was the same person.

Even before the door closed behind him, his gaze swept the room, searching.

When he found her, she shivered, but she didn't look away.

Those eyes. A light blue-gray and ringed with short, dark lashes. It was the one part of him that hadn't changed, though the hard expression was new. At the moment, they were mostly blue. That used to mean he was thinking through a problem, or he was angry.

God. She shouldn't remember why his eyes changed colors.

Over the years, when she felt like tormenting herself, Bree searched for articles on Marcus Keller, Silicon Valley wonder boy. There were hundreds of photos online, and not one of them did justice to the man standing before her. His shoulders were broader, his stomach flatter, his thighs more muscled beneath the expensive suit. His thick brown hair fell perfectly into place.

And she was wearing beat-up old clothes and hadn't bothered to brush her hair or remove last night's makeup. Awesome.

For a breath, no one moved. Then the man standing behind Marcus stepped forward with a smile, and time started again.

Marcus walked to their table. No, walk was the wrong word. He glided toward her with assured steps, not a hint of uncertainty.

How nice for him.

Bree leaned back into the booth and waited. She might not share his confidence, but she could damn well fake it.

When he reached the table, his sharp expression lightened into an easy smile—for Maddie. "It's good to see you. I heard you lost a hundred and ninety pounds since high school."

Maddie shook her head. "No way. Charlie was one-eighty, tops."

"I was sorry to hear how that turned out."

She shrugged. "It's what happens when you get married straight out of high school for all the wrong reasons."

Tension shot through Bree, but Marcus didn't glance in

her direction.

Maddie kept talking. "Things are fine now. They're great, actually. So what brings you guys to town?"

Marcus relaxed. Her friend had asked just the right question. "I'm officially opening the campus this week, and the IPO is in a month. Tommy's my soon-to-be CFO."

Bree nodded at Tommy. Though they were both locals, they hadn't crossed paths often when they were younger. He was shorter than Marcus, maybe six feet, with brown eyes peeking out below a mop of blond hair. While Marcus wore a suit, Tommy was in loose jeans and an untucked shirt. To look at them, it would be easy to mistake Marcus for the moneyman and Tommy for the programmer.

"He's here for the campus," Tommy clarified. "I'm here because he pays me enough that I forgot I vowed never to come back."

"You're in good company," Maddie said. "Bree used to make that same vow at least once a week."

Bree longed for telepathy, if only so she could give her best friend a mental slap. Marcus stilled, but he didn't turn to face her.

Maddie smiled as she made the connection. "Wait, campus. You're the one building on the old Stanwick Ranch? The whole town's been wondering. Some great theories were thrown around. I heard everything from paintball course to medical marijuana farm."

His smile turned a little wicked. Even in profile, he was breathtaking. It wasn't fair that he should be so damned perfect.

Bree's cheeks grew flushed. He was so close. If she leaned

forward just a few inches, she'd sense the heat rising from his skin, learn if he wore cologne these days.

"I was cruel," he said. "I created a shell company just to hide that I bought it. I knew it would drive people crazy. Though now I want to build a paintball course." He glanced at Tommy. "What do you think? Is that in the budget? It'll be cheaper than medical marijuana. Less harmful to productivity too."

Maddie glanced at Bree, uncertain. She was finally noticing the strange undertones of their conversation. After their initial eye contact, Marcus hadn't glanced at Bree again, and the snub was becoming obvious.

Obvious, infuriating, and easy to end. Bree rested against the padded booth. "Why not option three? At least one person thought it was a government brainwashing facility that would turn the entire town into mindless zombies."

There. At last he turned toward her. "Old man Harper?"

One side of her mouth quirked up. "Who else?"

An awkward silence fell, long enough for her friend to rush in. "You remember Bree, right?"

The waitress appeared at their table with a large basket of mozzarella sticks. Bree was vaguely aware of Maddie thanking the woman, asking for a side of ranch, requesting a beer. The whole time, Bree said nothing, all of her attention focused on Marcus as she braced for his response.

Marcus blinked once, as if she were a stranger he needed to place. "Of course. A man shouldn't forget his first wife."

MARCUS HADN'T PLANNED ON DROPPING THE W-BOMB. HE definitely hadn't meant to say something in front of the waitress, who was already back at the bar and whispering to her coworkers.

By the end of the day, everyone in town would know he'd been married to Bree Rogers.

He'd returned to town to celebrate his success, not his failures—and their brief marriage was the biggest, most humiliating failure of his life.

But she'd just been sitting there, cool as ever. Slouching against the booth with one leg pulled up on the seat, perfectly at ease and as disinterested as she had been in high school. She needed to know things were different now. *He* was different, and it had been a long time since anyone ignored him.

"First…wife?" Maddie Palmer spoke the word cautiously, like it might have a second meaning.

Over the years, he'd occasionally allowed himself to imagine this meeting. He would appear in a tailored suit that cost more than most cars, with gold cufflinks and a Rolex that would have covered his first semester at Berkeley. In his daydreams, he delivered the perfect indifferent greeting, proving he no longer cared. Bree would be reduced to stammering out an apology.

Well, at least he had the clothes. Bree, of course, didn't follow the script. She gave an easy shrug and didn't stutter once. "Shit happens," she told her friend.

Marcus forced himself to stop grinding his teeth. They were good teeth. They didn't deserve to be ruined because his ex was an unfeeling shrew. "Can Bree and I have a minute alone?"

She scowled at Maddie, demanding her friend refuse the request, but the other woman smiled sweetly. "Sure. Take all the time you want."

There was a solid thunk, and he was pretty sure Bree tried to kick Maddie and hit the bench instead.

"Tommy, can you order me a salad?" Marcus asked. "The chicken Caesar."

"You got it." Tommy turned toward the bar and froze. "Get your own. I'll meet you at the car when you're done."

His friend rushed through the front door. Marcus tried to figure out what had spooked Tommy.

"It's Stewart." Maddie nodded at the old man at the end of the bar. The guy had a mostly empty glass in front of him. Though he was braced on his forearms, his head drooped forward like he could nap at any second.

Shit. Tommy's father. "I didn't know he'd gotten this bad." Over the years, Marcus asked his father for updates, but Quentin and Stewart barely spoke these days.

Stewart had lost his hand in the same accident that destroyed Quentin Keller's legs, and he never really recovered. Marcus had no idea the man was getting drunk in the middle of the day. He wondered if Tommy had known.

Maddie kept her voice low, though Stewart was too far away to hear. "He's in here most days, though I've heard Gavin waters his drinks to slow him down. He'll kick him out eventually, then Stewart will move on to the Capital's bar and start all over."

Every town had their resident drunks. Marcus just hadn't expected it to be someone he knew.

It could have been his dad. Both men had been disabled, their lives changed forever. It had been bad enough that Marcus left Berkeley halfway through freshman year to help his family. These days, Quentin got by, though Marcus hated the way his dad was drifting through life. Looking at Stewart, he realized it could have been so much worse.

And while he'd been doing everything he could to care for his father after the accident, Bree wouldn't even answer her phone. He'd been falling apart, and she'd been waiting for him to sign the divorce papers.

Something of his anger must have flashed in his eyes, because Maddie hesitated.

"It's okay." Bree's smile was mocking. "Marcus and I need to catch up."

Maddie reluctantly slid out of the booth. "I'll call you." Her parting glare was meaningful, and he suspected Bree would be answering a lot of questions later.

But he got to ask them first. For the first time in years, Marcus was alone with Bree.

He took the seat across from her. Marcus used to live for moments like this. Not sitting across the table—that wouldn't happen, not in high school—but near her. Two seats behind her in AP math. The row across from her on the school bus. God, he'd been pathetic.

She looked the same, more or less. Still kept her chin lifted and her shoulders set, permanently informing the universe that she was ready for anything it handed her. He thought she was a little thinner, the softness of her eighteen-year-old self vanished, though she was wrapped in a large, beat-up sweater that made it difficult to say for sure.

"What do you want?" She glared at him.

Over the years, he'd convinced himself that her eyes couldn't be as remarkable as he remembered. No one could have eyes that enormous, a warm brown with so much depth they reminded him of melting chocolate, and surrounded by the longest damn lashes he'd ever seen. Guys weren't supposed to notice things like lashes when a woman had a body as great as Bree's, but it was hard not to. They were almost cartoonish, a ridiculously soft feature on a woman who otherwise looked like a rock star coming off a bender.

Once, her eyes made him think that there was more to Bree than a big brain and bigger attitude. He learned the hard way that warm brown eyes could hide a cold heart.

Marcus leaned back against the padded booth. "You changed your hair."

She tugged on one shoulder-length strand. It was platinum now, a wild mess of bleached hair.

"It hasn't been blue in a long time."

"Or purple or green?"

She groaned. "A friend wouldn't mention my green period." She winced, like she wanted to bite back the words.

"Friends also answer emails and phone calls." A bolt of energy shot through him at the memory. "Doesn't sound like we were ever friends."

Of course Bree avoided that subject. "Back in town, what, five minutes before mentioning we were married? It's like you couldn't wait to tell people."

Marcus laid his palms flat on the table to avoid fidgeting. Her gaze dropped to his hands.

Images arose, unbidden, of his hands on her body. Long, careful strokes, learning every detail of the curves he'd fantasized about his entire high school career. The memory was seared into his brain, and not just because it had been his first time. For years, he'd examined the memory from every angle, searching for any indication she hadn't felt what he did. Warning signs he should have spotted before she shattered his heart.

Marcus wrenched his mind back to the present. "Maddie's your best friend. I figured she already knew."

"Like Tommy knew? He was as surprised as she was."

Marcus mimicked her careless shrug from earlier. "I was embarrassed. No one wants to admit they were a lovestruck kid who trusted the wrong woman."

Her lip curled. "And maybe I was embarrassed to admit I got drunk and married a man who wouldn't know a boundary if it jumped up and licked his face. A man who didn't know me at all."

He mirrored her relaxed pose, but his anger rose to match hers. "That's one thing we agree on. It's hard to know someone who only lies."

"I didn't lie when I said I didn't want to be married. You just didn't want to hear it."

"Oh, I heard it. I heard every fucking word you ever said to me." He inhaled sharply, waiting until he was calm enough to sound unaffected. "You also said you were never, ever coming back to Lost Coast Harbor, so there was no point staying married. How did that work out for you?"

Her pause was a second too long. "What can I say? Life is full of surprises."

"Is it? You didn't look surprised."

Bree took a bite of mozzarella stick and followed it with a long swig of beer. "How long are you in town?" she asked.

"Didn't I say? I'm not here for the opening. I've moved

back to Lost Coast. Permanently." Marcus stood. "Surprise."

Her already enormous eyes rounded, and Marcus felt a sharp bite of pleasure. No, she wasn't clutching his ankles and gushing abject apologies, but any conversation that left Bree Rogers speechless counted as a victory.

And now that he was back, he had time for many such victories. He'd waited for them long enough.

CHAPTER THREE

Three days later, Marcus was pretty sure he had his life completely under control.

The buildings were completed, and a press release had gone out that morning announcing Hours's move to Lost Coast Harbor. The labs in outbuilding number four were up and running. The first wave of employees would arrive the following week. It would take time to fill the offices, but soon it wouldn't feel like a ghost town in the redwoods. Already, he had a role picked out for his father, one that would get Quentin out of his damn recliner for several hours a day. The company had just finished the third and final SEC review, which meant Tommy would spend the next few weeks hopping around the country, convincing people to give them lots of money.

Everything was on track. He'd done it.

Thoughts of his ex-wife rarely popped into his head. And when they did happen to appear, it was only to remind him that her heart hadn't grown a single size since graduation. She might be a beautiful bitch, but she was still a bitch. It was a relief to discover that time and distance had finally cured his addiction to Bree Rogers.

His computer pinged, and a chat window popped up in the lower right corner. *Just heard from a couple of investors who think you've lost your mind.*

Marcus peered over his computer. "Tommy, you're fifteen feet away. Get in here."

His friend scrunched his face in mock protest, then crossed the hallway that separated them. They had matching corner offices on the east end of the third floor. Marcus believed hierarchies and petty in-fighting were poison to creativity, and he included himself in that. Everyone's offices were the same size—though, admittedly, he gave himself the best view. He'd spent too much time staring at concrete not to take full advantage of the forest setting.

All he really needed was a desk and a computer. Too much additional space and people might try to hold meetings, as he'd discovered in the Mountain View office. Marcus did everything in his power to avoid meetings, as any right-thinking person would.

Tommy dropped into one of the two chairs on the other side of Marcus's desk. "The *Times* wrote about the move today."

Marcus leaned back and waited.

"Someone found old photos of the LCH town square and ran it alongside pictures of the Silicon Valley headquarters. Nice compare and contrast. The general tone of the piece was that you're doing something brand new, so you're either a fool or a genius, and only time will tell."

"It could be worse."

Tommy grimaced. "It's easy to sell the Silicon Valley wonder boy who made more money every year. A bit harder when the pitch is 'genius or idiot, take your pick!'"

Marcus laughed, though he knew Tommy wasn't entirely joking. "And this is why you get to handle the roadshow. You're good at those questions."

"The investors are getting cold feet, Marcus. They don't understand why you had to move the company out here."

Marcus considered their options. "Then we'll have to show them. Get them out here."

"What's your plan?"

He glanced around his quiet, peaceful office and winced. "Though it pains me to say this, to the deepest core of my being..."

"A party?" Tommy perked up.

"A party," Marcus confirmed. "Let's impress them with our glorious wealth and success. Let them see the campus, not the town. We'll need Rae for this. When is she scheduled to arrive?" Like Tommy, Rae had been with him from the beginning. It didn't feel right opening the campus without her.

"Later this week. She's already reserved one of the dorms."

"Is there any hope of people calling them apartments?" Outbuilding number one was intended to provide temporary housing when his employees first arrived. Afterwards, he would use the building as guest lodging for the overnighters and long-term contractors. It was better than forcing people to stay at the ancient Capital Hotel in the town square.

Tommy was unimpressed. "You gave them a common room and a Ping-Pong table. It's a dorm."

"I'm firing people at the first sign of a keg stand."

"Duly noted." Tommy glanced down and picked at an invisible piece of lint. "There's something else. You're not going to like it. Oliver Hastings approached me about investing."

"No."

"I get it. You know I do. But the family has money, and we could use a backup plan."

"Are you serious?" Marcus didn't hide his disgust at Tommy's suggestion.

"Oliver wasn't in charge when the accident—"

"Not the Hastings. Anyone but them, Tommy."

The phone on his desk chirped. For once, Marcus welcomed the interruption.

Rae got right to the point. "We have a problem."

He sat up straight. Rae didn't call him about problems. She fixed them, then emailed Marcus to remind him how amazing she was and point out that it was time for a raise.

"Tell me."

"There's been a data breach."

Marcus put Rae on speaker. "Define breach."

"Someone's trying to break into the user accounts."

Panic threatened to overtake him. Not now. Not when he was so fucking close. "Have they accessed any information?"

"Not yet, but the attacks aren't stopping. They come in waves."

His mind raced. They couldn't risk shutting the whole thing down. Few things made a company look weaker than an app that couldn't stay connected—except for a data breach.

That was the kind of thing that took down companies.

Tommy bent toward the phone. "Are we talking ransom-ware?" More and more, hackers were freezing company's systems, just so they could unfreeze them once a ridiculous sum of money had been paid.

It was their best-case scenario. Those hackers wouldn't go public, not if the ransom was paid.

Rae exhaled, and in that sound he heard all the stress and exhaustion of the last hour. "I don't know. Right now, we're just trying to keep up with the attacks, but it's only a matter of time till one of them slips through."

"But you helped design the system. Block them." Marcus didn't bother to soften his order.

She snapped back at him. "And I told you at the time I'd be better in product design than IT. You ignored me."

He glared at the speakerphone. "I didn't *ignore* you. I needed you—"

Tommy cut them off. "Fight later. What do you need, Rae?"

"Any chance you can help with this, Tom?"

His laugh was rough and directed at himself. "It's been a long time since I've touched a line of code. You don't want me."

"Well, we want someone. Whoever's doing this, they're busting through every firewall I set up. And every time they knock down a brick wall, we're putting up a plastic tarp to hold them off. If we don't get this under control, they'll get everything. We need to block them, then rebuild the damn system."

"Get Rick in," Marcus said. The consultant was expensive, but he did solid work and was more experienced than Rae.

"Stick him in an office, and don't let him leave."

"He's already working, but he thinks, considering the situation, you need the best."

Marcus scowled at the phone. "I thought he *was* the best. That's why we use him."

"Rick says there's someone better—and she lives right down the road from you."

BREE WOKE AT TWO IN THE AFTERNOON AND GOT TO WORK.

She needed to stay busy. Otherwise, she might think about Marcus, and that was a terrible idea.

Her cabin was a rental, but she'd made it her own. After a couple of years living in Maddie's house, it had been a relief to have a whole place to decorate. The small living room was overpowered by the enormous sofa she'd bought the day she signed the lease. It barely fit, but if a person found a super-soft teal couch big enough to double as a bed, that person would be a fool not to buy it. She'd put no conscious thought into decorating, merely picking out items she liked, but somehow her preference for bright furniture, garish pop art, and soft textures came together in a warm, playful room.

Her dining table was no exception. When it arrived at her cabin, it was a beat-up piece of pine. A bit of sanding and a whole lot of paint later, it was fire-engine red and covered in a Ms. Marvel poster. She'd taught herself decoupage just for that project. At the moment, Ms. Marvel was hidden by three desktop computers and one laptop, which were all running complicated scripts designed to ferret out weaknesses in a new operating system.

It was her space, and it was the safest place in the whole

world. Only a few people were allowed past the front door. A few months ago, Erin's new boyfriend kept popping by unannounced, and it had taken reserves of strength Bree didn't know she possessed not to throttle him. She made wisecracks and did what she could to help Will and Erin, and neither of them ever knew she couldn't draw a full breath until her house was her own again.

Every time she thought she was making progress, it happened. Something disturbed her, and the damn pill bottle grew a little lighter. She was so fucking sick of it. She knew there was more to life, and it was passing her by, one panic attack at a time.

While the machines compiled data, Bree grabbed her other computer, Dolly. It was the only one she ever bothered to name or decorate—in this case, with a cow-print decal across the front—and it seldom left her house. Most of the time, it didn't leave her safe.

The security work was fine. It might not have been her first choice, but Bree had given up on her first choices long ago. The consultant jobs paid well, and she kept her expenses low—low enough to put thousands of dollars each month into her own project.

The money wasn't stretching as far as it once did. She'd applied for a loan the week before and was waiting on approval. Once she had that, she could port the files from the laptop to a virtual-reality device.

Bree stretched across her couch with a green pillow supporting her lower back. She placed the computer on a lap desk and opened a file she'd barely glanced at since the construction began on Marcus's campus.

A flash of anger pulsed through her. It was bad enough that he'd disrupted her work. Ever since she ran into him at Donnelly's, he'd disrupted her thoughts, until she caught herself playing the *What If?* game far too often—and no one ever won that game. Their past was already written. She could only worry about the future now.

And once she got Wanderlust up and running, she might be able to rewrite her future.

Bree opened her cloud storage and double clicked on a recently uploaded file. At first glance, it was a film shot from the point of view of someone cruising down the Grand Canal of Venice in a water taxi. But with a small adjustment of the mouse, the camera panned right, revealing the enormous Rialto fish market. Another adjustment turned it left, showing the Gritti Palace where Hemingway used to write. The video was filmed in three hundred sixty degrees, both horizontal and vertical, and patched together with some film technique Bree couldn't begin to understand. It was also why her bank account was currently empty.

Her sigh was a mix of happiness and longing. Venice felt like a fairy tale to her, a magical land of history and beauty unlike any other city on Earth. She couldn't wait to be surrounded by the mosaics in the Basilica or ride in a gondola piloted by a surly Italian man.

The program was limited. No film could capture the air rushing across her face or the rhythmic bumps as the taxi hit the wake left by other boats. Life was made of five senses. With the current technology, virtual reality only excelled at two of them.

At that moment, Bree wanted to focus on the visual. She

turned off the sound, silencing the chatter of voices, and pulled up her music library. Yet another benefit of living on her own. Maddie would make a face when Bree played modern music too loud, but her friend played the "my house, my rules" card when Bree reached back a century—or five.

As the first notes of Monteverdi's *L'Orfeo* flowed from her speakers, Bree let the music wash over her. Notes formed by nothing but ancient instruments and the human voice. Only when she felt the music inside her, breathing for her, did she begin to work.

The water taxi was crowded. Even looking at it made Bree tense slightly, and she wasn't there, surrounded by dozens of people. Trying to track everyone's movements. Aware, constantly aware.

She took a calming breath. It was just a video. She was here, in her cheerful cabin, with a glorious tenor soothing her very soul. Her warm sofa was beneath her. The door was locked. She was alone. She was safe.

She adjusted the camera until it focused on a group of female friends. She marked the three women who would need to be erased in the multiple versions of the video that would eventually be created, then panned to a large family. She winced at the overexcited children and marked the entire family to be removed in the first version. The parents and one child could be added in the second one.

A notification popped up, and her fingers stilled on the keyboard. She'd requested an email, rather than a phone call, but she'd expected it to take a few more days.

Her future lay in her inbox.

Bree's hands shook a little as she clicked to open the message from the bank.

Lack of collateral. Freelance income too unpredictable. A business plan out of a sci-fi movie. Assessment: try again next year.

"Fuck." Bree spit the word, tasting venom in her mouth. Without that money, the project was stalled. *She* was stalled.

She set down the laptop and paced her living room. The familiar weight pressed on her chest, this time near her clavicle. It showed up when she was struggling against a deadline or unable to repair a system. In other words, when she was afraid she wasn't good enough. When she was failing.

Bree braced her hands on the back of her sofa and bent over, taking long, slow breaths. In through her nose, out through her mouth, repeat.

There had to be a way. Hell, Maddie's boyfriend Gabe had been in prison. Maybe he had tips on the best way to rob a bank.

She snorted at the thought, and the panic began to recede. She would find a way. If there was one thing at which she excelled, it was learning to live within limitations.

Her instant messenger pinged. She was going to ignore it until she noticed the name. Rick had come through with a lot of great projects for her, and she was in no position to turn down work.

The craggy bastard smiled at her. "Hey, Bree darling. Marcus Keller needs you at his office, pronto. He'll pay you the GDP of a small island nation."

It was money. She needed money. She'd practically summoned this call through pure force of will.

And accepting a job from the ex-husband who hated her

was probably a stupider choice than bank robbery.

"I'm on my way," she said.

CHAPTER FOUR

Of course he kept her waiting.

His company was under attack, and it was more important that he remind her who was in charge. The Marcus she used to know didn't play games.

And she was one of the reasons the old Marcus no longer existed. Though she couldn't have ruined his life too much, not if this was where he ended up.

The inside of the building was as beautiful as the exterior. Whoever the designer was, they'd earned every penny. Everything was in the same palette as the outside world—rich greens, reddish browns, and the pale gray of a cloudy Lost Coast sky.

She paced, unable to sit still. When he didn't appear, she wandered down the nearest hallway.

As expected, she found several conference rooms, but she paused when she reached a dark room. Unlike the others, light didn't pour through floor-to-ceiling windows. Her hand groped for a switch, and she gasped when the room was illuminated.

"It's a movie theater."

Bree spun to face Marcus, who'd apparently taken ninja lessons over the last decade. She hadn't sensed him approaching, and her heart beat double time for a second too long.

His gaze was as unnerving as it had been at Donnelly's. Once, he'd worn his heart on his sleeve. Now his expression was locked tight, giving nothing away.

"Yeah, the giant screen and cushy seats gave that away. Why do you have a movie theater in your office building?" Her voice was steady. Good.

"Because sometimes you need to take a break in the middle of the day and watch *Batman*."

She snorted. "You always were a DC fanboy."

There was a tiny hitch in the conversation, a moment when she knew they remembered the same thing. A drunken debate at two in the morning about the relative merits of DC versus Marvel.

Marcus broke the silence first. "You haven't seen the error of your ways yet?"

"Do we really need to talk about DC's *New 52?*"

Marcus opened his mouth to protest, then gave up. Smart boy. The DC universe reboot was a gateway to another hours-long debate that she would, without doubt, win.

"I liked the new *Batgirl*," she admitted. One should be gracious in victory, even if it was only presumed.

"If she gets her own movie, we can screen it here." Marcus gestured inside. "You know how it is at tech companies. People work too hard. They get obsessed with a project. You need to let them blow off steam and relax. That goes double in a small town like this."

Bree nodded, pretending she had any idea what he was

talking about. After graduation, she hadn't been capable of interviewing at a tech company, let alone working at one.

"You want a tour?"

Bree shook her head. "It's not necessary. Let's get to work."

He studied her a beat too long, just enough time to make her think that was the wrong answer, then led her up the wide staircase next to the reception desk. He was two steps above her, giving her a perfect view of the way his thigh muscles bunched and released under the expensive fabric. Her skin prickled in awareness, and she glanced down, focusing on her combat boots as they took one step after another. She should absolutely, under no circumstances, be thinking of Marcus's thighs.

She made a mental note to not accept jobs when she'd seen her boss naked.

The second and third floor were identical. Both consisted mainly of offices that ran along either side of the hallway. Each office was the same size—and they all had glass walls.

"So this is what hell looks like," she murmured.

"What's wrong with it?" The words were sharp.

"Nothing. Throw in a large wheel, and you'll complete the hamster-cage effect. Is this so you can spy on your employees?"

Instead of answering, Marcus opened a glass door near the end of the third-floor hallway. "You'll work here."

"Uh-uh. Nope. Also, fuck that."

He raised a single eyebrow and waited.

Bree stepped into the room. The minute she was surrounded by the glass walls, she felt simultaneously trapped and exposed. Across the hall, Tommy watched both of them with a little too much interest. No way was she working here.

"First of all," she said, "I work at home. Always have, always will. This is partly because my house is warm and cozy and filled with the best junk food currently approved by the FDA and partly because I won't get a damn thing done if I'm distracted by other people."

Marcus pressed a button next to the light switch. The glass darkened to an opaque smoke. "We're experimenting based on recent studies. Some say an open floor plan increases creativity and a sense of community. Others say that if you make an introvert work in those conditions, they'll imagine killing you in your sleep. We plan to spend half the day in traditional offices, half the day in an open plan. If that doesn't work, we'll let people self-select." He hit the button a second time, and the walls returned to clear glass.

It was an interesting idea, in theory. "I'm not getting paid to be your lab rat. Trust me. I work best away from people."

The way he studied her was unsettling, like he was weighing every word, then considering all possible meanings and assigning unintended subtext to every sentence.

"How's your equipment at the cabin?"

"The best." She didn't ask how he knew about the cabin. The info was easy to come by if one bothered to ask around.

Marcus strolled across the room and popped open a set of cabinets on the far wall. Five monitors appeared alongside three CPUs with a variety of operating systems.

Bree moved forward and stroked the machines. "Okay, second best." She crouched to read the numbers on one unit. "This isn't supposed to be out until next year."

"I have connections."

She glanced up at him. "I thought you were just the king of love. Since when do dating-site gurus require this kind of equipment?"

"Because only a fool turns down something amazing when it's freely offered."

It was a direct hit. Maybe she should have been paying more attention to Marcus's subtext.

Bree rose. "No matter how amazing the equipment, it needs a solid connection."

He didn't bite. He was too busy looking smug. "Will 1.2 terabits do?"

Bree gaped. She was a little turned on at that moment, and she didn't think it had anything to do with the man in front of her. "One point two. Terabits. In Lost Coast Harbor?" One thing was for sure. She needed to reevaluate her deal with Coastal Telecom.

"The head of the FCC has a new son-in-law thanks to Hours. He was happy to help with my application to install new network cables out here. And before you ask, no, you can't access it from your cabin. If you're doing the work, it'll be in this office."

Though it pained her to give up without a fight, she pictured the check that would be deposited at the end of this week, the one with all those extra zeroes. That kind of money bought a lot of compromise.

She'd still make Marcus work for it. "Fine. I'll need my own assistant. I run on caffeine and sugar, and you can't expect me to drop my work every time I need a bowl of mini Snickers."

Marcus glanced at her waistline.

"Snark burns a lot of calories," she told him. "I want a keycard, because I set my own hours, and most of them will be after midnight. If someone needs to contact me, they will, in order, email, text, instant message, and then video chat. I'll growl at anyone who knocks on my door without an appointment, and I don't pick up the phone for anyone but my best friends and people who share my DNA. Also, I want a private screening of *The Princess Bride* in the theater."

"As you wish." The man didn't skip a beat. "But I expect daily timecards, so I know when you're working. We have an on-site cafeteria and a juice bar, so try to consume a few vitamins every day. If I call, you'll pick up. If you don't, I'll come looking for you, and I don't care if you growl at me. I seem to recall enjoying that."

For a second, his intense stare softened, and she caught her breath. That man, right there. That was the one she remembered. The one who, after an all-nighter spent drinking and talking, convinced her to head to a small chapel on the Nevada side of Tahoe.

Just as quickly, the mask was in place. "This is important, Bree. If we don't stop this attack, it's not just the IPO at risk. The entire company could fall."

"I won't let that happen." She hoped he saw her sincerity.

Marcus returned to his office. It was right next to hers. He smiled at her through the glass, though there was no humor in it. It was a challenge.

She punched the button, throwing the room into darkness.

He was the boss. If he wanted to lighten the windows to check on an employee, he had that right.

Particularly if it made her growl as promised.

God, Bree was exactly as he remembered her. Seeing her for the second time just drove that home. He couldn't remember the last time he had to work to keep up with someone.

If anything, he thought she might be more than she used to be. On occasion, there were hints of a depth he didn't remember. A little more weight behind the eyes. In high school, she'd been too reckless for her own good, but she'd been raised in comfort. She'd been fearless because she had nothing to fear.

He wondered whether that was still true, and then he wondered why he was such an idiot. Trying to figure out what Bree Rogers thought or felt was an exercise in futility. She'd done what she did best—closed the door and locked him out. Nothing had changed.

That wasn't true. *He* had changed. He was smarter now, smart enough to not fall for her a second time.

He buzzed Levi and asked his assistant to grab him a carrot-ginger juice from downstairs. Later, he'd go for a run. Nice, healthy habits, unlike his ex-wife.

Tommy dropped into the seat across from Marcus. "Ex-wife?" The words burst out of him. "I could pretend to ignore it at Donnelly's, but now she's in the office across the hall. Tell me why this isn't a terrible idea."

"It'll be fine. It's been so long, she might as well be a stranger."

"How long?"

Marcus paused to give the impression he needed to recall

the information. "About eight years." Eight years and two weeks since the divorce was finalized.

"You were twenty."

"I turned twenty a week after the divorce. I was almost nineteen when we got married."

Tommy folded his hands across this stomach, like he was settling in for a wait.

Marcus gave in and offered his friend the CliffsNotes version. "Every year, the Lost Coast Harbor High graduates have a class trip. Usually, they go camping in June, but that year someone's dad got a deal on some rooms in Lake Tahoe. We ended up going in late August, right before everyone headed off for college. The first night, Bree and I got drunk, then we got married. We sobered up, we divorced. The end."

"It took you a year to sober up?"

That question led to the long version. The long, painful, humiliating version. "There were complications with the paperwork."

Tommy glanced at the opaque wall between them and Bree. "And this won't be complicated?"

Marcus shrugged. "It's not like we had a drawn-out custody battle or arguments over alimony. It just didn't work out. Not much different from any other breakup."

"She's gorgeous. Debbie Harry in her prime gorgeous, if Debbie Harry was an IT goddess."

"Please don't hit on the freelance employees while they're under contract." Marcus's gut tightened at the thought.

"She's not my type," Tommy said. "But is she yours? Combat boots and bleached hair? Is that why all those Palo Alto princesses never interested you?"

Marcus braced his arms on the desk. "Like I said, it was a long time ago."

"Yeah, I heard you. Maybe you should listen to me. Double her pay, double her hours. Do whatever it takes to get her to rebuild the system and get out of here in the next week. Because that look on your face, it's not the expression of a man in control."

"Rebuild the system in a week? She's a security expert, not a wizard."

A door slammed, and Bree appeared in the doorway. Her cheeks were flushed, and she was grinning. Something inside him tilted at the sight of that smile.

"I shut the leak down," she announced.

His jaw dropped. His best crew had worked on it for hours, and she figured it out in twenty minutes.

"Is it a permanent fix?" he asked.

"Not even close. You need to upgrade your entire system. I have a base program I can adapt for your network, but it will take a couple of weeks."

Those words shouldn't please him as much as they did. IPO, he reminded himself. Professional credibility. The sanctity of personal data. Those all mattered more than the chance to torment his ex-wife for a few more days. "What's the situation?"

She sat in the chair next to Tommy and stretched out her legs. He could see the outline of strong quads underneath the worn-out blue denim, and a hint of pale skin peeked through a tear in her knee. "Don't blame your tech crew. They were doing their jobs. The problem is they were too trusting. That's a bad habit in a security consultant. My default setting is paranoid."

Tommy's brows drew together. "Are you insulting us by saying we're not paranoid enough?"

"Doesn't matter whether you are or not. People are still out to get you. Your people were searching for external cracks. I checked the inside first. The hacker is using a bunch of redirects, but there's no question about the origin point."

That sure as hell got Marcus's attention. "You're saying that…"

"Yep. The call is coming from inside the house."

Tommy leaned forward. "I'm pretty sure I know what you mean, but could you use plain English so there's no doubt?"

Marcus's hands tightened into fists. "It means we have a spy in the company."

Chapter Five

Marcus stared out the window and tried not to grind his teeth to dust. A fucking spy. An Hours employee—someone he trusted—had attempted to access confidential user data. It didn't matter how they planned to use it. It was a betrayal. For it to happen right before the IPO was a disaster…and he doubted it was a coincidence.

If Bree hadn't stopped the hacker the day before, he might have lost everything he'd worked for.

Someone spoke his name, loud enough and exasperated enough to make him think it wasn't the first time. Marcus spun around, and his dark mood instantly lifted.

"Rae." He smiled, rising to hug the petite force of nature. Barefoot, she was an inch or two over five feet, but he'd only ever seen her in heels. Even in college, she ran between classes on three-inch wedges. These days, his head of tech was more likely to wear Jimmy Choos. "About time you got here. Hours isn't the same without you."

"That's not true. Until all the employees are here, Hours remains in Mountain View." Her dark brown eyes studied him. "Do I want to know where you were just then?"

"Just mentally reviewing some IPO details," he improvised. It was what he *should* be doing. Bree was rewriting his security protocols and doing her best to find the hacker, though she warned Marcus that the person had covered their tracks well. Still, she was on top of it, leaving him free to focus on the SEC report on his desk.

And every time he read it, his vision blurred.

Rae's mouth tightened. "Let's talk about the IPO."

He blinked in surprise. Rae worked hard, but she was also his friend. It wasn't like her to skip the small talk. Before she sat, she darkened the walls and shut the door. Marcus raised an eyebrow in question.

"If Tommy knows I'm here, he'll want to say hi, and we need to talk alone."

Unease stirred. The three of them had been a team for years, and that meant no secrets.

Rae sat down. "I don't want to go through with the IPO." He didn't realize he was gaping until she tapped her long fingernails on the desk. "You can close your mouth, Marcus."

"No, I don't think I can. I thought you supported it. What changed?"

She took a deep breath. "I tried to get another job."

He didn't react. He didn't give any indication the news stung, though it felt like a betrayal. "Why?"

"Let's get one thing straight. I love Hours, and I don't want to leave, but it's been a long time since I loved my work. When we started, I took the tech side because Tommy didn't want it. I believed in this company, so I was happy to help however I could. But there are plenty of people who can do my job, and I'd be better at something else. The security breach is proof of that."

"Is that what this is about? It could have happened on anyone's watch."

She leaned forward, her expression intent. "Maybe, but you shouldn't need to hire an outside consultant to cover my ass. I'm good, but I'm not great. I could be, though. I've been telling you for years that I want to work in product development. There are so many different directions this company can go. Expand to non-English-speaking countries. Offer online chat dates for people who don't live in Hours cities. Organize second and third dates. You're playing it safe, Marcus."

He fingered the button on his left wrist. The cuffs felt tighter than usual. "I took your hologram idea."

"You mean my drunken suggestion that you turned into an overpriced toy?"

An *amazing* overpriced toy, but he didn't think Rae would appreciate him pointing that out.

She wasn't wrong. For at least a year, he'd avoided the subject of her changing departments whenever Rae brought it up. The company was on a straight path to the public offering, and he hadn't wanted to do anything to risk that. It was his crowning achievement. The moment he could finally say that he'd arrived in the business world.

"I'm sorry. I didn't realize how important this was to you."

Marcus probably deserved the *Are you fucking kidding me?* look she sent his way.

"We'll talk about your role. Really talk," he promised. "But explain why you're against the IPO now."

"Because I tried getting another job," she repeated. "And

no one would hire me."

He boggled. "That's ridiculous. You helped build this company. They should be begging you to work for them."

"I got a few tech offers. Every single one was a lateral move or a demotion. I want more."

"We'll work something out. I promise. As soon as things settle down."

Her expression suggested she was envisioning his grisly death. "Do you know what people say? That Marcus Keller made me. That he did all the original programming and I just maintained it. I hitched my cart to the right man, but I'm nothing more than glorified tech support. Some people think I slept with you to get my spot."

"That's bullshit."

"Of course it is, but it's the reality of this business. You've seen the hiring stats for women. They're abysmal. If you bring in outside investors with strong opinions about who should be in charge of what department, that's more people I need to convince I can do the work. They'll ask me questions they wouldn't ask Tommy."

"I'll be the majority owner," Marcus said. "And you'll own a huge chunk of the company."

"And we'll both answer to the board if profits drop. You think they won't narrow right in on the inexperienced woman who thought she could handle development?"

"I'll protect you," he insisted.

"I don't want protection. I want to do a job I'll be damn good at, at the company I love."

He couldn't give her the answer she wanted. Instead, he flicked his gaze over her shoulder, in the direction of Tommy's office. "Why didn't you want him to hear this?"

"He supports the IPO. He'll be happy rolling in all that stock-options money. If the board fires him, he'll land on his feet. You know this. And it's not his call, Marcus. It's yours." Rae stood, having said her piece.

Marcus exhaled. This was the part of the job he hated, drawing a line between friends and business. Rae's request was completely reasonable...for her.

"You're asking too much. Hours is my company, and this is the best thing for it."

Her resigned expression felt like a gut punch. "Maybe it is, but it's not the best thing for me. And considering the work you're doing in outbuilding number 4, I'm not sure it's the best thing for you, either."

"You're married?"

Bree set down Dolly and turned to find her brother standing in the doorway.

Adam was the one person in the world allowed to open her door without knocking, and he was only allowed because he refused to hear her frequent protests. Even her threat that she was going to wander around naked, thereby scarring him with the sight of her bare ass, wasn't enough to deter him.

Because Adam knew her better than anyone else, which meant he knew that sometimes she needed someone to check on her. Adam had been the one to find her six years ago. The one who'd figured out his little sister wasn't just being stubborn when she refused to come home. The one who studied the credit card statements and wondered when Bree started having groceries delivered every week and developed a worrying Amazon habit.

Adam stepped through the door, all six-foot-six inches of him filling her space. Bree was hardly a shorty, but she took after their mom while Adam was clearly their dad's son—and the family joked that their dad was descended from grizzly bears. Adam might not be that hairy, but he sure as hell seemed that big. They had the same coloring, except Bree hadn't seen her natural hair color since eighth grade, and Adam's skin was tan from days spent in the sun while hers was pale from years of keeping the same schedule as a vampire.

He was her favorite brother, and he probably would have been even if he wasn't her only sibling. The way he glowered at her, she might not be his favorite sister at the moment.

"So you finally heard the gossip? That took longer than I expected." Bree curled her feet under her, making room for Adam to sit on the couch. "I *was* married, barely. By a technicality. I've had colds that lasted longer than my so-called marriage."

That wasn't technically true, but it was close enough.

Adam waited. Her brother was the only person who could hold his own against her in a staring contest. She both loved and hated that about him.

"Look," she said at last, "we were young, drunk, and in Nevada. A dangerous combination. I knew it was a mistake right away. It's why I didn't tell anyone. It was like if a walk of shame came with an official document."

Her words bothered her. Yes, she and Marcus had been a bad idea, but she wasn't ashamed of him.

"My point is, it's in the past. Can we leave it there?"

At last, Adam broke eye contact. "Tell me you have beer."

"A growler from Donnelly's. The red lager. Grab me a glass too."

Her brother headed for the kitchen. "Do you *have* two clean glasses?"

Oops. For the last two days, she'd either been at Hours or working on the Grand Canal video. She'd had even less time—or inclination—to clean up than she usually did. "Check the cupboard over the fridge. I think I put some extras up there."

Since he was planning on staying, she slid the laptop under her sofa, next to her phone, a guidebook on Venice, and a souvenir snow globe that didn't belong anywhere else in her house.

A second later, he returned with two glasses. "You really should get someone out here to help. I know you make enough."

Bree grimaced. "But then someone would be in my house. Like, moving and talking and breathing."

"I was reading the other day," Adam began, and Bree knew this was going nowhere good. Adam probably spent more time than she did reading about anxiety. "It was about how environments impact mental health. The more control you have, the less chance of an attack." He pointed toward her kitchen. "That is not under control."

"I know environments affect my anxiety. That's why I live here."

She didn't mean the cabin, and they both knew it. Adam was the one who'd fetched her from Boston, who loaded her boxes and furniture into the U-Haul when she began shaking on the sidewalk, the cars and sirens and nearby construction noises feeling like an assault. He drove with her cross-country and saw her visibly relax as they left the city behind and entered the long stretches of farms and ranches.

"You were okay living with Maddie," he pointed out. "And I have it on good authority she both talked *and* breathed."

"Maddie is my best friend. She's safe. Plus, she needed me." And as soon as Maddie no longer depended on Bree for rent, she was out of there.

"How about this? The next time you go out for drinks with Maddie or Erin, call me. I'll get a cleaner over here, and I'll watch them the whole time to make sure they don't push the wrong button on one of your machines and accidentally blow up South Dakota or something."

Bree squeezed his hand. "I know you mean well, but you can't take care of me like this. I'm okay. I get out of the house all the time. No one else even knows, because there's nothing to see."

"Really? Then why did Maddie tell me you were on a business trip last month?"

Crap. Busted. "I needed some quiet time."

Adam looked skeptical, probably because Bree went on "trips" when she needed the world to leave her alone—and she only did that when coping in public took more energy than she possessed. Adam knew she'd barely crossed the town line since returning from Boston.

"Are you doing the most you can to help yourself? When was the last time you went to your therapist?"

Bree glared. "You're skating dangerously close to condescending, big brother. I had an appointment two weeks ago.

I'm doing yoga, even though it bores me stiff. I'm getting out of the house regularly. I know what I'm supposed to do, but sometimes my brain wants to freak out. And until you're inside my head with me, you have no room to judge."

"You're right. I'm sorry." The words were so sincere that her anger faded immediately. He only wanted the best for her, and she couldn't be mad that her brother cared about her happiness, even if he had a clumsy way of expressing it.

"Now," he said, "about your ex-husband…"

She was saved from answering by a knock on the door. Bree stood with a smile. Only Maddie or Erin would think to visit her uninvited.

She swung the door open to find her ex-husband standing on her porch.

CHAPTER SIX

Years ago—right around the time the divorce was finalized—Marcus decided it was time to change his life. He returned to Berkeley, submitted dozens of grant applications, and wrote out a five-year plan so detailed and precise even Rae was impressed.

Then he picked up a dumbbell and forced his skinny arms to do their first biceps curls. When he returned to Lost Coast, Marcus was startled to discover all the guys who'd been huge in high school no longer intimidated him, because he was now the same size or bigger.

Except for Bree's brother. Adam Rogers was still enormous, and for a second Marcus was pretty sure he was about to get his ass kicked.

"I hear you were my brother-in-law for a time," Adam said.

Bree shoved her brother, trying to push him through the door Marcus had just entered. Adam didn't budge.

"It's not a big deal," she muttered.

"Maybe not to you, because you don't answer your phone. I've been fielding calls from Mom. She's complaining because she missed her only daughter's ceremony. If you don't fix this soon, Bree, she'll make you get married again just so she can throw you a delayed reception."

Bree squeezed her eyes shut, grimacing. She looked like a teenager embarrassed by her parent, and it was unexpectedly adorable.

Marcus needed to help before he found himself at that same reception. "I can take out an ad in the LCH *Gazette* to clarify that I didn't say Bree was my first wife. She was my first *knife*. I hired her when I needed to take out a rival developer." Wait. Was he…joking with her?

A smile tugged at her lips, and Marcus's heart did a small flip.

"That'll work," she said. "If it helps, I can assassinate someone this week. I've already got a few candidates in mind."

Adam shook his head at his sister's version of humor.

She shrugged. "What? It beats a wedding reception."

Her brother pointed at Bree. "There's more to discuss." As Adam passed, he whispered to Marcus, the words too quiet for Bree to hear. "Hurt her and I'll drop you in the middle of the forest with nothing but a blanket and a sharp rock."

Once they were alone, he wasn't sure what to say. "Your house is warm. I mean, compared to outside."

Yes. That was the genius IQ Bree competed with all through high school.

"You've been in Mountain View too long if that's your idea of cold." She didn't offer him coffee or ask him to sit down. She stood there, her arms crossed, and waited. "Why did you decide to come back?"

His father. The cost of real estate in the Silicon Valley.

Homesickness. It was all true, but the words disintegrated in his mouth, dry as ashes. He was in Lost Coast Harbor because he'd stayed away as long as he could, and now he needed answers.

"What about you?" he countered. "You swore you wouldn't come back to Lost Coast Harbor."

"Things change. So what brings you by? I made it clear unexpected visitors aren't welcome."

She wasn't joking. The woman he knew in high school loved being social. She went to all the parties and constantly hung out with Maddie. "I didn't realize you were a hermit now."

She shrugged. "If you move into an isolated cabin in the trees, it's required. Hermit or oracle. Those are the choices."

"You haven't tried telling the future yet?"

"I foresee that I'll kick you out if you don't tell me why you're here."

"Can we sit?" He gestured at her couch, and after a second she nodded. "Where does one find a velour couch, anyway?"

"The internet, of course."

He settled onto the teal sofa. He'd be covered in blue lint later. "Your house is very..." He glanced around the living room, noting the bookshelves stuffed with graphic novels and the walls covered in movie posters and cheerful art.

"Bright? Obnoxious?"

"You," he finished.

"So, obnoxious."

He bit back a smile. "I came over to talk to you about the spy."

She held up her hand. "Nuh-uh. This is my home. You

want to talk to me about work, you've got to email or text me."

Marcus pulled out his phone. *Let's talk about how to catch the spy*, he typed.

A beep came from under the sofa. He reached down to grab her phone.

Bree leapt forward. "Don't do that. Leave it."

His hand wrapped around the device, and his knuckles brushed a paperback book and the edge of a laptop. He pulled both from underneath the couch. Bree immediately grabbed the machine from him and clutched it to her chest. She appeared relieved when he leaned back into the couch cushions. He eyed the machine, curious, but decided to let it go.

"Venice, huh?" Marcus cracked the travel book open. It was a full-color guide to the Italian city. The photographs were stunning, but a quick glance showed the descriptions were a bit lacking. It was hard to do justice to a city like Venice. "Gorgeous place. Are you planning a trip?"

Bree looked uncertain, though he couldn't imagine why. She sat on the other end of the sofa, keeping several feet between them. "Have you been there?"

"Twice. I visited after the company made its first million, because I wanted to backpack through Europe and didn't know when I'd get the time again. I went back a couple years ago for the film festival."

"That's right. You were dating that actress."

He studied her over the edge of the book. "You keeping tabs on me, Bree?"

"Please. Anytime you switched girlfriends, someone

brought it up in town. You gave them plenty of chances to gossip."

"You didn't have to listen."

"Did I have to avert my eyes when I was at the checkout counter so I wouldn't see the tabloids? Or stop reading social media when my city friends posted about their dates from your app?"

Marcus turned the page. "Wow. It sounds like you haven't been able to forget about me."

She didn't respond, and he was forced to look up to gauge her reaction. Bree tucked her computer under a couch cushion, then pulled her knees to her chest and wrapped her arms around her shins. She nodded at the book. "What's it like?"

He glanced down, barely noticing the shots of Piazza San Marco. He wanted her to respond to his jab, not ask about Venice.

"It's amazing. It's hard to believe a city like that exists." Marcus relaxed into the memory. "The streets make no sense to Americans. All twists and turns and alleyways. You have to accept 'lost' as your default setting, but that's the best way to discover the shops. Some of the restaurants in the tourist sections don't try very hard, but there are treasures if you know where to go."

Bree rested her cheek against the top of one knee. Her expression was soft, like she was trying to experience the memory with him. "What about the gondolas?"

"I didn't ride in one."

"Why not?"

"Well, the first time I was there on my own. The other time was in August, and the canals don't smell very nice in late summer." Also, Mimi hadn't been able to stop talking about taking a sunset ride, and how they absolutely needed to travel underneath the Bridge of Sighs. Marcus might have given in, at least until he learned about a local legend that promised eternal love to those who kissed beneath the bridge at sunset.

He hurried on. "It's not like any other city you've visited. I'm surprised you haven't gone yet. You used to talk about how much you wanted to travel. Didn't you say Venice was at the top of your list?"

He'd said the wrong thing. The dreamy expression she'd worn as he talked about the Italian city vanished, and the easy moment passed.

Bree sat up straight. "What's so important you had to stop by? You can't force me to work in your office and then show up at my house when I'm off the clock."

She was right. During the short drive to her house, he'd tried to think of a reasonable excuse for a visit instead of a text. There wasn't one, except that he wanted to see where she lived. For the last few years, his life had felt like an open book. His dating life in the tabloids, his professional life splashed across the business pages.

Bree, on the other hand, returned to Lost Coast Harbor and practically disappeared. Even her business was conducted under an LLC it took him time to discover. Marcus needed more information. He needed a reminder of who Bree really was, because his libido had forgotten. The last two days, he'd been constantly aware of her presence. Every time she walked down the hallway, he listened for the soft rustle of her jeans. He learned her coffee schedule the first day, and soon he found himself in the break room at the same time she was.

Marcus rose from the bright couch. Her home was warm enough that he took off his jacket and rolled up his shirt sleeves as he wandered through the room. She was doing okay for herself. She didn't flaunt her wealth. She might wear combat boots instead of designer heels, but he recognized some of the original artwork, and the shelves of collectibles would be the star attraction at any nerd auction. Nothing from the last couple of years, though.

As comfortable as it was, it wasn't flashy. Her money wasn't going into her house. The mystery of Bree Rogers deepened. "Why *did* you come back?"

She stretched her legs across the couch. "Because a lot can change in nine years. I shouldn't need to tell you that."

"That's not an answer."

She shrugged. "You haven't told me why you're back, either."

"A lot of reasons. I'll tell you mine if you tell me yours."

Heat rose in Bree's cheeks, and a memory slammed into him. Her teasing words from years ago.

I'll show you mine if you show me yours.

BREE TRIED VERY HARD NOT TO REMEMBER. IT WASN'T THAT the memory hurt too much, though it did. It was the kind of memory that made others pale in comparison.

She'd had a good life. Dated a few guys in college, before things got too bad, and a few more when she returned to Lost Coast Harbor after graduation. She liked sex and was glad to have the experiences she'd had. It was just unfortunate that none of those experiences ever lived up to her first one.

It had been early evening when she and Marcus first woke up as man and wife. They lay in bed, tangled in the sheets and each other's arms, and remembered at the same time. They remembered the hours spent sharing stories and secrets they hadn't thought to tell anyone else. Remembered how Marcus proposed, and how it felt wild and ridiculous and somehow right to run to the chapel across the Nevada border. How they had no rings, so they drew them on with Sharpies. And how they returned to the hotel, exhilarated and tired and a little too drunk to go any further, and they fell asleep together.

As they woke, they became aware of their bodies, still dressed, lined up together. Of his hard cock pressed against her hip, her thighs wrapped around his. Time stopped, waiting for them to make a decision. In that moment, they could chalk it up to a drunken lark and arrange an easy annulment.

Instead, Bree smiled. She tugged on his waistband. *I'll show you mine if you show me yours.*

Some memories were best forgotten, but this one was stubborn. It showed no sign of fading.

She'd said those words to the boy, and she knew the man in front of her remembered them too.

Marcus rested his hands on the back of the sofa. He had gorgeous hands, both strong and graceful, but she didn't remember his forearms being quite so…lickable. They were tan and powerful, covered in a light dusting of dark hair. She imagined her mouth on his warm skin, tracing the tendon with her tongue.

Marcus watched her, and she prayed she hadn't accidentally licked her lips while distracted by his forearms. His fucking perfect forearms.

"When did you decide it was a mistake?" His voice was low and controlled, giving nothing away. "It wasn't that first morning."

No, not then. Not when he stroked her entire body like it was a treasure he longed to uncover, when his mouth found every sensitive inch of skin. Neither of them had really known what they were doing, but they figured it out together, and Marcus had been so careful. So sweet.

The second morning hadn't been so bad, either. It turned out they were quick studies, and they learned it didn't always need to be sweet.

"That week was one of the best of my life." Her voice was steady as she spoke the truth she'd once whispered to him on late-night phone calls. If she spoke any lie, it was that other weeks competed for the title. "It wasn't a mistake. Our mistake was making a lifelong commitment after one night."

"Bullshit."

Bree rose, eyes blazing. This was what came of trying honesty. "Are we seriously doing this again?"

Marcus boggled at her. "We didn't do it the first time. I tried to talk to you, and you refused to answer. You filed divorce papers, then you pretended I didn't exist."

"And that's where we can never get our stories straight. I remember telling you, quite clearly, why I wanted out. I didn't want to be married to a man who lived three thousand miles away with no plans to change that. You wanted to build a marriage on a one-week relationship!"

"Bullshit," he repeated. "Sure, you got the scholarship, but I was figuring it out. You didn't even give me six months to pull together enough money to transfer schools. It was fucking MIT. I couldn't pay for it with a summer job."

Bree threw her hands up. "And what? I was supposed to wait while you applied for every scholarship? Put my life on hold because we had a good week in Tahoe?"

He began pacing her small living room, casting dark glances her way as he did so. "A week? It was four years. Four years of competing with each other for that alumni scholarship. We were constantly aware of how the other person did on tests. How many extracurricular activities they were doing. I knew when you flaked off studying to watch a Doctor Who marathon, because that was the week I passed you, and you knew when I snuck away to BayCon, because you reclaimed the lead. For four years, we were in each other's brains. All that week meant was we were finally together in the same place." His gaze raked her body. "And naked."

The smug bastard. "Rewrite history much? Yeah, I knew I had to keep my GPA above yours, but I didn't think about you every damn day. I had friends. A social life. I wasn't the one with a crush all through high school."

The words sounded harsher than she intended, and his lips thinned. "Sure. I saw a smart, funny girl who liked comic books and understood computers as well as I did, and I was a fifteen-year-old with a permanent hard-on and no interest in cheerleaders. Of course I had a fucking crush."

"Which you tried to turn into a marriage. You can't stand here and say you felt nothing but a silly crush while also telling me I should have tried to make it work." At some point during their argument, she'd walked to Marcus, and he'd stopped pacing long enough to glare at her. They were nose to nose.

"You *said* you'd make it work. You changed your mind. God, sometimes I think I imagined that. I came to Boston, and you changed your mind. That is what happened, isn't it?"

"It was a mistake."

Marcus put his finger under her chin, tilting her face up. Electricity raced across her skin at his touch, like her body was waking up after a long nap. "You didn't try," he said. "It was a marriage. That *means* something."

She called on the bravado that had served her so well over the years. "Vows made under the influence of fortified wine mean nothing."

He took in a ragged breath. "Maybe not, but this sure as hell did."

Before she understood what he was saying, his hands were on her cheeks, and his lips were on hers.

The kiss started soft, a gentle reminder of what happened when they connected. The way they fit together, it was like his lips had been made for hers. He held her loosely, giving her space to draw away, but she couldn't. The fighting and the anger and the lost years disappeared until it was just the two of them, kissing each other the way they were meant to do. Her eyes grew wet with tears she'd held in for years.

But Marcus wasn't satisfied with soft for long, and when she opened her mouth to his, Marcus's tongue slid inside. She stroked her tongue against his and felt such relief at the familiar touch that a small sob escaped.

His body was both known and strange. Marcus's taste was the same, as was the feel of his lips below hers. He cupped her face when he kissed her, like he used to. His strong fingers curled gently into her skin. She'd always loved that, the way it felt like he was both adoring her and holding her to him.

When her fingers strayed to his waist, she found it wider than before, his once narrow oblique muscles thickened with exercise. Her fingers gripped a hundred-dollar shirt instead of a worn-out tee.

But the hunger…that she knew. She'd known it from the first time he kissed her. But now, there was more. Marcus's need was mixed with determination, even anger. Anger that she hadn't stayed with him. Anger that he still wanted her. He punished them both with the desire that rose between them, a desire that cared little for betrayals and unforgivable silences.

Bree pushed on his chest and staggered backwards. She spun around and scrubbed her face before he could notice the tears.

"I don't think you're paying me for this," she told him, her voice unsteady. "I'll see you in the office tomorrow."

CHAPTER SEVEN

As the days passed, Marcus began to notice the whispers in town. The averted stares. It had nothing to do with the gossip about his and Bree's past. Rather, some of the people he'd grown up with appeared unsettled by his return. Marcus was born and raised in Lost Coast Harbor, and sometimes he felt like an outsider. He spent more time on campus, and not just because he wanted to be near Bree.

The kiss had unsettled him. No matter how many times he'd sworn he wanted nothing from Bree, his lips found their way to hers pretty damn fast. The kiss had been electric, a jolt of energy that woke every cell of his body. He couldn't forget it. Just as often, his mind returned to her face in that split second before she turned away. It made no sense, and he was probably hallucinating, but he could swear her eyes had been bright with unshed tears.

Forget about her. She's a distraction.

What mattered was the IPO. Finding the spy. Getting settled in town. That last one bothered him more than he expected it to. To both their surprise, Tommy was having an easier time than Marcus. It helped that Tommy didn't appear in the Page Six gossip column, and he wore jeans, and he drove a Prius rather than an Aston Martin. Tommy might resent every day he spent away from the Bay Area, but the town didn't resent him.

Marcus, on the other hand, had returned with more money than the Hastings and Donnellys combined. They'd been the wealthiest families in town for centuries, and it only took him a few years to supplant them. His arrival was upsetting the natural order—and Lost Coast Harbor wasn't fond of change.

He had to believe they'd come around once the job postings went up. The local unemployment rate was about to drop significantly—and he was ready to hire his first new employee.

"You know," his father said, tilting back farther in his overstuffed recliner, "I'm grateful every day that my accident came after on-demand video. It spared me any number of *Judge Judy* reruns."

Marcus moved his father's leg braces out of the way and took a seat on the large brown couch. The family room held the same furniture it had for Marcus's entire life. The couch stopped being comfortable when he was in high school, but it felt like home—sharp springs, threadbare cushions and all. He swallowed past the lump in his throat. He should have come back sooner.

For the last few years, he'd arranged trips for his parents every December. They were flown first class to Aspen or Whistler, and an award-winning chef prepared their Christmas dinner. His parents were skilled at pretending Marcus only wanted to share his success with them. No one ever mentioned that his sudden reluctance to return home coincided with Bree's return from Boston.

"Mom says you watch a lot of TV."

Quentin adjusted the heavy blanket that covered his frail legs. "I've got a lot of time to kill. Let me have my cop shows."

Onscreen, a gruff cop with a soft spot for widows and orphans studied that week's crime scene.

"Is this how you're exercising your brain these days? Trying to figure out a fictional mystery?"

"An hour or two a day isn't going to rot my brain."

"What are you doing the rest of the time?"

His father huffed out an exasperated sigh and hit the remote control. The screen turned black. "Marcus, it's way too soon for us to reverse roles. You don't need to be the parent. I'm fine. I read the paper every morning and do the entire crossword without using the internet. I garden with your mom."

"What about a social life? Friends?"

"Sometimes."

"I saw Stewart in town the other day. He's in bad shape."

His father frowned. "He has been for a while. We haven't spoken in years. He blames me, you know."

Marcus wanted to say that was ridiculous, but Stewart Cantor lost his right hand when it was crushed during an equipment failure—while he was trying to push Quentin out of the way of falling crates. Without his interference, Marcus's father would have died.

The accident broke something in both men, but Quentin found ways to keep going, though his life was quieter than it had once been.

"While we're on the topic of not speaking for years…" Quentin changed the subject a little too casually. "I heard you hired Bree."

Marcus didn't bother asking how. One did not question the Lost Coast Harbor gossip mill. One simply accepted it as a fact of life, as inescapable as gravity.

"I had a security problem even more important than avoiding my ex-wife. She's done great work too. It's fine, Dad."

"What about her? Is she fine?" Quentin's raised eyebrows told him he expected a real answer.

He deserved one. After the accident, Marcus left school to help care for his father, but they ended up taking care of each other. With every day that Bree didn't reply to his emails and phone calls, didn't reach out to him while his father suffered, Marcus felt the best parts of himself fade. They were replaced by longing and pain and an anger he could barely recognize as his own, as he hadn't felt anything like it before. Together, he and his father put themselves back together, but it took months. He would never forget his father's suffering, no more than Quentin would forget his son's.

It was a memory he needed to hold onto. No matter how soft her lips, this was the woman who ignored him while his father lay in a hospital bed, waiting to learn if he'd ever walk again.

"She's Bree." He tugged at the knot of his tie. The room was too warm. "Same as always."

"Son…"

Marcus hurried to change the subject. "When are you coming out to tour the campus?"

"Soon. Your mom's busy trying to keep the shop afloat, and it's a forty-minute drive there and back."

His parents lived twenty minutes south of town, and the campus was twenty minutes to the north. Just far enough to be inconvenient, especially when his father didn't drive.

"Why don't you move closer to town?"

"What, and rent a one-bedroom apartment from Hastings Properties? That's all we can afford on our income." His father sneered in disgust.

Marcus shared his father's anger. After the accident, Hastings Fishing had its equipment inspected by two separate experts. Both swore there was nothing wrong with the machinery. They chalked it up to user error, and neither Quentin nor Stewart had a hope of suing for negligence. Instead, they received workmen's comp, then disability. His mother needed to quit her job to take care of her husband while his mangled legs healed. These days, she ran a small Etsy shop out of her home. Between that income and the disability checks, his parents got by, but it was a struggle.

A completely unnecessary struggle, considering their son was a freaking millionaire.

"Dad, I'll buy you a house. Any house you want, or I could build one on the campus. There's plenty of land. I'll hire you a car and driver. There's no reason for you to be stuck out here."

Quentin picked up the mug of coffee on the side table and took a long sip. "I know you mean well, but there's something about living in a place you earned, one way or another. It means more than a palace someone gives you."

"Fine. I'll tell them to stop building the castle." His father nodded in satisfaction, then Marcus moved the conversation where he'd intended it to go all along. "You'll earn it, then. Work for me."

"That's just a different form of charity."

Marcus blew out a heavy gust of air. He could be proud, but he was an amateur next to his father. "Dad, you're one of the smartest people I've ever known. You should have gone to college. You should have lived in a place with nonindustrial jobs. This isn't charity. I'm being a selfish bastard, because I know my dad will have ideas some Silicon Valley twenty-something wouldn't consider."

"That's really your pitch? A man who owns a flip phone will have a fresh take on technology?"

Marcus knew his father was tempted. He sounded like a man who wanted to be convinced.

"I don't program anymore," Quentin reminded him. "The medications they put me on…well, they help with the mobility, but my mind isn't as sharp."

"No programming. I built a holographic imaging lab."

"Like…in *Star Trek*?" He sounded both intrigued and concerned for his son's mental health.

"Sort of. Limited by twenty-first-century tech, of course. You'd be mainly testing the images, adjusting the parameters for large-scale projects. You wouldn't have to be on your feet too much, either."

Quentin's expression grew wistful. "It sounds great, but you'd need my brain. It plain doesn't work as well as it used to."

Marcus refused to accept that. "This is a safe way to test that. No machinery that requires all your attention. You can't break a hologram, Dad."

"But I don't have that kind of training." His father's protests grew weaker.

"I know. That's why you'll be a paid intern. You'll learn on the job. I've already hired a department head, and he's agreed. There's no reason to say no. Unless you're scared you can't keep up with some young kid…"

His father gave him a wry look. "Oh, the old bawk-bawk gambit. You think I'll fall for that?" Marcus waited. "If it's an entry-level job, I'll want entry-level wages."

Marcus didn't let the victory show. "Agreed, but you and Mom get full benefits. That's standard for all new employees, so don't even bother arguing. You'll take your health insurance and 401k and like it—and you'll use the insurance to find a doctor that will prescribe a better medication for you. Agreed?"

Before his father could sputter a response, Marcus clasped his dad on the shoulder and hurried from the room. "I'll have a car here next Monday," he called back, then closed the door before Quentin could change his mind.

Chapter Eight

It should have been a quiet day. Tommy was meeting with possible investors in Miami, and Rae had taken the helicopter back to Hours to solve an unexpected crisis with the latest app update.

Someone tapped on his open door, a solid, confident sound, and Marcus cursed under his breath. He was supposed to be left alone today, damn it.

His entire body tensed when he saw the man standing in his doorway, and Marcus half rose. It took more control than it should not to leap across the desk and wrap his hands around the guy's throat.

Oliver Hastings's smile faltered. "Sorry to show up like this. Your assistant wasn't at her desk."

"I gave Levi the day off."

"Sorry. All my assistants have been women, so I assumed—"

"What do you want?" Marcus made no effort to temper the hard edge of his voice, and he didn't ask the other man to sit.

Oliver's expression was determined. "I want to talk to you

about your father's accident."

Marcus leaned backward in a perfect facsimile of calm while an emotional tornado destroyed him from the inside. "What about the accident?" he managed.

Oliver moved to the chair. "Can I sit?" Marcus gave a curt nod, and Oliver settled across from him. "It shouldn't have happened."

"Didn't you hear? It was user error." Marcus spat out the words.

Oliver grimaced. "It doesn't matter. It shouldn't have happened."

A Hastings, admitting the accident was preventable? Someone was ice skating in hell.

"We had a few accidents earlier this year," Oliver said. "User error. That's the problem. It's always user error. The equipment is inspected regularly. We haven't had a machine fail in over fifteen years."

"Did you come here to reiterate that the accident was my father and Stewart's fault?"

"No! No. My father ran the company very differently than I do." Oliver's features, so clean and classic, darkened. A crack in the perfect facade. "I've hired someone to investigate all accidents from the last decade."

Marcus pressed his palms flat on the desk before he could start fidgeting. "What are you saying?"

Oliver's face was open and guileless. "If my father paid off the inspectors, I want to know. If equipment needs to be replaced, I'll do it. And if your father's accident was our fault, I want to make it right." He slid a business card across Marcus's desk. "This is the man I'm using. Feel free to double-check his credentials and contact him yourself."

Marcus tapped the card against his desk. "Why are you doing this? From what I hear, Hastings Enterprises damn near went bankrupt the last few months, and now you're risking a huge settlement?" It smelled wrong. Another Hastings trick.

Oliver rose. Though he wasn't much older than Marcus, the movement was slow, like Oliver was simply too weary to move faster. "I'm doing this because it's the right thing. I'll send you the report when it's completed. You can tell me then how you want to proceed."

As he left, Marcus couldn't think of a single thing to say. Somehow, he'd woken to an alternate universe, one where Oliver Hastings wasn't an asshole.

Of course, if it was an alternate universe, maybe Bree wasn't a bitch in this one. He ought to check. Yes, the excuse was flimsier than tissue paper, but he didn't care. She'd avoided him since their kiss in the cabin, a fact that bothered him more than it should.

He strode from his office to find hers empty. Of course it was.

He tugged at his tie. The damn thing was too tight.

Marcus returned to his office, but instead of getting back to work, he stood at the window. The sight of the redwood trees usually calmed him, but today it wasn't enough to peer at them through glass.

What was the point of being home if he was only going to see it through a window during breaks in his seventy-hour weeks?

Marcus hurried to outbuilding number three, which

housed the still-empty human resources and IT departments on the first floor—and his own apartment on the second floor. He yanked off the suit and pulled on a T-shirt, shorts, and running shoes. A hard five-mile trail run should clear his head. Give him time to figure out what to do about Rae, Oliver, and Bree.

Maybe a ten-mile run would be better.

TECHNICALLY, SHE WAS ON KELLER PROPERTY. THEREFORE, she was working on site.

She was also working on a large rock and surrounded by redwood trees. An opera by Gluck filled her ears, and she stood on the deck of a ship in the middle of the ocean, trying not to vomit.

The new virtual-reality headset had arrived that morning. It was the latest model, far more responsive to small movements than the last one, and the graphics included in the sample programs were spectacular. To her great annoyance, it did nothing to resolve her nausea issues.

It was a common problem. A lot of people's minds struggled to reconcile what their eyes saw and what their bodies felt, but it was a problem she needed to overcome. Not just so she could produce the software, but so she could use it and get the hell out of Lost Coast Harbor, if only for a week.

Ideally, before Venice was consumed by the sea.

Disgusted, she ripped the headset off, then yelped when she found Marcus standing in front of her.

The rustle of wings filled the clearing as several birds took off, unsettled by the noise.

She swallowed. Marcus could wear a suit like no man she'd

ever seen, but the expensive outfit made it easier to feel the years between them. In a pair of shorts and a zip-up hoodie, he didn't just look younger. He looked familiar.

He also looked insanely hot. His arms were covered in a thin sheen of sweat from his run. Warmth filled her body as she imagined licking his neck, the salt of his skin on her tongue.

She'd avoided him since the kiss, hoping a little distance would dim whatever spark leapt between them. With any luck, the attraction was just sense memory, her body recalling what they once shared even as her mind compiled a list of reasons they should keep three feet between their hands and lips at all time.

"How long have you been there?" she demanded.

Instead of answering, he nodded at the headset. Music poured from the headphones, though the sound was small and tinny.

Marcus opened and closed his mouth twice. "Opera?" he said at last.

She hit a key on the laptop, and the music cut off mid-note. "That surprises you?"

"Surprise is starting to feel like my default position." He sat next to her on the rock, close enough for her to feel the heat of his body, smell a hint of sweat. She squeezed her thighs together.

"A test program is installing as we speak, and I'm not charging you for time I don't work." The words came out too fast.

"I didn't think you were."

His glanced at the headset, and she hurried to cut him off

before he could ask another question. "You know I don't like being in the office. And not just because you never knock."

"I don't knock because I'm hoping to catch you doing something."

"Something?"

"You know. Demon summoning. Satanic ritual."

Bree bit back a snort. "Because I'm a witch?"

"I'm just saying. If it walks like a soulless she-devil and talks like a soulless she-devil..."

A smart woman would ignore the comment, and she was a smart woman. Despite this, she lifted her chin and said, "You were more than willing to tangle with the devil the other night."

He gave no sign that her words discomforted him. "The most dangerous devils are often attractive. They tempt you, then destroy you." The words were level, like he was repeating an inarguable fact.

He was taunting her, she knew, trying to provoke a response. This time, she wouldn't give him the satisfaction. "I've been searching for weaknesses in your original code, but it's pretty damn solid. I'm impressed."

His lips thinned at the change in subject. "A compliment?"

She tilted the laptop so he could read the screen. "This section, right here. It's genius in its simplicity. It's a shame I have to get rid of it for the new system."

He scanned the lines she indicated. "Much as I'd like to take credit, that's all Tommy."

"Really?" Bree didn't bother hiding her surprise. She knew Tommy used to program—it was how he and Marcus ended up in the same department at Berkeley—but given his current role in the company, she'd assumed he wasn't very good at it.

"It was from his senior project. Considering he spent his first three years of college sleeping late and forgetting to do his homework, it's the only reason he graduated. Then he handed it over to me in return for his role in the company."

"If he can program like this, why is he in finance?"

"He said he was burned out on code. When he didn't bankrupt us the first year, and Rae didn't crash the systems, we settled into our new jobs. Now he's having too much fun making money to ever go back."

Bree grimaced, though she understood the appeal. Money was tidy. Placed in expenditures and income columns, it made sense. Programming languages didn't behave themselves. Bugs popped up in random places. Clever hackers were never more than two steps behind. Though lines of code appeared orderly, nothing about the work itself was neat.

But those lines of code added up to something. With letters and numbers, she could create entire worlds.

Bree switched to a different program, and a blueprint filled the screen. "What's in Asgard?"

"Huh?"

"Until you come up with a better name than outbuilding number four, that's what I'm calling it. If you're wondering, the main building's Olympus, and the others are Narnia, Oz, and Cleveland."

"Cleveland?"

"I ran out of ideas. So what's in it? The specs are vague, but the building eats a tremendous amount of power. If you weren't using solar panels, I'd give you grief about being wasteful."

"You hacked…"

"Of course I hacked your building plans. I was bored. The less information I found, the more I wanted to know."

"And you're annoyed because I don't knock?"

She shrugged without the slightest hint of shame.

"Why did you want the building specs?"

"Because I don't know what's there, and I don't like not knowing things. Give me a tour."

"No."

"Why not?"

Marcus rose, and his hand twitched toward her, like he was going to offer to help her up and remembered at the last moment that he no longer helped her do anything. A pang of disappointment cut her.

"How badly do you want to know?"

He was trying for leverage. She said nothing, but the way he studied her, with a hint of amusement lurking in his eyes, he knew exactly how curious she was.

"I'll make you a deal," he said at last. "I'll show you outbuilding number four if you answer one question for me."

Bree thought quickly. "What question?"

"I haven't decided yet. You'll have to risk it."

One question, for the answer to a mystery. Over the years, Bree had become an expert at honestly answering direct questions without revealing a single truth.

She rose and brushed off her jeans. "Show me what you've got."

CHAPTER NINE

The building specs for Asgard had been frustratingly vague. Bree half-expected a rock-climbing wall or a dumping ground for leftover construction materials. Instead, she found a building made with such advanced tech it could have come from the future.

The first room was filled with computers, projectors, and a collection of glass panels, some of which had been combined to form a single piece. "This is where my dad will work. Only half days at first."

She stepped into the space. Lines formed between her brows as she spun around in confusion. "What is this?"

One of the computers was left on. Marcus punched a few keys, and a perfect 3-D image of a puppy filled the center of the room.

Bree squeaked at the sight. "That's not even fair. I want to pet it."

A second later, the puppy morphed into a gorgeous chestnut horse. She crouched and peered at the image, trying to find any flaw, but there were none. Bree would never mistake it for a real animal—without the sound of hooves shuffling on the ground or the unmistakable smell of horse, her mind couldn't be fooled—but the appearance was remarkable.

"Why on earth do you have a lab for holographic animals?"

Marcus turned off the image. "It's not just animals. We're working with a lot of holographic images."

"But why?"

"You'll see," he said, frustratingly vague.

"What's your dad's role here? I know you learned a lot from him, but isn't this outside his specialty?"

"It is, but the stubborn bastard refuses to work with machines now, and the meds they put him on to manage his pain make his brain too fuzzy to program. That's what he says, anyway."

"You don't believe him?"

"I don't think he's lying. I just don't think he's tried very hard after the accident. He needs a push. He'll do simple tasks to start, but he used to love a mental challenge. I'm hoping that once he understands what's possible, he'll want to do more."

He walked away, and she followed him to the lab across the hall.

In the next room, she pointed to a red button. "What does this do?"

"Don't push that."

Bree didn't bother to hide her amusement. "You have a big red button that you tell me *not* to push? Does it blow something up? Because if not, you know I'm pushing it as soon as your back is turned."

Marcus's expression was long-suffering, but she thought

she caught a hint of a smile. Because come on. It was a big red button. Anyone would want to push it.

"Fine." He made a few adjustments on a console, then stepped outside. "Do your worst."

She knew she was walking into a trap, but she couldn't help herself. With a grin, she pushed the button, then shrieked as the temperature in the room plummeted. She hit it a second time, but nothing changed.

Bree rushed from the room, sighing in relief at the warmth of the hallway. Marcus leaned against the wall with an evil smile. "Feel better now that you know what it does?"

She shivered and glared at him. "It's going to be hard to finish the work when my fingers fall off due to frostbite."

"It's not usually that cold. I tweaked it a little. But you wanted to push the button…" He removed his hoodie and held it out to her. "It's only a little sweaty, I promise."

Bree knew exactly how sweaty Marcus had been from his earlier run. "I'm fine."

Now he only wore shorts and a white T-shirt that stretched tight across his chest and biceps. She dropped her gaze, only to discover it fit just as well across his abs.

He pressed a button on the wall, and the hallway grew silent as the room's equipment stopped working. "It would have turned off on its own in another few seconds," he assured her. "Employees complain if their work conditions cause hypothermia."

She cautiously stepped back to the doorway. "What the hell does this have to do with a dating company?"

"Nothing at all. I'm playing with climate controls. I want to replicate a range of environments."

"Why?"

"You'll see."

"I don't get it. I know you planned to hire Quentin, but why didn't you create a separate company? Because you have got to be the first dating app/hologram company in the world."

"A company should diversify." Instead of elaborating, Marcus led her upstairs. "Come on. I only have an hour before I need to shower and change for my next meeting."

She walked several steps below him. Her libido took over. It was a damn fine view. His legs were tanned from regular runs and dusted with a light coating of hair. In an hour, those legs would be wet, rivulets charting a course across his hamstrings, over the soft skin at the back of his knees, down his rounded calf muscle...

Bree stumbled, and she cursed herself. She had to get a grip. Yes, he was hotter than the surface of the sun, but they had too much history for her to think about him like this. It couldn't lead anywhere good.

It might lead to another kiss.

No. The first kiss had been a mistake. Her brain and her body really needed to get on the same page. "I thought you tech guys dressed down. Why are you usually in suits?"

"Because I look good in them."

"I know I'm behind you, but you heard my eyes roll, right?"

Marcus reached the top of the stairs and waited for her to join him. "Early in my career, I was invited to some political fundraiser. There were lots of networking opportunities, so I wore the most expensive suit I could afford. That was the first photo that got picked up by the AP. It was when I stopped being just another tech guy and became Marcus Keller."

"You say that like there should be a trademark symbol after your name."

"Might as well be. The suits became part of my brand."

"Like Jobs's turtlenecks or Zuckerberg's gray hoodie."

"Exactly."

"But even in Lost Coast Harbor? There aren't any paparazzi hanging out in The Sweet Spot or Donnelly's."

"I guess old habits die hard." The air between them seemed to thicken. Marcus swallowed and gestured for them to walk down the hall. "It also became part of the Hours brand, a small distinction in the casual Silicon Valley environment. This afternoon I have a video conference with some New York guys who expect to see me in the suit."

"For the IPO?"

"Yeah. If I'd known how many meetings this would require, I don't think the company would have ever left my dorm room."

"It's video, right? If you stay seated, you can do it in your underwear." It was the wrong thing to say. She wondered if wealthy Marcus still wore white boxer briefs, or if he'd moved on to designer silk.

Marcus glanced over his shoulder, his eyes more gray than blue. She wasn't the only one whose thoughts had derailed.

Mentally, Bree dressed him quickly. "Then why are you doing it, if it means a life in suits and endless meetings with New York moneymen?"

"Because in two weeks, I'll quadruple my fortune."

That wasn't news. "Aren't you already richer than God?"

"I do okay," he said. "Though I lease my helicopter."

She snorted. "Such deprivation. Seriously, why? You'll end up with a board that tries to make decisions for you, and every decision is based around making more money. What happens when that goes against the spirit of Hours?"

Marcus turned to face her. "What, exactly, do you think is the spirit of Hours?"

Bree recognized the challenge, the suggestion that she couldn't really know what he cared about. She lifted her chin. "The belief that we're never more than an hour away from a true connection. That the smallest things—a fondness for modern art and a free Tuesday afternoon—can change someone's life forever, and sometimes people need to be pointed toward that connection. Have I got it about right?"

They'd reached a closed door at the end of the hallway, but Marcus didn't open it. "That's not going to change. No one's going to buy stock in a company, then dismantle its cornerstone product."

"No, but they might find for new ways to monetize dates. Make sponsorship deals with chain restaurants, for instance."

"That's ridiculous." Except it wasn't out of the realm of possibility, and his uneasy expression suggested she'd hit a nerve. "It doesn't matter. I'll be the CEO."

Unless someone mounted a hostile takeover. Unless the board pushed him out because they believed profits could be higher. If it could happen to Steve Jobs, it could happen to anyone. She said none of this. Marcus knew the risks.

"God, wouldn't that be awful?" He shook his head. "A go-kart date sponsored by Chevrolet? Someone would try to make it happen, wouldn't they?"

"Without a doubt."

Marcus withdrew a small notepad and pen from his pocket, and jotted something down. "Note to self: talk to Rae about ways to prevent farmer's market dates sponsored by pesticide companies." He glanced at Bree. "Satisfied?"

"Not even close. I shouldn't have been the one to remind you of this. It should have been your first thought when you planned the IPO. Why are you doing this?"

A muscle ticked in his jaw. "It's time. This is what I've been working toward for years. The company's ready."

"Are you sure? Because from what I can see, you're trying to create a whole other company here in Asgard. Whatever's waiting behind that door, I'd bet my signed copy of the first Harry Potter book it has nothing to do with a dating app."

His expression relaxed. "That's where you're wrong." Marcus pushed open the door.

Bree stepped into the room and tried to understand his excitement. It was a large, white room. No furniture. No equipment. There appeared to be speakers and vents in the ceiling, but otherwise the room was entirely plain. "What am I supposed to be seeing?"

"The official name is the Programmable Reality and Immersible Space Mechanism." He tapped on one of the wall panels, and it sprang open to reveal a complicated collection of monitors and switches. Marcus flipped a few levers and tapped the screen. "Or Prism."

The room darkened, and the temperature dropped. Bree gasped as the walls transformed into the night sky—but this was no planetarium. She wasn't simply viewing the stars. She was viewing the stars as they would appear from the moon.

Not too far away, Earth hovered in the middle of a black sky. The floor appeared to change, rising and falling until it created a more rugged surface.

Marcus's voice stretched to her through the dark room. "I can't manage zero gravity. Yet." He was joking, but Bree wouldn't be surprised it was on his to-do list. "There's a Mars sequence too. These are the defaults. They're pretty useless, because I don't plan on creating products for Martians, but they do impress people."

She heard the beeps of buttons being pushed. The moon vanished, the temperature rose, and she found herself standing in the middle of a farm, surrounded by animals—including the dog and horse from downstairs. "How did you do this?" she marveled.

Marcus joined her. "I've been working on it for three years now, whenever I got a chance. I had a lot of help, of course. This is what the tabloids didn't see."

She wandered the room, her hands outstretched. She knew the wall existed, but the image was seamless, and she could almost imagine that the pasture stretched as far as the horizon. "Projectors, temperature controls, adjustable surfaces…not a bad start."

A project like this, it wasn't the sort of thing one did on a weekend. Even if Marcus had only been the project manager, in charge of overseeing other people's work, it would have been a full-time job.

It wasn't just that the tabloids didn't see Prism. The life the tabloids reported couldn't have existed, not if he was working on this. No one had time to gallivant with models and hang out on a yacht in the Mediterranean if they were trying to reinvent holographic technology. All those articles, all the mentions on gossip pages… "They were photo ops," she murmured. Bree waved off his questioning look. "One more time, how does this connect to Hours?"

"Not everyone wants to date in their hometown." Another couple beeps, and the farm disappeared, becoming a cafe in Paris. The images didn't only fill the surrounding screens. Three-dimensional holograms projected all around her. Tables filled with food, waiters weaving between the patrons.

The scents hit her first—chocolate, the faint hint of cigarette smoke, a burst of exhaust from a passing bus—and then the sounds. Voices. Horns. The squeal of brakes surrounded her, until she couldn't identify where the noise was coming from. There were too many speakers. They were everywhere. Bree felt the creature that lived inside her claw at her chest.

"Also audio and scents." Marcus sounded so pleased. "They have their own rooms downstairs. Imagine being able to hit a few buttons and have your dream date on command. A limited version of it, but still. It's hard to beat that view." Marcus spun her toward another wall, where the Eiffel Tower rose above the Seine.

She tried to keep a smile on her face. It wasn't real. She passed her hand through the chest of a man laughing uproariously. He didn't exist. None of this was really here. In that way, it was no different from her work on Venice, but on a much larger scale.

Except the point of her work was to start slow. A single waiter. One other table. This was everything, all at once. Too many voices, too many people, too much noise. Too much.

Bree took long, open-mouthed breaths, but it wasn't

enough. The weight grew on her chest, spreading and tightening with every honking car. Every excited shout. Someone passed by her, so close she felt the person brush her sleeve. Her nails dug into her palms. Bree tried telling herself it was just a fan hitting her shirt, but her body no longer cared. Adrenaline punched through her, demanding she run. Hide.

"Turn it off." Her voice sounded small in her own ears. "Turn it off," she repeated, louder.

Paris disappeared, and once again she stood in a white room with Marcus. When she was able to school her features into a calm mask, she turned back to him.

"That's impressive," she said. "Though you've got a ways to go before you can program Klingon battles on the *Enterprise*." She slid her hand into her purse, trying to appear nonchalant as she searched for the medication bottle. Just half a tablet would do. Enough to ease the stress and the sudden fear assaulting her.

Marcus's jaw tightened as he watched her hand dig through her bag. "We're nowhere near the technology to create mass. A holodeck is a long way in the future. I'm having a range of furniture created, though. That's one of the projects downstairs. The holographic imaging lab will create the visuals, and they're working on mirrored chairs and tables that will project whatever the program requires. I'd say it's a pretty impressive toy."

There was a hint of defensiveness in his tone, and Bree knew her reaction was too muted. What he'd shown her was extraordinary. She should be exclaiming over his accomplishments, bombarding him with questions. Instead, she was trying to keep breathing.

"It's amazing." Her voice was level. Controlled. If she'd learned anything over the last decade, it was how to cover up when she was falling apart. She dug a thumbnail into one of the pills, cutting it in half, then palmed it and withdrew her hand from her purse. She spun away from him long enough to pop it in her mouth and swallow it dry. "It's a lot more than a toy."

The device was remarkable. It would be wasted setting up dates for people who wanted to pretend they were in Paris for an hour.

"For now, it is. After years of only thinking about building the company, I wanted something that felt like fun again."

She barely heard him. Bree peeked at her phone, noting the time. Fifteen minutes till the pill would kick in and her chest would loosen. Fifteen minutes until her body would stop expecting an attack. She needed to go home. Lock the door, turn off the phone, and hit the reset button on her overloaded brain.

She glanced around the room stark white room. It was safe. She knew it, but she couldn't believe it. "You're lucky to have the opportunity to do this." The words sounded artificial, like she didn't even know the language she was speaking. "Most people don't get what they want."

She managed a weak smile in his direction, then walked away, trying to outrun the monster that had chased her for years.

CHAPTER TEN

With a curse, Marcus wrenched off the black bow tie. "Tommy, how the fuck do you tie these things?"

His friend emerged from the walk-in closet. At some point, Marcus meant to buy a house in town, but he was also realistic enough to know there'd be many nights he didn't come home. Hence, the large apartment on the second story of Narnia. *Outbuilding number three,* he reminded himself.

"First," Tommy said, "you remember that you're not thirty yet and stop trying to wear a classic tux." He handed Marcus a thin silk tie and a different shirt. "You're supposed to be impressing these guys with your youthful energy."

Marcus took the clothes with a grimace. His friend was right. Never before had Marcus even considered wearing a traditional tux.

But when he'd picked his outfit, some stupid part of his brain remembered that Bree used to love Bond movies—especially the old ones with Sean Connery, who knew how to wear a classic tux.

Obviously, he was a masochist. She refused to give him a single hint that she was impressed with everything he'd accomplished. Here he stood, in the middle of an apartment filled with the kind of luxuries found in a Fifth Avenue condo, desperately trying to impress a woman who lived in a small cabin, and she plain didn't care. His money meant nothing to her. Even worse, his achievements meant nothing to her. He'd finally won, and it turned out victory didn't matter if he was the only one who noticed.

When he showed her Prism, she'd called his baby "fun," and then she checked her damn phone. *Checked her phone.*

He was fucking done expecting something from her that she was incapable of giving. She'd agreed to answer a single question if he showed her the holographic labs, but he had no idea what to ask. He doubted she could tell him why she was so evil or how he could fucking forget about her once and for all.

Marcus tore off his shirt and replaced it with a silk one with just a hint of blue. He knotted the slim tie. "Does this feel as surreal for you as it does for me?"

Tommy shook his head. Not in disagreement, but in bewilderment. "It's bizarre. Three guys from high school grabbed me in the market and asked how they could get an invitation."

"Were you friends?"

"They used to give me wedgies in gym."

"Next time, tell them they're welcome to come. We could use more cater waiters."

Tommy's bark of laughter contained little humor. "I just can't get used to it. I know you love this town, God knows why, but I left tire tracks on my way out."

"It's home. I don't know how else to put it. It helps that

my parents are here, but I think I'd want to live here even if they didn't."

"Are they coming tonight?"

"My dad is. My mom isn't a big fan of parties." He hesitated. "Have you talked to your dad yet?"

Tommy tensed. "No."

"You used to be close, right?" Marcus tried not to push, but it pained him to know Tommy was struggling. He couldn't imagine how he'd feel if Quentin was hurting as much as Stewart clearly was.

Tommy gave a noncommittal shrug and moved toward the window. "People are arriving. You should get downstairs."

Marcus gave himself one last look in the mirror. It wasn't James Bond, but bespoke Prada was a decent compromise. "Tommy, remind me who I need to impress tonight."

"Everyone, of course. This is about creating the impression that we have everything under control. We're building investor confidence right before the IPO. Just be the same asshole who got cover stories on national magazines. You know, the one who dates actresses and socialites. They'll eat it up."

Marcus's laugh was hollow. Tommy didn't notice. "But make sure you hit up the Gotham Investments group. They flew out to examine the campus, and they've been one of the louder skeptics about your plan. Where they go, the rest of the finance world follows. If you convince them of your brilliance, you'll be set. Plus, they sent Helen Barker, who's pretty easy on the eyes."

Marcus tried to muster some enthusiasm. He'd met Helen before. In addition to being attractive, she was smart and influential—and she'd made no secret of her attraction to him. Maybe if he dated someone new, Bree would stop assaulting his thoughts at all hours.

Because if he didn't get some peace soon, he'd be forced to admit that Tommy was right, and returning to Lost Coast Harbor had been a mistake.

THE PARTY WAS LIMITED TO THE MAIN BUILDING, THOUGH several tours were scheduled for those who wished to view the rest of the campus. The tours didn't include the interior of Asgard. This wasn't the time to confuse investors with holographic imaging.

Outbuilding number four, damn it.

He didn't spot Bree when he entered, but the party was already underway. That's what happened when you offered a bunch of twentysomethings a trip on a private jet, then provided free booze. No one was going to make other plans. Most of his employees from the Mountain View office were present, and two Los Angeles investors walked through the front door less than five minutes after he arrived.

Marcus set his shoulders and mentally turned his charm switch to on.

Before he could take a step toward the investors, the crowd parted and Bree walked confidently across the room. His heart leapt, his breathing grew shallow, and years of denial were obliterated in a single moment.

Damn it. He'd never be done. He might be able to move on, even create a satisfying life, but he'd never be done. No acknowledgment of his success, no apology, would ever be enough. Maybe closure wasn't an option for them. When their marriage ended, she hadn't left an open door, but she'd sure as hell left an open wound. The best he could do was affix a thick bandage and try not to poke at it too much.

She was perfectly, essentially Bree. Her hair was brushed to the side and curled under in a messy bun. Her black eyeliner was a little heavier than usual.

Her dress had a single strap that crossed her left shoulder, and the bottom was knee-length black tulle. If she'd stopped there, she would have been dressed appropriately.

But her top was black and white stripes in a sea of subdued colors, and the skirt was cinched in with a thick black belt.

Also, she was wearing combat boots.

Marcus bit back an amazed laugh, unsure if he wanted to throttle or high-five her.

The Los Angeles couple could wait.

Marcus's steps devoured the distance between him and Bree. He clamped his hand around her elbow and guided her from the room.

"What are you doing?" she demanded.

He kept his gaze straight ahead. "We need to talk."

They moved down the hall until he found an empty conference room. Marcus urged her inside, shut the door behind them, and hit the button to darken the windows.

"What the hell are you wearing? The party's black tie."

Bree shrugged. "This is Vivienne Westwood. More or less."

"And the boots?"

"Are comfortable." She kept her chin up.

Marcus tugged hard at his tie before remembering that

he needed to look put together. "Of course you ignored the dress code. Why wouldn't you?"

"I didn't ask to be invited to this party. I definitely didn't agree to cocktail dresses and high heels."

"I need you here. I'm announcing the new security system in two hours. I'm mentioning you by name and pointing you out. Hell, I might shine a spotlight on you. Tonight, you represent Hours. Everyone at the party will know our network is being updated by one of the country's foremost security experts. That's the kind of thing investors want to hear."

He swore Bree shuddered at the thought. "I won't be here in two hours."

"Why the hell not?"

"I don't need to be present. They'll know my name. Just say I designed it."

"Stay until the announcement. Two hours. I'll throw in a mint *Ms. Marvel* #1," he added, when she remained unconvinced.

She gnawed on her lip. "Which variant?"

"Any of them."

Her chest rose on an inhale, and his gaze dropped to the skin revealed by her dress. Shoulders, clavicle, the hint of cleavage.

Bree didn't notice his slip. If anything, she withdrew, disappearing into her thoughts. "Can you make the announcement in thirty minutes?"

Something was off. "Bree, what's going on?"

The door was thrown open. "Marcus, if you don't get your butt out here, Helen Barker is going to leave early with your head of marketing. Come save our money, please." Tommy gave Bree an apologetic half shrug.

Marcus gritted his teeth at the interruption. "I'll be right out."

Tommy walked away, but he left the door open.

Bree wore her default expression. Strong and determined. Ready for whatever the world threw at her. Whatever weakness he thought he'd glimpsed a moment ago, there was no sign of it now.

"Thirty minutes," she reminded him, and left the room.

CHAPTER ELEVEN

A quarter of an hour later, Bree wanted to crawl out of her skin. With every passing minute, more people arrived through the front door. Some were sedate, gliding across the room with the calm confidence of old money, but far more were upbeat, even exuberant as they greeted friends and exclaimed over the new buildings.

The volume rose, voices and music, the clink of glasses, and it became harder to navigate between people. For the first time, she regretted not wearing heels, six-inch platforms that would help her see over the crowd. At five-seven, she wasn't short, but she was surrounded by tall men and women in towering stilettos. As the room filled, she began to feel trapped. Caged.

Before she'd agreed to attend, Marcus had assured her a few locals would be present, but she didn't spot any familiar faces. Strangers surrounded her.

She wasn't drinking, though she knew a glass of wine would help. It would relax her body and calm her mind until she was no longer aware of every single sound and smell and touch. She would stop trying to identify all possible threats.

But Bree did her best not to use alcohol as medication. She'd done that her first two years of college. Hell, even high school. She would drink enough to forget her reservations and have a bit of fun. No one ever noticed she was self-medicating—including her. She figured that out years later.

When all this was over, she'd call Maddie and Erin and arrange a girls' night at Donnelly's, complete with large cocktails and tipsy conversation, because that was safe. Donnelly's was filled with people she knew. They were predictable, and they would take care of her if anything went wrong. It wasn't so hard, being out with friends. This roomful of strangers was anything but safe.

Bree pinned a smile on her face and tried to focus on the person in front of her.

He was the sixth guest to accost her since she emerged from the conference room. She was well-known in the tech world, and too many people wanted to meet her. They were all nice, but each additional minute of small talk wore on her shields a tiny bit more. Every nerve felt raw. Exposed.

There was no way she'd make it another fifteen minutes. She needed to find Marcus. She felt ill, or she needed to help a friend, or Adam was locked out and needed her spare key. Bree had dozens of those excuses lined up, because over the years she'd used all of them at least once.

Even in the crowded party, she found Marcus straightaway. It wasn't just that he was one of the taller men, or that his shoulders took up a little more space than the others. He moved with a confidence few possessed, the absolute certainty that he mattered. It wasn't just here, where he literally owned the room. He'd carried himself the same way at Donnelly's, or even when he worked quietly in his office. Despite everything that had passed between them, she was happy for him, that he'd found such confidence after his years as an uncertain teenager.

He was talking to someone. Bree found an empty corner away from the speakers, and she allowed herself the rare pleasure of watching Marcus when he wouldn't know. The tension didn't vanish, but it eased a bit. She tried finding a sense of calm in his profile, with its strong nose and firm chin.

Unbidden, a memory hit her of the exact moment she'd realized Marcus Keller was beautiful. Before that, she hadn't thought of him as ugly. She simply hadn't noticed him as anything other than a rival. Throughout high school, she and Maddie had been proud members of the bad girls' club. Maddie dated Charlie, the kind of guy who wore black leather and rode a motorcycle, and Bree hung out with a few of Charlie's friends. Most of them were older guys, because Bree was certain she was too smart and mature to date some high school kid.

By Tahoe, Marcus was no longer in high school.

August in the Sierras could be hot, and Bree had spent most of that first day napping in an effort to avoid the high temps. By the time she woke up, her friends had wandered off to a nightclub on the south shore, ready to test their fake IDs in a town where no one knew them.

She didn't mind the quiet. Bree grabbed a book and an iced tea and headed for the rooftop deck.

Marcus had already been there, reading the same book. Without thinking about it, she took the seat next to him. He nodded at her, silently acknowledging her presence, though she thought he gripped his book a little tighter.

"Why aren't you with the others?" she asked.

He appeared vaguely horrified at the thought. "Because at some point, one of the popular girls will decide to be magnanimous and flirt with the nerd to prove high school cliques no longer matter. Then they will make me dance."

Unexpected laughter burst from her. "They're not all bad." She glanced at Marcus, chuckling at the idea that a cheerleader would pity flirt with him, and she stopped laughing as quickly as she started. For the first time in years, she looked at him. Really looked.

It turned out Marcus Keller was a late bloomer. Sophomore year, he was so short he could have passed for a middle school student. Then he'd sprouted ten inches over the next two years. Puberty hadn't been kind to him. He wasn't just skinny. He'd been gangly, a stretched-out boy whose muscles hadn't begun to catch up to his bones. His gait was awkward, like he was a stranger in his own body, and he was terrible at every sport he was forced to play. Once his hormones began working, they tried making up for lost time with a face covered in acne.

And because everyone knew Marcus had a crush on Bree, she did her best not to encourage him. She only talked to him when a school project required it. She avoided any scenario that might lead to him asking her out, because Marcus was a nice enough guy, and she preferred not to hurt him.

This time, Bree saw someone new. His skin had cleared, only leaving behind a small scar or two. With no red bumps to distract her, she finally noticed his face, with its bold cheekbones and solid jaw and eyes that looked like a winter sky.

Though no one would call him buff yet, he'd lost his scarecrow appearance and finally figured out how to move in his own body. The man he would become was beginning to emerge, and he was stunning. When Marcus smiled at her, for the first time she thought it might not be so terrible if he asked her out.

When Maddie called the hotel that night to ask Bree to join the group, Bree told her she was too tired.

Twelve hours later, she was married.

These days, there were few signs of the boy he'd once been. There'd been a delicacy to his younger self that was missing now. Back then, she could hold her own when they play wrestled together. There was nothing gentle about the man standing across the room, and Bree imagined she'd need to spend a year in Niall Donnelly's martial arts studio before she had a chance of pinning Marcus again.

Not that she wanted to spar with Marcus. Or wrestle. Or fight for who got to be on top. Her body warmed at the thought, but her body was a notorious liar.

His cheekbones were just a little too sharp, even with the added weight. Her gaze drifted past the brown hair to his neck, following the curve of skin as it disappeared into his collar. Across his shoulder, down his arm to the hand that was…touching another woman?

If she were a cartoon, steam would have emerged from her ears. Marcus showed up in town, announced they were married, kissed her, brought up every memory she'd worked so hard to bury…and now he wandered around with his hands on some woman's back? Not just the back, either. The lower back, his fingers splayed dangerously close to her ass.

Her eyes narrowed as his hand pressed against the woman, guiding her toward another group of people.

Did he invite a *date*?

It was a slap in the face.

The world silenced. The noise of the party dimmed. All she could see was Marcus's left hand on some brunette's back, his third finger completely bare.

It was wrong. Everything about that image was wrong. This moment, this life, the choices she'd made. They were all wrong.

She blinked, and the world roared back. Her brain picked out every sound, every movement. Nothing was too small to catch her attention. Her mind overloaded. She was under attack.

"Excuse me." She pushed past the group standing near her. Her words were barely audible, a small burst of breath as she moved away.

If she could get to her office, she'd be safe. It was empty. It had dark walls and a door that locked.

Bree navigated the maze of people, her breathing shallow as she searched for openings between the bodies. One person rested a hand on her forearm, trying to draw her attention. She managed a weak smile and didn't wrench her arm back, and that small act of acceptable behavior felt like a battle won.

At last she reached the stairs. A few people strolled past her, and she slowed her pace until she neared the top. As soon as her path was clear, she picked up speed, jogging up the final steps. She turned the corner to the next flight and sprinted to the third floor.

It was deserted. She raced for her office, slamming the door behind her and leaning against it, breathing hard. Adrenaline pounded through her body, and she fought tears of both desperation and anger.

She was Bree fucking Rogers. Certified badass. She went after what she wanted and she got it. Everyone knew that.

And she couldn't make it through an entire party without triggering the fight-or-flight response.

A bottle of antianxiety pills was in the top drawer of her desk, but she didn't want to take another so soon after the incident in Prism. She was trying to decrease her dependence on the damn things.

Twice in one week. Goddamn it. She needed to make an appointment with her psychiatrist to confirm she didn't need to adjust her meds. It was a pain in the ass, driving out of town each time, but it was better than another panic attack.

She slid to the floor and inhaled through her nose, long and slow. She pushed the air through her lips, listening to the gentle hiss, and repeated the action.

Five breaths later, the panic began to recede. The breathing exercises didn't heal her, not exactly, but the weight on her chest lessened. The shot of adrenaline was exhausting, and she knew the crash was on its way.

There was a soft rap on the door. "Bree? Can I come in?"

Her heart leapt, her raw nerves bursting to life at Marcus's voice. She wiped under her eyes in an effort to clean up the smeared liner, then rose to standing. She was pleased to find that her legs were steady.

With one last deep inhale, she swung the door open,

afraid of the anger she'd see. She'd agreed to wait a measly thirty minutes, and she hadn't even been able to manage that.

Instead of rage or even irritation, there was only concern. "Tell me what's wrong," he commanded.

Bree opened her mouth, ready to offer the same denial she always did. The same promise that she was completely fine.

But the way he studied her made her think this man would see straight through her lies, though he never had before.

It would almost be a blessing to tell someone else, but she hesitated.

Then he cupped her cheeks and tilted her face up with such tenderness, and he whispered, "Whatever it is, you can tell me. We agreed I could ask one question. This is it. What's wrong?"

When Bree opened her mouth, the truth rested on her tongue.

Wailing filled the halls. Lights flashed. She stumbled backwards, the little calm she'd managed to gather vanishing in a rush. Bree shuddered, her shoulders folding in, trying to protect her upper body.

Noise came from outside the building, voices growing louder. Marcus hurried into the hallway.

"Goddamn it." He bit out the words, each one coated in thick rage. He called back to her. "We have to go, Bree. It's a fire."

CHAPTER TWELVE

Bree appeared frozen. Marcus strode back to her office and held out his hand. "We have to leave," he repeated.

She snapped into motion, but instead of moving toward the door, she spun toward her computer.

"What are you doing?" he demanded.

"It's Cleveland. I mean, outbuilding number one. The dorms." She turned the monitor to face him, and his stomach clenched. Flames were consuming the first floor. "It shouldn't spread beyond the building. There's no wind, and the sprinklers will suppress it. The fire department is on their way, but…"

"But they won't get here for fifteen minutes."

"There could be people inside. The last tour left twenty minutes ago."

Horror pressed on him. "I need to go."

The fear in her eyes matched his own. "I know." She stepped around the desk and took the hand he held out. Bree squeezed it a little too hard. "Be safe. No heroics, okay?"

Marcus returned the squeeze. "Stay here. Please."

To his surprise, she didn't argue.

He raced down the hall and from the building. The dorms were more than a quarter mile from the main building. Even from here, he could see the crackling flames. They were beginning their assault on the second floor. The door to the common room was open, and as he watched, the draperies, the couch, even the Ping-Pong table turned black.

Two figures emerged from the front door. "Tommy!" He ran toward his friend, who was stumbling away from the building with his arm wrapped around Rae. Her dark hair was wild, and her skin was slick with sweat. Marcus moved to support her other side, but Tommy pulled away.

"Get your dad." His friend's voice was rough. "He was in the kitchen."

Marcus didn't remember making a decision, or moving, or even crossing the threshold of the burning building. Behind him, people shouted warnings. The voices were distorted, like his head was underwater. Grasping fingers tugged at his sleeve, but he wrenched free and stepped into the flames.

Heat assailed him, unbearable in its intensity, but the smoke was worse. He crouched, trying to get below the worst of it. Flames rose on either side of him, and he squinted through the haze, searching for a safe path.

There wasn't one. Flames danced gleefully through the common room. An ear-splitting crack was the only warning he got before a bookshelf on his right collapsed. Marcus was covered in a shower of sparks, and a hungry flame licked at his leather shoes. Water poured from the sprinklers in the ceiling, but it was a drop to the vast swell of flames.

The corridors on either side led to emergency exits, but the fire ran down the length of the hallway.

Through the thick smoke, he could just make out the kitchen door ahead. It was closed. Marcus wrenched off his jacket and used it to cover the metal door handle. He pushed it open. The flames hadn't consumed the room yet, but they pounded at his back, eager to follow him. "Dad?" he rasped.

A noise came from his left. His father had maneuvered himself to a floor-to-ceiling window and was bashing one of his crutches against the glass. The room was soaking wet from the sprinklers, and his father's hands were slippery.

Another loud crash. Marcus spun as another row of shelves toppled. Books sacrificed themselves to the fire, the flames growing more ravenous with each page devoured. There was no path back. He slammed the door shut, locking the flames on the other side and buying them a few more minutes.

Quentin's shoulders drooped when he caught sight of Marcus, relief for himself mingled with fear for his son. "Marcus…"

"It's okay, Dad." He grabbed a fire extinguisher from the wall. "No one's dying today."

They didn't say anything else. Smoke was creeping under the kitchen door, and they saved their oxygen.

None of the downstairs windows opened because of security concerns. Marcus thought that might have been the stupidest building decision ever made. He bashed the butt of the fire extinguisher into the glass. Each time he hit, the impact slammed into his arm and shoulder, the bones and muscles shuddering.

Panic welled in his chest. Double-paned energy-resistant secure glass. What the fuck had he been thinking?

He'd been thinking the sprinklers would do their job, but

this fire was immense. It had grown too fast. Unnaturally fast.

With a wordless scream, he swung the fire extinguisher. A small fracture appeared, the size of a quarter. Over and over, he pounded the metal into the glass. The crack widened, then became a cobweb of broken lines. At last, it shattered.

Air rushed in, and both men took long, ragged breaths. Marcus climbed through the window. A jagged piece of glass tore his pants. He reached for his father's hands and half carried, half dragged him outside. Quentin groaned as the cool air hit him.

A siren wailed, growing louder with each second.

"I smelled…" Quentin broke off, coughing.

"I know. It's okay, Dad. I've got you." He placed one hand under his father's knees and lifted. His father was heavier than he remembered. By the time they made it around the building, his arms were straining with the effort.

"Bring us water," he called as soon as others came into sight. A large group of worried onlookers had gathered to observe the building burn.

Rae reached them first. "Are you hurt?" she asked. "I was showing your dad the dorms, and he wandered off to find the common spaces, and then…" Her voice was wild, guilt and panic mixed together.

"We're fine." He didn't go into more detail, but he rested his hand on Rae's arm, a small gesture to assure her she wasn't at fault. Her grimace told him she wasn't convinced. "What about the last tour?"

"They were in outbuilding two. No one was hurt."

"Oz."

"What?" She peered at him like she was worried about oxygen deprivation.

"Never mind." A fire truck barreled up the main drive, and Marcus guided Quentin toward it. He didn't recognize the first guy off the truck, but he grabbed the man's wrist. "Take care of my dad," he ordered.

The firefighter blinked at him, but the next one off was Captain Davis, who had enough brains to help his father to the side of the truck. "I've got him, Marcus."

You better. It took restraint, but he didn't say it aloud. He didn't care if the building burned to the ground while the firefighters confirmed his dad hadn't been harmed in the fire.

Tommy stood at his side and watched as they wrapped a blanket around Quentin. He breathed a heavy sigh of relief. "Thank God." He repeated the words several more times.

Marcus clapped him on the shoulder. "Get Rae checked out. You too."

"What about you? You look like hell."

He turned his head just enough to stare Tommy down.

His friend shrugged. "Or be really macho and do nothing."

"Could anyone else still be in there?" Given the height of the flames, it would be suicide to go back in.

Rae overheard. She wiped sweat from her forehead, leaving a long smear of ash. "The entire party is standing behind us. No one's unaccounted for."

"What the hell happened?" Tommy shook his head. "I thought the building went through every safety check known to man."

"Fire the builder. Or sue him. Or feed him to lions. I

don't give a fuck, but make him pay. The sprinklers didn't do a damn thing."

"You think it was electric?"

"No." Marcus ground his teeth. The fire was too large and too tidy. A single line of flames from one side door to the common room, and from there to the second exit. Like someone had run through the ground floor with a can of gasoline. He'd talk to his father once he was checked out, but Marcus thought he knew what Quentin had been trying to say. He'd smelled gas.

Tommy glanced over his shoulder at the throng of investors. "It's going to be hard to convince them everything's under control now." The words were casual, but his expression was hard. "I better do damage control." He headed toward the group, determined to salvage whatever they could of the company's future.

"Rae, can you make sure we get that fire report before anyone else sees it?"

"Of course." She walked away, probably to charm a firefighter. He didn't doubt she'd succeed.

Whoever set this fire hadn't destroyed just any building. They'd picked the one that would house most of his employees for the foreseeable future. Without Cleveland, he couldn't staff the new offices. This fire would set the company back at least a month.

Tomorrow, he'd be on the front page of every business section in the country—and none of the news would be good.

CHAPTER THIRTEEN

It took too long to get back to her.

Even after the fire was extinguished, Marcus needed to stick around to answer questions. Ethan Ford, the local police chief, arrived soon after the firetruck, and it took him a while to study the scene. Marcus was fine with the cops catching the arsonist—so long as he got to slam his fist into the person's face before they spent several years in the local prison.

By the time Marcus calmed the remaining guests and arranged for transportation for all the employees back to Mountain View, he was vibrating with unspent energy. He wanted to run, or scream, or punch something.

And it wouldn't be enough, because what he wanted was Bree. He wanted to bury himself in her and forget every awful thing that had happened that night.

Her truck was still here. The valets had stuck it in a far corner, like the beat-up old thing might give rust cooties to the Mercedes and Jaguars that filled the rest of the lot.

As soon as he was free, he rushed to her office. It was empty. The computer screens were black. The other offices on the third floor were unoccupied. A few displaced employees were on the second floor, arguing about who would get the couches that night. Marcus knew he ought to help them get settled. Instead, he hurried to the ground floor.

The band was hauling their equipment off the makeshift stage, and the caterers were cleaning up, but otherwise the first floor was empty. A few now-homeless employees milled about, grabbing the leftovers.

He checked every room he passed, but Bree wasn't in any of the conference rooms or in the cafeteria.

He forced himself to stop and think. If she hadn't left, and she wasn't in front of a computer, there was only one other place Bree would be.

A thin beam of light fell into the theater as he opened the door. She sat alone in the dim room, staring at the white screen.

Her head whipped around when she heard him. She reminded him of a skittish horse just waiting for someone to hurt her. She hurried to him. "That's your idea of no heroics?" She rubbed his cheek hard, then held up a finger covered in soot.

Marcus caught it. "I'm okay. No one was hurt."

With her free hand, she shoved his shoulder. Hard. "You got lucky. What the hell were you thinking?"

He gaped at her. "I was thinking it was my father. What was I supposed to do?"

She glared. "Exactly what you did. That didn't make it easier to watch you run into a burning building and not come out for five minutes." She tried tugging her finger free, but he didn't release her.

The cameras. She'd seen everything. If their positions had been reversed, he wasn't sure he would have survived those five minutes. "I didn't mean for you to worry."

"I know." She exhaled. "Is Quentin okay?"

"He is. I sent him home in the company car."

A pause. "Are you okay?"

"I sound like I've been smoking three packs a day for a year, but I'm assured that will pass. I'm fine. No damage done." He drew in a deep breath, as if to prove he could. "The cops are going to follow up with the building's security footage. It might tell us how the fire began."

She dropped into one of the soft seats. Her shoulders slumped forward. "No, it won't. Two minutes of footage are missing."

He yanked off his tie and tore at his collar, needing to breathe, then ripped off the jacket that reeked of smoke and hurled it across the room. "What? How?"

"It's a completely different system, and not that difficult to get into. You should fire the designer."

"I want to fire everyone right now," he muttered. "Do you think it was one of our own? The same person?"

Bree gave a helpless shrug. "I have no idea."

It was too much. The fire, the betrayal, the doubt. Marcus sat in the chair next to her and simply let himself feel every emotion. For a time, that was enough, to sit at her side, their shoulders touching, while they breathed together in the same space. It made things easier, though he couldn't explain why. That wasn't a question he wanted to ask.

Instead, he gave her a sidelong glance. "Why are you sitting in a dark theater?"

"Because I couldn't figure out how to play *The Avengers*."

He didn't believe her, but he let her have the lie. "How many times have you seen that movie?"

Bree gave him a sidelong glance. "Probably as many times as you've seen *The Dark Knight*."

"I never saw it in a theater, you know."

"Seriously?"

"Yeah, the year it came out, I was..." He caught himself. He was living with his parents and trying to get through each day. He spent that summer acting like he was in a damned country song. "I was in Lost Coast, taking care of my dad." That much, at least, was true, but it tore the scab off an old wound. His father had been hurt, and she hadn't been there. He didn't know if he could ever forget that.

Bree pulled one knee to her chest. Her foot rested on the cushion. At some point, she'd removed her combat boots.

"I'm sorry," she said.

He searched her profile for more information. "For what?"

"I should have been there. I should have called."

The words found the last chink in his already depleted armor and wormed their way inside. "Why didn't you?" His voice was so rough, he barely recognized the broken sound that came from his throat.

She swallowed. "I didn't know."

He shook his head, disgusted with himself. He kept hoping for answers, and even Bree didn't know why she'd acted the way she did.

"It's in the past," he said.

"Is it really?" She waved at herself, then at him. "Because this doesn't feel like the past. You're here, and you hate me, but you're also kissing me, and then you go and you almost die, and I couldn't breathe until I knew you were safe. If I could go back to the past, I would. I wouldn't walk on that path. Then I would have picked up the phone, or I would have read email, and I'd have known what happened to Quentin. I'd have known you needed me, and I would have been there. I would have." She said the words like she was desperate to believe them.

"What path? Bree, what are you talking about?"

She waited a long time to answer, and when she did, her voice was a monotone. "I was attacked. Mugged."

His muscles tensed. "When? Why didn't you say anything? The cops were just here."

"The second week of February. Our freshman year of college."

His mouth went dry. Two months after she filed for divorce. She was already out of his life, by her own choice, but his heart cared nothing for logic. He should have helped her, saved her, killed whoever hurt her.

She must have sensed his horror, but she didn't acknowledge it. Bree told the story in quiet, level words. "I was walking home from the library. There are a lot of dark paths on campus, and I wasn't paying enough attention. Three guys surrounded me. They were average height. One was a little heavy, and one was skinny, and they all had short hair. The tallest one had a piercing in his left eyebrow. I don't know why I remember that. Anyway, they had knives, different lengths. They asked for my bag, with my laptop and tablet in it. I didn't argue. I handed it over, then they made me get on the ground. I was wearing your gray sweater, the one you forgot on your last visit."

Marcus hadn't forgotten it. He'd deliberately left it because he loved the thought of Bree curled up in clothes that smelled like him.

"It was a gravel path, and the sweater tore. One of them told me to count to one hundred before I moved, but the other two decided to make sure I couldn't get up. They kicked me. Once they got started, they didn't want to stop. They were enjoying it too much. They kicked my ribs, my hips. Wherever they could reach. The sweater was covered in mud stains shaped like the soles of their shoes."

Her breathing grew shallow, and she stopped speaking. It felt natural to bridge that small distance between them, so Marcus covered her hand with his and squeezed. She clung to his fingers.

"After they left, I couldn't move. Someone found me, eventually. I don't know how long I lay there. They called an ambulance. Fractured ribs, lots of bruising. Nothing permanent." Her voice twisted on that word. No, her scars weren't on the outside. "I gave a statement. The cops told me they'd be in touch if they found the guys, but they never did. That was the end of it."

"Except it wasn't."

"No, it wasn't," she agreed. "I went home. I closed my door and locked it. I took off your sweater and shoved it in a black garbage bag. Same with the jeans I was wearing. I threw away my shoes. It felt like, if I could remove all evidence of the attack, it wouldn't have happened. And that meant not talking about it to anyone."

He provided the unspoken words. "Including me."

"I'd already stopped talking to you. I know you remember. But that was different. In January, I didn't answer the phone because I knew if we talked, I'd change my mind about the divorce. After the attack…" Bree drew in a long, shuddering breath. "You were the one I wanted to talk to, but I couldn't. It was like someone sewed my mouth shut. I could ask questions in class, or make small talk in the grocery store, but the words that filled me all day, I couldn't speak those aloud. Not to anyone."

It took every ounce of willpower not to wrap her in his arms. He wanted to soothe her now, to make up for the time he wasn't there when she needed him. "What did you do?"

"I waited. I figured it was a matter of time until I got over it. I mean, I lived in a city. I was walking through a park at night with headphones on. I might as well have had a 'mug me' sign on my back. Shit happens, right? Lots of people get mugged, and they all manage to get on with their lives. But I couldn't."

His heart ached. His Bree had been indomitable. Something like that would have shaken her entire sense of who she was. "Did you get better?"

At last, she turned to face him. Tears hovered on her lower lashes, but there was nothing weak in her expression. "Of course I got better. I was a mess, and now I'm awesome. But it took a long time, and some things didn't go back to the way they were. By the time I felt like I could talk to you, it was too late."

She wiped her eyes with both hands, and her liner smudged a little. She looked perfect.

She stood and stretched. "Anyway, I thought you should

know. I've wanted to tell you for a long time."

Marcus struggled to find words. He knew what Bree had just given him. Vulnerability. Trust. Two things at which she didn't excel. It was important for him to acknowledge that.

But it felt like his body was rewriting itself with this new knowledge, as if the anger and pain had been temporary poison his cells were eager to purge. Bree wasn't a monster. Not now, and not eight years ago.

He reached for her hips, his touch gentle as he curled his fingers to hold her. She didn't protest. Marcus gave a gentle tug, and she stepped between his legs.

"You're wrong," he told her. "It's never too late. Not for us."

CHAPTER FOURTEEN

Marcus didn't move toward her. He didn't cup her cheek or stroke her hair like he usually did. He simply waited to see what she would do.

Telling the truth after so many years of silence felt like her own trial by fire. It wasn't the whole truth, but it was a start. A lightness grew within her, an empty space that had harbored her secret for so long.

The fire that purged her wasn't extinguished, not yet. It moved into that newly created space, a growing need that blazed through her body. The ache centered between her legs, and her breasts felt heavy, as if they longed to be cupped in his palms.

Marcus's hands were on her hips. Only inches separated them.

Bree ran a tentative finger over the soot on his forehead, and she swallowed a sob that appeared out of nowhere. They were so fragile. One choice could change everything. If she hadn't walked down the wrong path at the wrong time. If he'd been trapped in that fire just a minute longer. Everything would be different.

But at this moment, it was just the two of them. No matter what choices they'd made before or would make in the future, they were together now. She couldn't waste that.

With one hand, she traced the curve of his shoulder. That disconnect between her memories of the man he used to be and the man he'd become was fading, and she wanted to fully bridge the distance between then and now. She wanted to sweep her hand across every muscle—his wider chest and rounder biceps, his flat stomach—and discover what had changed and what had remained the same.

His lips…those hadn't changed at all. Bree placed her thumb in the center of his full bottom lip, depressing the soft flesh. She traced it, relearning every curve. She waited for him to suck the tip of her thumb into his mouth.

Marcus didn't move. If she kissed him, it would be her choice.

"This is a terrible idea," she said. "You and me, we don't end well."

"Are you saying we ever ended?"

"Yes. No. This is…" She considered her options. "It's a time-out. From everything."

He narrowed his eyes, dissatisfied with her answer, but she forestalled any argument the best way she knew how.

His muscles tensed as her lips found his. Even now, Marcus insisted she take the lead. Later, she would have no out, no chance to pretend she didn't want this as much as he did.

Bree slid her mouth across his, then took his lower lip between hers. She placed her hands on him, feeling the rise and fall of his breath and the quick beats of his heart. With tentative fingers, she outlined the smooth muscles of his chest. Through the thin fabric of his dress shirt, she felt his small nipples. She pinched one, drawing a gasp.

She pushed her hips to his, and she both felt and heard his sharp inhale. Marcus's control snapped, and he dragged her closer. She groaned, and his tongue swept inside her mouth.

One of his hands moved down to cup her ass and the other tightened in her hair, holding her in place as he deepened the kiss.

His hips lifted and his erection pressed against her. A low, insistent throb pulsed between her legs, and she shifted enough to raise the damn tulle out of the way. She rarely wore skirts, but at that moment she understood their appeal. Bree resettled on Marcus lap with one less barrier.

Thought abandoned her. All she knew was his lips and body. Their hot breath mingled as their tongues danced together. They gave and took in equal measure, testing and challenging, pushing each other further than anyone else ever had.

It was Marcus, and in that moment, he was hers.

His hand tightened on her ass, fingers digging into her flesh. He tore his mouth from hers long enough to drag his lips down her throat in a trail of open-mouthed kisses. He made a small complaining noise when he hit the top of her dress.

"Off," he muttered, tugging at it with one hand.

"You're the one who's overdressed." Her fingers worked the buttons of his shirt. As soon as the top two were open, her hands slid inside. She sighed with pleasure as her palms met hot skin and the line of hair that bisected his torso. It was thicker than it used to be, and she gave one of the strands a playful tug.

Marcus's teeth nipped her, then he soothed the bite mark with his tongue. Bree gasped and pressed her fingernails into the hard muscles of his chest.

He worked his hands beneath the fabric of her dress, then pushed the tulle up her bare legs. His thumbs massaged her inner thighs.

"Touch me," Bree begged. "I want your fingers inside me."

Marcus growled and shoved her panties aside, groaning when he found her drenched and ready. He stroked her clit once, but she was already repositioning herself to give him better access.

Bree groaned when he slid two fingers into her. This was right. This was how it was supposed to be. She clenched her muscles tight around him.

His gaze was hot, demanding. Possessive. A look she remembered too well, and one that didn't lead anywhere good.

But that would be tomorrow. Tonight, she wanted him inside her in every way.

Bree tore the button on his pants and wrenched the zipper down. His dick sprang free, warm and heavy. She wrapped her hand around the length and brushed her thumb over the sensitive tip, spreading the beads of pre-come that had already formed.

His fingers inside her stilled. "God, Bree. Just like that." It sounded like a prayer. He pulled his fingers from her, but before she could protest, his hand brushed hers as he painted the tip of his cock with her juices. "I want you on me," he said. "I want to feel you and taste you and be covered in your scent." The words fell from him, fast and hungry and uncontrolled.

Bree rose on her knees and positioned him at her entrance, moving in a slow circle. The head of his cock spread her open, and he slid in a single inch.

Marcus winced, and she felt his pain. She longed to sink down, to impale herself on his shaft as much as he wanted to plunge into her wet heat.

"Tell me you have a fucking condom," she said.

"In my jacket." The words came out in a rasp that had nothing to do with smoke inhalation.

Bree didn't even care why he was prepared. All that mattered was getting Marcus's perfect dick inside her. She withdrew the foil packet from his inner pocket and tore it with her teeth.

A thin beam of light spilled into the theater.

"Marcus? Are you in here?" It was a woman, and she was making no effort to be quiet. Bright light flooded the room as she flicked on the overhead lights. Disappointed rage hit Bree, and she needed to remind herself that coitus interruptus wasn't an acceptable murder defense.

Considering Marcus's glower, Bree thought he was telling himself the same thing. He rearranged her skirts with unsteady hands, covering them both, though his erection pressed against her aching core.

Rae turned the corner and drew to a halt. She blinked several times, but otherwise gave no sign she'd caught her boss making out with his former wife and current security consultant. "I'm afraid there's a problem."

Bree wanted to hiss at the woman, and Marcus's expression wasn't much kinder. "It can wait," he bit off.

"Gotham Investments has withdrawn its support. If you don't fix this now, the IPO is dead." Bree got the feeling Rae wasn't that bothered by the news.

Marcus took a deep breath. He waited long enough to answer that Rae shifted and began tapping her fingernails on the back of a seat. "I'll be right there," he said at last.

MARCUS STRODE INTO THE CONFERENCE ROOM, MAKING no effort to disguise his foul mood. "What the fuck do they want?" he asked.

Tommy didn't back down from his glare. "They don't trust the company's new direction," he said. "The campus was a mystery, but they were willing to give it a chance—until the fire. It's not the kind of thing that fills investors with confidence."

Marcus paced the room. Unspent energy coiled in his gut, needing an outlet.

Fuck that. It needed Bree, but he couldn't jeopardize years of work because he had an epic case of blue balls.

Tommy leaned against the wall with his arms crossed. He'd cleaned up since the fire, but his face was drawn and pale. Marcus's anger faded.

"Tell me what to do. You wouldn't have summoned me if you didn't already have a plan."

"You're going to hate it," Rae warned.

Tommy shot her a dirty look. "He'll hate losing hundreds of millions even more. We all will."

Groaning, Marcus collapsed next to Rae. In theory, he wanted to be a billionaire, though he couldn't say how it would make a difference. He already didn't know what to do with his money.

For years, the IPO had been the cherry on the sundae of his success. The absolute proof that his pathetic twenty-year-old self no longer existed. At the moment…well, now he felt a bit like a pathetic twenty-eight-year-old who would throw away millions if it meant he could kiss Bree again.

Some things never changed.

But it wasn't just about him. His friends' futures depended on this deal going through. Even if Rae didn't want it now, her soon-to-be astronomical wealth should be sufficient comfort.

"Whatever it is, I'll do it."

Tommy leaned back in his chair. "You need to be Marcus Keller. The public version."

Marcus groaned. If Tommy had said he needed to crawl naked and covered in honey over a hill of fire ants, Marcus would have been more enthusiastic.

"What possible reason would that help with investor confidence?"

"Two reasons, actually. First, it will prove that you're committed to Hours, and this whole cabin-in-the-woods thing you have going won't interfere with that."

"And the second?"

"It will raise the company profile. Put us in the news for reasons others than burning buildings."

It sounded unpleasant, but manageable. "Why are you saying I'll hate it?" he asked Rae.

She passed a tablet to him, opened to his schedule for the next week. It was covered in red. Morning shows, newspaper interviews, evening talk shows, podcasts. Every form of twenty-first-century publicity was displayed, and he was booked for all of it.

"What did I ever do to you?" he muttered.

"You wanted this?" Rae said. "This is how you'll get it. You have one week to remind investors why they want to give you all their money. Your plane leaves for Los Angeles tomorrow. See you in a week."

CHAPTER FIFTEEN

It should have felt strange, not hating Bree, but Marcus woke up the next morning feeling lighter than he had in years. It wasn't just that a weight had been removed. It was like a parasitic growth had been excised, and the creature could no longer feed off his anger and doubts.

Bree wasn't a horrible person. She hadn't simply laughed an evil laugh one day and decided to break Marcus in two.

His mind flashed to images from her story. Bree on the ground, being kicked by three sociopaths who didn't deserve to keep breathing. Helpless. In pain. And he hadn't been there.

While he was trying to convince himself that Bree was fickle and cruel, she was wearing his sweater, two months after filing for divorce.

If he wasn't an idiot—and that was up for debate—he'd remember that Bree Rogers was trouble. There were too many gaps in the story and pieces that didn't add up. Whatever happened next, he needed to proceed with caution. The fact she was willing to sleep with him didn't erase the past.

Willing? She'd been burning up. God, the feel of her wet

opening around his fingers, his dick. When Marcus finally climbed into bed the night before, he couldn't sleep. He tormented himself with the memory of her soft flesh spreading around his cock, taking him in just one inch. He relived the moment over and over until the tease wasn't enough, and he mentally rewrote the night so they weren't interrupted. Marcus jacked off hard to thoughts of thrusting upward, her pussy tightening around him as he drove deep into her body. Even now he stiffened at the memory.

Marcus pulled into a parking spot in the town square and took a moment to think about programming languages. C++. Java. Objective-C. HTML5. When his cock softened enough for him to be seen in public, he stepped from the car.

He was leaving in two hours. Three interviews were already scheduled for that afternoon, both little more than puff pieces, and he was supposed to take the Gotham Investments representative to a popular local restaurant. Tommy's logic was, if it was reported that Helen Barker was talking to him, everyone else would fall in line. He even promised to call the paparazzi if necessary.

Marcus grimaced. When had he started acting like a reality TV star?

He had plenty of work for the flight, but he planned to use the time to read.

Marcus stepped into Lost in a Book. The owner, Declan Donnelly, nodded at him. A pink bakery box rested on the counter. Marcus had interrupted him mid-éclair.

Marcus skipped small talk. Though he'd come to know Declan's brother Niall fairly well, the quietest Donnelly was little more than an acquaintance. "Do you have a section on mental disorders?" Marcus asked.

To his credit, Declan didn't even blink. "I only keep a few books in stock. I've found that most people buy those books online."

"It's not for me. I mean…never mind."

Declan shrugged, unconcerned. "A good bookseller's like a pharmacist. We don't gossip about what you bought, but people want to order their Rogaine and self-help books online."

Marcus had to respect a man who didn't give a fuck what anyone else was into. "The books?"

"They're over by Pablo."

He glanced around in confusion. There was no one else in the store.

Declan pointed to a large orange cat keeping watch from the highest shelf.

It really was a small selection, and most covered the extreme disorders that made for juicier reading. Schizophrenics, sociopaths, and narcissists. There were a few on addiction and one on depression. Nothing on PTSD. The best option was a general mental illness resource, so he took that to the counter.

As he was paying, the bell above the door rang. Oliver Hastings stepped inside. Marcus tensed.

"I was sorry to hear about the fire. Is there anything I can do to help?" Oliver's green eyes were painfully sincere.

"I don't suppose you have any spare bedrooms on the docks?"

Oliver seriously considered the question. "Not the commercial ones, no, but I have a bedroom on my yacht. Couches too, if people aren't too picky. You're welcome to use it."

As before, there was no indication he didn't mean every word—but Oliver Hastings was still a man who thought sleeping on a couch on a damned yacht required sacrifice.

"I think we'll be okay." That wasn't remotely true. All his employees were heading back to the Bay Area, where they'd remain until another housing option was sorted out. Even so, Marcus wasn't prepared to be indebted to a Hastings.

"Let me know if you change your mind. While I have you, the investigator thinks he'll wrap up the report on your father's accident this week. Should I mail it to your office?"

Marcus withdrew a business card and handed it him. "Email it." He nodded at Declan, then left the store without acknowledging Oliver Hastings again.

He checked his watch. Enough time for lunch. He could go to the bakery for a hummus sandwich and bowl of vegetable soup, but he'd been living off quinoa salads and green juice for the last week. Marcus was starting to think he'd brought a little too much of the Silicon Valley with him to Lost Coast Harbor.

Today, a burger sounded good. He crossed the square to Donnelly's and stepped into the cheerful pub.

Marcus spotted her immediately. Her platinum hair was like a beacon, demanding his attention. She sensed him at the same time and glanced up, and she…smiled.

A weight lifted from his chest. It was a small thing, the corners of her mouth quirking upwards, but the smile was meant for him. He used to live for those smiles.

Then the smiles had abruptly stopped, with no explanation, even before she was struggling with PTSD. He should try harder to remember that.

Marcus crossed the room and took a seat before she could invite him.

"Working?" He indicated the computer in front of her. "I thought we agreed you did that in the office."

"*You* agreed," she reminded him. "But don't worry. This is my breakfast. I'll be over this afternoon."

Marcus didn't bother pointing out the time, or that her breakfast consisted of a plate of cheese fries and a ginger ale.

He snagged a fry, and she gave him a dirty look. He returned a shameless smile and tried not to remember how she'd looked the last time he'd seen her, writhing on his lap. "What are you working on?"

Bree studied him, like she was trying to figure out if they would pretend the previous night hadn't happened.

He shifted in the seat and adjusted himself under the table. It had definitely happened. He just had no idea yet what he wanted to do about it.

Other than throw her across the table and finish what they'd started.

"It's a side project," she admitted at last. "It's not ready yet."

He snuck another fry off the plate. "Let me see it. God knows I need could use a distraction." And not only from the way her T-shirt clung to her body, though he really needed to stop noticing that.

Bree shrugged, too casual.

"Does this have anything to do with the VR helmet from the other day?" He tried grabbing another fry, and her hand was a blur of speed as she slapped his away.

"Get your own."

"But I like the way yours taste."

For the space of a breath, they studied each other. Weighing. Assessing. No, they weren't pretending the night before hadn't happened. They were waiting. Processing. The table sat between them, a distance neither was ready to cross.

Marcus shook it off. "So what is the project?"

"It's VR, but it's got a long ways to go." The words were reluctant. He gestured for her to continue. "It's something I've been working on for a while. It's based on virtual-reality exposure therapy."

Marcus brushed his knuckles against his jawline as he tried to recall why that sounded familiar. "I think I've heard of that. Some veterans groups are lobbying to include it as part of…" He trailed off.

"As part of standard PTSD treatment, yes. You can say the word, Marcus. But I'm not doing anything like that. Nothing medical, I mean. It's not intended as treatment. But I was interested in the general idea."

He sensed there was something held back. Some part of the story was missing.

Marcus leaned forward. "So what are you doing?"

Bree hesitated, then closed her laptop. "It's not ready. It needs more time."

"Are you doing it on your own? That's a huge project, too big for one person. Why not get some investors? I could hook you up with some guys in Palo Alto who are doing great VR work."

"No." The word was out of her mouth almost before he stopped speaking. "No," she repeated, softer. "I don't want to go to Palo Alto."

"Why not?"

She took a deep breath. "Marcus, do you still want to hate me?"

He blinked, confused both by the question and the sudden subject change, but he gave her a direct answer. "No. I don't want to hate you. I don't hate you."

There it was again. That smile. "Good. I was thinking, if you don't hate me anymore, maybe we could be friends."

"Friends." He repeated the word, his voice flat.

She gave him an exasperated look. "Yes. Friends. Because until last night, you couldn't be in my presence without some kind of jibe, and we went straight from anger to me attempting to mount you in a movie theater."

"You will never hear me complain about that sequence of events. I'm all for mounting. I say we do more of it."

Her chuckle was low. "I'm not taking mounting permanently off the menu. But maybe we could pause for a couple of weeks on the friends setting."

"Friends." He said the word again, this time with more warmth. It wasn't as good as mounting, but it had its appeal. "We skipped that step before, didn't we?"

She tilted her head in acknowledgment of his point.

"Well, friend, I'm glad I ran into you. I'm traveling to L.A. and New York to do a bunch of horrible press things, so I won't be around this week. I know you're working on the security breach, but be careful."

Her mouth twisted. "I'm doing what I can, but don't hold your breath. It's a lot harder to catch someone after the fact. The best solution right now is to strengthen the network, which I'm doing."

"That'll help, but this isn't some basement hacker. I'm pretty sure the fire was arson."

"That makes sense, with the missing footage. What doesn't make sense is how these things are connected. A data breach and arson. That's a pretty diverse criminal skill set."

There was one common thread. Both threatened the IPO. "The important thing is to protect the company."

Bree nibbled another fry. "With everything going on, are you sure it's the right time to go out of town?"

"I have to."

She didn't fight him. "You need to be careful too. No more running into burning buildings, not unless it's filled with orphans and kittens. Even then, check if there's anyone else who could do it. I get rather protective of my...friends."

Marcus didn't feel ready to leave, and he lingered a second too long, trying very hard not to say something stupid. *Will you think about me? You can call me. Text me. Send naked photos.*

"I'll come back," he said instead.

Chapter Sixteen

Since Marcus wasn't around to insist she work in the office next to his, Bree spent the day in a corner of Maddie's nursery, putting the final touches on the Grand Canal video. She claimed Maddie's WiFi was superior to hers, which was a blatant lie. Really, she wanted a bit of company. Even a recovering agoraphobe got lonely.

While Maddie had given her more than one pointed glance as she worked, she had yet to ask any follow-up questions about Marcus. Her friends were being remarkably patient. The questions were coming, if Bree didn't spill on her own, but they were giving her room to do it on her terms.

Bree saved that day's progress. She was almost ready to port the first video from the relative safety of her laptop to the far more immersive VR headset. At that point, she'd include sound, and then she'd discover how much therapeutic exposure she could actually handle.

The helmet might make might her feel ill, but that was a small price to pay—if the program worked.

Screw that. She'd invested too much of herself into Wanderlust for failure to be an option. It wasn't just another project. It was her future.

Her computer dinged, alerting her that the latest test of Hours's network was completed. Reluctantly, she closed Venice for the day. Time to get back to the work that paid the bills.

The security rebuild wasn't difficult. She'd done enough of them over the years that it was mainly a matter of adapting her base program to the company's needs. What was frustrating was how little luck she'd had identifying the hacker. Maybe she needed to try a different approach.

"Mads, you're a business expert, right?"

Maddie stopped sorting seed packets to give Bree the scornful look she deserved. Not long ago, Bree hadn't been a fan of Maddie's pursuit of a business degree. In fact, she spent years explaining why Maddie's choice to be a business major was foolish, ill-advised, and downright stupid. In the end, Maddie gave up her corporate aspirations, but it turned out she needed the degree to run her beloved nursery. In other words, Bree had been wrong. It had to happen occasionally, she supposed.

"I've been known to balance a checkbook," her friend noted wryly.

"Have your professors covered corporate espionage yet?"

"Yes. It was business plan, tax preparation, and corporate spies. In that order."

Sometimes, it was a pain in the ass having friends almost as snarky as she was. "Well, MIT didn't require it for a computer science major either. Can we talk it out, see what we come up with?"

"Of course." Maddie stashed the seed organizer on a top

shelf and crossed the room. She sat on the floor near Bree, unconcerned about the dirt. "I'm sure two uninformed opinions are the equivalent of an MBA."

"You haven't met many MBAs, have you? Those fancy letters don't mean as much as you think they do."

"Why aren't you asking Tommy these questions? Isn't he Marcus's right-hand man?"

Bree's mouth twisted. "I can't. The only person I know isn't involved is Marcus. Everyone else is suspect, even if he doesn't want to admit it."

"Even Tommy? He's local."

"True. Because no locals commit crimes. Especially not recently."

Maddie acknowledged the point. Of late, Lost Coast Harbor had been contributing more than its share to the local prison population.

"It sounds exhausting, being that paranoid."

"It helps that I have a long history of not trusting anyone but my friends," Bree pointed out, only half joking. "It's probably not Rae, since she was the one who called attention to the leak and had the good sense to recommend me."

"That's not enough to fully exonerate her?"

Bree shook her head. "I wish it was, but Marcus let slip that she's not a huge fan of the IPO. Maybe she's trying to sabotage it."

Maddie sputtered. "That's ridiculous. What percentage does she have in the company? She'll make bank if they go public." Her friend sounded disgusted. Once, Maddie thought of money as security. Gabe might have changed the way she viewed the world, but that didn't mean she thought people should walk away from millions.

"Yeah. I should probably check into her reasons for that." Bree made a note.

Maddie leaned backwards. She kept her voice conversational. "So, Marcus."

Bree made a noncommittal noise.

"You've said his name twice," Maddie pointed out.

"So have you. He's not Voldemort. I can talk about him, especially since he's my boss."

"It's more the way you say his name. Your voice softens."

"That's ridiculous. You know you're biased, right? You view everything through Gabe-colored glasses these days."

Her friend couldn't help her small smile, and Bree hated the twinge of jealousy that briefly hit her. Maddie deserved every bit of happiness she could grab. It wasn't her fault Bree had absolutely no idea how to be in a relationship.

"We're just friends," Bree insisted. "It's an improvement over where we were a couple of weeks ago, so I'll take it." Though...shouldn't a friend have called her to check in by now? It had been two days. The night before, she'd resorted to checking his Twitter feed and Facebook page, but they only contained news of his next appearance.

"Friends. Is that why you've checked your phone six times in the last hour?" Maddie kept her voice light, but her eyes were serious. Even hurt.

Bree had avoided this long enough. With steady hands, she closed the laptop. "It wasn't just you. I didn't tell anyone about the marriage. Not even Adam."

She could tell that Maddie was trying to be neutral and understanding, but her friend wasn't a great actress.

"Just say it." Bree raised both hands, palms up, and waved her fingers. *Bring it on.* Whatever it was, she deserved it.

"I've been your best friend since second grade, and I found out you were married from your ex-husband. In the middle of Donnelly's, almost a decade later."

"I get that you're angry…" she began.

"I've been through angry, though I should warn you that Gabe had to listen to me rant. He's still angry by proxy."

Bree bit back a groan. Maddie remained fiercely independent, but now Gabe had her back. They were a package deal.

"He took the LSAT last week, right? Tell him to back off, and I'll find a way to boost his scores," Bree offered.

Maddie wisely ignored her. "Why didn't you tell me? Did you think I'd judge you?"

Bree winced. "No, not at all. But I didn't think the marriage would last. We were drunk and in Nevada. When does that ever work out? Then he somehow convinced me we didn't need to rush the divorce. It's not like we could get any more married. It would be the same as any other long-distance relationship."

Her friend blinked at her. "He convinced you to do something you didn't want to do? Is he a superhero?"

Bree responded with her middle finger.

"But seriously. Long-distance relationships suck. Why would you sign up for that?"

"Because divorce required paperwork." Bree wrinkled her nose at the thought. "It was easier."

"I don't believe you. If you stayed married, it was because you wanted to be married."

Bree took a deep breath. "You're right," she admitted. "It

was real. I didn't want it to be, but it was. That week in Tahoe was like a goddamned dream. Every day was better than the one before. When it was time to go our separate ways, Marcus asked me to try, just a bit longer. I agreed, but I insisted we keep it secret. I knew it was a long shot, and I didn't want to be stuck answering hundreds of questions when it didn't last."

Bree remembered the last night before she left for Boston. She and Marcus drove about thirty miles out of Lost Coast Harbor and parked near the cliffs. They sat on the hood of his dad's Taurus and watched the ocean. They didn't speak much, because neither wanted to say goodbye. Marcus cupped her cheek and whispered against her lips. "I'm not going anywhere, Bree Rogers, so you better come back to me."

It had been the easiest thing in the world to agree, though she'd always sworn she would leave town and never look back.

"And then there was college," she told Maddie. "And dorms and parties and too much homework. I didn't work so hard in high school to half-ass it at MIT. I studied, and I tried adapting to life in a big city, and in between I was making friends. I was doing what I said I would do—taking the first steps toward a bigger life. Marcus was at Berkeley, doing the same. Our phone calls were interrupted by people banging on our doors. Roommates limited the dirty talk. This was before decent video chat, especially considering how bad LCH internet used to be. We could only do so much with email and phone calls."

"That doesn't sound like you," Maddie said. "You weren't the sort to wait by the phone."

"Exactly. I wanted to have fun. It was the first time in my life I could get wild without the whole town knowing about it the next day. Without my parents knowing about it. I was a college freshman with a husband I barely knew. And the worst thing was how much I wanted him. This awful part of me wanted to throw away everything I'd worked for and run back to him."

"Did you love him?" Trust Maddie to get right to the most important question.

There was no point lying. "Yes. As much as you can love someone after a week. But I didn't *want* to. Loving Marcus meant I didn't get to be a college student, not really. I didn't get to flirt with the water polo team or go on group dates with the people in my dorm, because I was waiting for Marcus to call. I turned nineteen a month after I got to MIT, and there was no one to celebrate with. Look at you and Gabe. Love's supposed to make you happy, and I was miserable."

Maddie nodded in understanding. There wasn't a hint of judgment on her face.

"I didn't have money to come home for Thanksgiving, and that's when I knew. We weren't going to make it. I informed Marcus it was time. We tried, but it wasn't working for me. I told him everything I just told you, though I left out the part about the water polo team. A week later he was at my door. He spent his entire savings account on that plane ticket, and the minute I saw his face, I didn't want him to leave. He fucking bought wedding rings, and we wore them for his entire trip. It was wonderful, and it was awful. Every day, I'd explain why the marriage was hard for me, and every day he talked me out of a divorce. He wouldn't go home until

I agreed. He convinced me to wait till summer, when we'd both be in Lost Coast Harbor. Then he left, and I was so damned angry at him."

The memory was still there, a single layer of emotion in the complex mess that was her and Marcus. She'd told him what she needed, and he ignored her—and then he left. Nothing changed between them, except her heart was broken all over again.

"A week later, I filed for divorce. I stopped answering his calls and his emails. He'd proven that he couldn't hear what I said, not really, so I stopped saying anything. I was scared if I answered, he'd change my mind like he did before. He's really good at that. And I kept having fun, and I kept partying too much, and it was obvious I wasn't meant to be married."

"You didn't come home that Christmas."

Bree shook her head. "I should have been there, Maddie. With everything you were going through, you needed your best friend, but I wasn't ready to face him. Marcus refused to sign the papers until we spoke, and I didn't trust myself to talk to him. It takes nine months to get a contested divorce in Massachusetts. Six months for the official Judgment of Divorce, then ninety days when the parties can change their minds."

"Were you scared you would change your mind?"

Bree closed her eyes, remembering. One week after the divorce was finalized, she received a small package, delivered to the apartment she was already having difficulty leaving. The box held a glass snow globe from Lake Tahoe and a handwritten note. She'd traced the letters, each one formed of harsh lines and bold circles. She could picture him gripping the pen as he wrote. The words were so quintessentially Marcus. Open and honest, his heart laid bare, but they were coated in a bitterness she'd never seen before.

I bought this at a gift shop the night we married. I looked at it whenever I missed you. I imagined it in our home. I imagined the two of us, warm in a cabin, the promise from our week in Tahoe growing into our entire lives. Maybe I imagined it all.

The tears came then, and they didn't stop for hours.

"No. By then, I had other things on my mind." She knew this was the moment. Right now, she should tell Maddie everything about her final years in Boston.

The words stuck in her throat. Maddie wouldn't judge her, but she wouldn't see her quite the same way. Bree wasn't weak, and she refused to let other people view her that way.

Instead, she opened her laptop. She hadn't checked Marcus's Facebook page in a few hours.

She read the news feed, then read it again.

"Motherfucker," she growled.

Bree shoved her laptop in her bag, muttered a quick goodbye to her confused friend, and drove home, cursing the entire way.

The bastard was trending.

CHAPTER SEVENTEEN

B ree refreshed her Facebook news feed for the third time. He was still there, between an article about a politician's secret affair and one about a new movie trailer.

The paparazzi had snapped him exiting a high-profile sushi restaurant in West Hollywood—with his arm wrapped around Helen Barker. The same woman he'd been touching at the party.

Helen's fingers were pressed lightly against Marcus's chest, and she peered up at him with a secret smile. The woman had full lips, gravity-defying breasts, and legs that reached her shoulders. A New York investor had no business looking like a supermodel. Bree supposed she couldn't blame Helen for that, and tomorrow she'd remember she wasn't an insecure bitch who tore down other women because they were pretty. Tonight, she'd call it a victory if she didn't hack the woman's phone.

She hit refresh, willing the story away. Lead sat in her stomach. When she'd said they should try being friends, she hadn't meant he could go off and be naked friends with another woman.

Tech guys rarely trended on social media, at least not for personal reasons—but most tech guys didn't look like Marcus. He'd already been in the news all week, and here he was again, with a powerful woman who wouldn't be out of place on the cover of *Vogue*.

Bree gnawed her lip. Did Helen really need her credit rating?

Bree clicked on the story. *New Power Couple? Tech Superstar Marcus Keller Caught Canoodling With Fabulous Financier.* The headline was nauseating. The picture made her want to kick something. Like Marcus's balls.

No, she didn't have a claim on him, but she thought they had an understanding, one he'd obviously interpreted differently than she had.

Bree had her pride, and that pride wasn't okay with Marcus canoodling with anyone less than a week after they nearly had sex in the theater.

Perhaps he needed a reminder of what kind of friend Bree Rogers could be.

THERE WERE TIMES MARCUS QUITE ENJOYED HAVING TOO much money, and being able to summon a private jet at will was one of those times. He'd need to plant a new rainforest the next day to offset the carbon emissions, but he couldn't spend another day away from Lost Coast Harbor and his campus.

And considering the photo that popped up on Facebook, he didn't want to spend another day away from Bree. Friends or not, considering the recent progress in their relationship, it was the kind of thing that required an explanation. It was an easy choice to cancel all of his New York appearances and return home two days early. Besides, his dinner with Helen had convinced Gotham Investments that Hours was stable, which meant the IPO was back on track.

The hard part was not stopping by Bree's cabin on the way in.

It was past midnight as he climbed the stairs of Narnia. His front door clicked open as he neared, the electronic lock sensing his approach. Marcus entered and flipped the hall light switch.

In the kitchen, his blender turned on.

"What the fuck?" He tried a second time, and the same thing happened.

The piercing screech of the security alarm demanded his attention. He stumbled through the darkened room, heading for the blinking panel. Marcus typed in the code. Nothing happened. He did it again, and a message flashed. *Invalid entry.* Once more, he punched in the code, hitting each number carefully.

Another message appeared. *System locked. Authorities notified.*

Marcus groaned. It would take the cops twenty minutes to get out here, all so he could explain that he was trying to break into his own apartment. Any second now, the alarm would start blaring, just for good measure.

Sound filled the entire house, but it wasn't the loud wail he expected.

His home security system was playing "The Macarena."

"What the fuck?" Marcus repeated, but even as the bouncy notes of the obnoxious song beat their way into his brain, he found himself smiling. Broadly.

Thirty minutes later, he'd filled out a police report and phoned his very confused security company. He'd also flipped several switches on and off and discovered that the switch for the gas fireplace now turned on his bathtub jets, the accent lighting appeared to control the printer, and the dining room chandelier only worked when the Blu-ray player was on.

Marcus collapsed onto his living room couch and attempted to think. At least he wasn't sitting in the dark. If he turned on his oven fan, the ceiling light came on. He had no idea how to turn on his oven fan.

When he'd set up an all-digital house, it hadn't occurred to him to Bree-proof it, if such a thing could be done. Every system—security, electric, heat, even water—ran through a single control grid. He should be happy he hadn't returned to a flooded house.

Not only had she rewired the entire apartment, but she'd transferred the system to her private server. He couldn't undo her work, not without taking everything offline and starting from scratch.

They were on good terms when he left. Marcus could only think of one thing that had changed—the photograph with Helen.

If he didn't know better, he'd say Bree was jealous.

His heart lurched. It wasn't possible. The world as he understood it didn't include his ex-wife acting like a jilted lover.

Marcus wanted to drive to her cabin and confront her. Only one thing stopped him—it was what she wanted. Her revenge was far from subtle. Hell, she would have heard the police sirens going past when the alarm was set off. She was probably sitting on her teal sofa right now, grinning her evil grin and waiting for him to pound on her door.

She was ready for him, and it was his turn to catch her off-guard.

If he could prove to Bree that he was no puppet who jumped at her command, even better. He had little doubt she was better at computers, but he possessed a few skills of his own.

BREE STRODE INTO OLYMPUS AT ONE IN THE AFTERNOON like it was any other day. She wore her favorite pair of beat-up jeans, a green hoodie, and her usual boots. In other words, she was dressed like a woman who wasn't trying to impress anyone.

Last night had been a lesson, that was all. She wasn't trying to get him back or anything like that, so it didn't matter that he hadn't called as soon as he discovered her creative reinterpretation of his home systems.

As usual, she entered her office and punched the button to darken the walls. In the second before they turned opaque, she spotted Marcus in her peripheral vision. There was nothing casual about his gaze. He watched her the way a predator observed his prey.

Excitement unfurled at the challenge. He was up to something. Her nerves went on high alert, but tension and fear didn't follow. She was having too much fun to be afraid.

She shut the door and followed the light of the monitors to the far wall. The computers would be the most likely object for his revenge. Cautiously, she flicked on the devices she needed that day. They all booted without a single error message.

If not the computers, what was he up to? Bree dropped into her chair and leaned back while she studied the computer array. It didn't look like Marcus had touched a thing. Her programs were safe.

Next, she checked her bank account and visited her various social media sites. They were all in order.

Biting her lip, Bree glanced at the dark wall separating their offices. He knew she was there, and he hadn't said a word.

Was he really going to pretend she wasn't holding his entire home system hostage? Ignore her like some naughty child? Was that his grand revenge? She had to admit it wasn't a bad choice. She would end up wasting the entire day waiting for his retaliation.

Maybe she'd gone too easy on him. Bree made a mental note to rewire his bathroom heat lamp and television switch that evening.

When Marcus didn't appear, she returned to work, though she had a hard time concentrating. She was too aware of the man on the other side of the dark wall, and all her attention strained toward him, longing to know what he was thinking. An hour later, her coffee mug was empty and she'd accomplished little.

Bree picked up her cup and headed for the door. The entire chair came with her, and she gave a loud yelp of surprise.

"What the fuck?" Already knowing what she'd find, Bree tested the seam between her jeans and the leather chair. It was sealed shut.

The bastard had glued her to her chair.

Her office door swung open. "Wow. You really bond with your work, don't you?"

Bree returned the chair to the floor and stretched her legs before her. "This was the best you could do?"

He leaned against the doorframe, way too pleased with himself. She would wipe that expression from his face—as soon as she could move without an office chair attached to her ass.

A smile played at the corners of his mouth, and despite her indignation—which was righteous and powerful—she almost smiled back.

"Admit it. You spent all morning checking every line of code twice, wondering where I was going to hit. How many passwords did you change?"

Her silence was answer enough.

Marcus moved into the room and shut the door behind him. He perched on her desk. "I beat Bree Rogers with a frat house trick. Someone should include that in my obituary."

"Which they will be writing later this week." Bree rolled backwards, putting space between them. "Are we even now?"

His expression said she should know better. "Let's see. I had to deal with the Lost Coast Harbor police, which took forty-five minutes, and I haven't stopped humming 'The Macarena' for the last twelve hours. Also, I still don't have control of my house. You've been glued to a chair for five minutes. Does that sound like we're even to you?"

She leaned back in the chair. "What do you want?"

"Let's talk."

Bree crossed her arms. "About?"

"What did I do to inspire novelty-song levels of rage?"

"Be grateful. I had 'My Heart Will Go On' cued up, but I chose mercy at the last minute."

He waited, far too patient.

"Also, I touched your dick before you left."

Marcus's mouth opened and closed several times, more like he was trying to get air than like he was trying to speak. "I remember."

"I would hope so. You seemed to enjoy it."

"So you touched my dick, then reprogrammed my entire house?"

His confusion was almost cute, except she had a hard time believing Marcus knew so little about women. He wasn't an idiot.

"Maybe the other night was a near miss. Maybe being friends is the most we can hope for, given our past. That doesn't change the fact that you were five seconds from being balls-deep inside me."

Bree dropped her gaze to his jeans and the growing bulge. Warmth flowed through her, need centering between her legs. But she'd started this, and she would brazen it out.

Bree leaned forward. "No woman, no matter the circumstances, wants to discover that a man can jump from her to another without taking enough time to change his clothes. I touched your dick, and a couple day ago you gave Helen Barker the same privilege. *Never* make the mistake of thinking I'm interchangeable." Bree glared at him, her breath coming faster. So much for keeping her cool.

She could practically see his mind turning as he debated

how to play this. "You're jealous." He said it like a statement of fact.

"No. I'm special, and I won't be treated otherwise." She really wished she could stand and stalk out of the room. It would have been a great exit line. Since she was glued to the chair, she had to settle for turning her back on him.

He didn't take the hint. "Do you plan to remain like that?"

"I'm fine."

"If you like, I can roll you to the elevator. Someone can drive you home. You'll have to ride in the back of a van, though. Maybe a cargo truck." He was enjoying this far too much.

Bree spun back around. "I can get myself home."

Marcus glanced at her thighs, which were firmly stuck to the leather cushion. "Uh-huh. So far as I can tell, you aren't going anywhere, so this is a good time to get a few things straight."

"What do you want?" She bit off the words.

He hooked one foot around the base of her chair and tugged, sliding her toward him. Marcus planted his legs on either side of hers, his hands on the armrests of the chair. Caging her. "I want to talk about why you touched my dick."

CHAPTER EIGHTEEN

B ree lifted one shoulder. "Well, it *is* a nice dick."
"You always enjoyed it before."

She licked her lips, and Marcus wondered if she experienced the same frisson of memory he did.

"Nothing happened with Helen," he informed her.

Marcus moved one hand to his half-hard cock. Her pupils dilated as he stroked himself through the fabric. His pants grew tight as the erection strained against the front, and Bree's lips parted.

"I don't want anyone else to touch me, but you said you only wanted to be friends."

Her cheeks flushed. "For now."

"Am I supposed to wait?"

"If you want to."

"That's not an answer."

Bree's hands clenched, like she was resisting the urge to touch him. "It's too complicated to be more. Too risky."

"Is that what you really believe? Or are you hoping I'll change your mind?" He stroked his length from the base to the tip.

"Undo your pants."

When Marcus hesitated, she raised a challenging eyebrow. "You're asking if I want your dick or if I want to be a friend. I think I need to see it again to fully understand my choices."

He knew she was fucking with him, but he didn't mind. He could fuck with her too. Marcus undid the top button and paused before tugging the zipper down. Her gaze snagged on the waistband of his boxer briefs. The tip of his cock peeked over the top of the elastic.

Marcus tugged the briefs down, one inch at a time. He reveled in the way her breathing grew shallow as more flesh was exposed. At last the whole thing bobbed free, the heavy length pointing toward his stomach. Marcus jacked himself once, twice. "Have you decided?"

Bree licked her lips. "I think I need more information." Her voice grew husky. "Maybe a taste test?"

Marcus's hand stilled. He didn't care if she was messing with him if it meant her hot mouth wrapped around his shaft. He braced his hands on the back of her chair and pulled it forward, until Bree only needed to dip her head to reach him.

Time stretched as he waited for her to act. Waited to learn if this was just a game.

Then her tongue darted out to clean the beads of pre-come gathered on the tip, and Marcus's knees threatened to give out. "Bree…" he murmured, unsure what to say next. He only wanted to speak her name.

She circled her pink tongue over the tip, wetting him, but she wasn't teasing. Her expression revealed only hunger. He whispered her name again, this time a plea, and she wrapped her lips around the head and sucked hard. Marcus groaned.

Bree slid down his length until he hit the back of her mouth, then she pulled back slowly, increasing the suction. He couldn't look away from the sight of his cock moving in and out of her soft lips. "That's so good. God, Bree."

She moaned around him, and his fingers clenched at the sound. Bree grazed his skin with just the hint of teeth, making him gasp. She knew exactly what he needed.

She was killing him. Not just her mouth, but the hunger in her eyes, the heat of her body, the hint of musk that was hers alone, because Bree had never worn perfume.

Ten more seconds, and he would lose himself completely. He'd watch her throat work, swallowing his come as he released hard in her mouth. His legs would shake, and for a few minutes he wouldn't think of anything else.

But then he'd remember he had no idea where he stood with Bree, or what she wanted. Marcus wasn't even sure he knew what he wanted, not anymore.

It took more self-control than he thought he possessed, but Marcus pushed her backwards with an oath. He yanked up his pants and stepped away, putting space between them. He might be the stupidest man alive. He'd just walked away from a perfect blow job.

It was necessary. He wanted answers, and every day in Bree's presence only led to more questions.

"What's wrong?" She blinked at him, confused.

"Nothing." Nothing at all, except the damn woman was glued to a chair and even now she managed to have the upper hand. "But friends don't play mind games with each other."

"Mind games? And here I thought I was just giving you a

blow job." She was a little breathless, but she was losing her dazed expression.

"Why?"

She sat back with a dissatisfied noise. "Are we back here? You have a nice dick."

"That's all it is?"

Her voice dropped. "What do you want me to say?" The words held a note of sadness.

Marcus returned to her. He dropped down, kneeling between her legs. He didn't remember making the choice, but there he was, supplicant before her—and still hard as a rock. "Maybe…that we can never just be friends."

"Even if you could forgive and forget the past—"

"I'm trying," he interrupted.

"I don't think I can be in a relationship. Considering those photos, neither can you."

"I told you, nothing happened with Helen. It was a photo op."

She continued as if she hadn't heard him. "And if we can't be in a relationship, and you don't think we can just be friends, what's left?"

"You mean, other than blow jobs?"

A corner of her mouth turned up. "I couldn't help it. Your dick distracted me."

He chuckled. Even when she drove him crazy, she made him laugh. "You want to know what's left?" Marcus placed his hands on her thighs and rose onto his knees, until he was at eye level. He leaned forward. His voice was low, the words just for her. "More. With you and me, there's always more."

"I don't know what that means."

"Don't you want to find out?" Marcus ran his hands up her legs. His thumbs grazed her core.

"It's not very sporting to do this when I'm trapped." Her voice hitched.

"Then tell me to stop." Marcus stroked her hips, then lifted the hem of her shirt. When he met warm skin, he hissed in a breath at the same moment Bree did. "Tell me you don't want this."

He cupped her breasts. She wore a simple bra of soft cotton. It was the sexiest thing he'd ever felt. Marcus ran his thumb across the nipple, then gave it a sharp pinch. She gasped and arched her back.

He remembered what she liked too. Marcus grazed his hands down her torso, digging in his nails to lightly scratch her sides. She writhed in the chair and arched her back. Marcus pushed her shirt up and dipped his head to run kisses across her stomach. The skin was flawless, so delicate beneath his lips. He bit it, applying enough pressure to leave a mark, and she exhaled in pleasure. Bree threaded her hands into his hair and held him against her.

"Are you thinking of the past? Or the future?" Marcus asked, running his hands across her ribs. "Or are you thinking of how I make you feel at this moment? What I could do to you with my lips and hands?"

When she didn't respond, Marcus nudged the shirt higher, following every revealed inch with his lips. He tugged her bra down, freeing one dusky pink nipple. He hungrily wrapped his mouth around it and sucked, flicking his tongue across the tip until it grew taut. He did the same on the other side.

It felt like her skin had been made for him, their bodies

magnets to each other.

He wound one hand into her hair, holding her in place. "Do you want me to walk away? Leave behind all this potential and just be friends?"

"Would you? If I asked you to?"

He searched her face, trying to figure out what answer she wanted. She gave nothing away, and he had no choice but to tell the truth. "Yes. But this time, you would need to tell me why, because I don't think I could stay away without a good reason. Not again."

"I had a good reason. I told you why."

"But you didn't let me answer."

Her eyes flashed for a second, then her jaw set. Bree leaned forward. "Do you want me to tell you want I want, or show you?"

"Both."

Her smile was pure sin. "There's only so much we can do at the moment. Hand me the scissors in the top drawer."

He did, and Bree lifted her waistband to slice through the fabric. The denim widened to reveal black underwear. Cotton, like her bra, and just as sexy.

It took her a minute to free the left leg. Marcus feasted on the sight as her pale skin was slowly revealed. Her legs were a little different now, more muscled than they'd been at eighteen, and his hands itched to trace the new lines.

He needed those legs wrapped around his hips like he needed to breathe. Marcus cupped her left calf, letting the muscle settle into his palm. He stroked her with his thumb. At that moment, he thought he might have lied. He was no longer sure he could walk away, no matter what she said.

She made the final snip, and the last bit of fabric fell away.

Bree stood. Marcus rose with her, his entire body aware of the woman before him.

She gripped his hips and tugged him to her. "You know what I want?" Bree brushed her lips across his jaw.

He held his breath while he waited for her to finish, then expelled it as she shoved him backwards. Unprepared, Marcus stumbled several steps.

"I want a man who believes me when I say I had a good reason." Before he could argue, she strode through the door, then walked down the halls of his company in nothing but a hoodie, boots, and a skimpy pair of black panties.

CHAPTER NINETEEN

Bree returned home only as long as it took her to grab a new pair of jeans. Her exit might have left Marcus dumbfounded, but he'd recover quickly.

Her beat-up old truck rumbled along the road to town. Town was full of people she knew. People who would be a buffer if Marcus showed up.

With others around, she was less likely to rip his clothes off in public. She couldn't have made the same guarantee if she'd stayed in her cabin. Part of her was pissed at him for not letting her finish sucking him off…and the other part was pissed at herself for pushing him away.

Equally loud was the part that wanted to scream at him for *still* believing that she didn't have a good reason for filing for divorce.

Donnelly's was surprisingly busy for a weeknight, but there was a free chair at a center table. "Can I join you?" she asked the enormous redhead.

Niall Donnelly broke into a grin. "Of course. Have a seat."

"Beat anyone up lately?" she asked, sliding into her seat. Niall owned the local MMA studio, so the answer was usually yes.

"No one who didn't deserve it," he assured her, signaling to Gavin. "Another IPA and one of those weird drinks Rogers likes."

A minute later, the oldest Donnelly brother appeared with a pale drink in a long, skinny glass. "I'm experimenting, so it's on the house." To his brother, he said, "Table service is only available to those who pay their bill."

"My name's on the sign," Niall protested.

"And mine's on the deed."

With a heavy sigh, Niall walked to the bar to pick up his beer.

Bree took a sip of the mystery drink and gave a happy sigh. Gavin was, at heart, a brewer, and Donnelly's was founded on his beers. However, he had a weakness for mixology and few willing guinea pigs, so Bree usually got first shot at drinks a lot of the town would barely touch—like a basil lavender Tom Collins, if her taste buds were accurate.

When Niall returned, he brought an ancient laptop with him. "How many lessons will it take to buy an hour of your skills?"

Bree gnawed her straw and considered. She took weekly classes at his studio, mainly because she liked hitting the heavy bag. It really was possible to punch out her stress.

But she also charged an exorbitant hourly rate. An hour of her time was worth a lot of free classes, and she knew her brother's finances had been strained ever since the Hastings stopped using contract employees. "Ten sessions. Give them to Adam and tell him there was a glitch in the system."

"My system of a pencil and a notepad?"

Bree shrugged. "There's math involved. He'll believe you messed up."

Niall snorted, but he didn't argue. An hour of her time was more than worth the chance to help her brother. Adam was too proud to take her money, but any self-respecting devious younger sister would find her way around that.

"So what do you need?" she asked.

Niall opened the computer and turned the screen toward her. It was the homepage for an upcoming MMA tournament. "I want every fucking thing you can give me on these guys. Anyone can be beaten if you know them well enough."

Bree gave him an exasperated look. "An hour?"

He blinked at her, far too innocent. "I heard you were just that good."

"Shameless flattery appreciated, but this is outside my specialty. I do security." And virtual reality, but he wasn't asking for an imaginary cage to test the fighters. "What you need is—"

"Data analysis."

Bree forced her breath to steady, then turned to face Marcus. It was like he'd followed her scent.

Or he just knew her that well. It was a discomforting thought.

Niall was already rising with a grin. "Keller! I've been wondering when you'd wander back in here."

The reaction was unexpected. Niall was several years older than Marcus. These days, the age difference was unimportant, but it meant everything in high school. Plus, Niall had been a champion troublemaker, while Marcus had been a nerd. Not a lot of social crossover. "You two are friends?"

Niall gestured to an empty chair. Marcus didn't glance at her as he sat. She tried to do the same, but with his long thighs only an inch or two away from hers, it was hard to ignore him.

"Hell yeah," Niall said. "Keller helped me get set up at the studio. Gave me a website that didn't look like a toddler designed it."

"I didn't give you anything." Marcus sounded more relaxed than he ever did at the office. While he talked, he absently loosened the knot of his tie and pulled it off. "Niall worked the hell out of me. He's the reason I have muscles."

Bree gave his chest a quick glance, remembering exactly how hard it felt under her hands. The quirk of his lips told her Marcus noticed.

Maybe Niall did too, because his expression was pure devil when he asked, "So you two are seriously married?"

"Were. Past tense." Bree answered quickly.

"How the hell did you keep that secret?"

"It helped that Bree refused to come home for years." Marcus's tone was dry. "By the time she did, I was gone."

"Yeah, I get that, but why not tell anyone?" Niall glanced between them, his smile widening. "Let me guess. Marcus didn't want to admit to anyone that he couldn't tame Rogers. You wouldn't be the first, man. Or wait…" Somehow, his smile grew even more dangerous. "Was it that Bree didn't want to admit someone tamed *her*?"

For someone happy to play the village idiot, Niall was dancing too close to the truth.

"So tell me about this project," she reminded him.

Thankfully, he didn't push the topic any further. "I want

the champion belt next year. These guys are my main competition."

Bree studied the pictures of five fighters, and Marcus leaned over to view them, as well. He was so close. If she moved an inch, they'd be touching.

You walked away from him, she reminded herself. *For good reasons.*

The growing ache between her legs couldn't remember a single one of those reasons.

With a shake of her head, she returned to the photos. They were all of humongous men. Several had faces that had suffered more than their share of broken bones.

Marcus whistled. "Damn. These guys make you look pretty in comparison, Niall."

"Oh yes." Bree rolled her eyes. "Tattoos and muscles. Girls hate that sort of thing."

Marcus coughed, and she bit back a grin. The truth was she didn't much care one way or the other. Tattoos or not, a hot guy was a hot guy, good for a bit of fun before she moved on.

A sexy man, the kind that lingered in her thoughts, had a big old brain to go with the muscles. Not that Marcus needed to know that.

Niall either didn't catch the undertones or chose to ignore them. "Most fighters have some kind of pattern. They'll play to their strengths. I've got to neutralize those strengths and exploit their weaknesses. A lot of that's about timing. When do the guys get tired? When do they shift strategies? That sort of thing. I've studied hours of footage, but the best guys are the hardest to predict."

Marcus tugged the laptop toward him. His brow furrowed, and Bree recognized his expression. It was the same one she wore when she identified a possible solution that would only require a few hundred hours of coding.

"It's not that different from the dating algorithm," he said. "For that, we enter everyone's interests. So far as people know, they get matched based on one or two items. They like aquariums, for instance, so we set up a date with someone else who likes looking at fish. But that's just on the surface."

"I don't want to date these guys. I want to beat the shit out of them."

"What the public doesn't know is how much work is being done under the surface. We're compiling all their interests to paint a big picture. I don't care if two people like hiking if one also likes skydiving and the other likes to visit English castles. We don't match based on shared interests. We check for similar dispositions. It took me a while to figure that out, but once I did, that's when Hours took off."

Niall appeared genuinely interested. "So you don't believe opposites attract?"

Marcus shrugged. "Maybe. I don't care. It's not my job. That kind of attraction is based more on chemistry. I can't program for that."

"How did you program for all those actresses and models?" Niall asked. "Because I'd sign up for that service."

"Easy. Make a couple million, don't be deformed, and be willing to appear on Page Six. It wasn't what it looked like. You want to hear the rest?"

Niall nodded.

Bree was happy to hear him be so dismissive of his dating

life. She'd already guessed it wasn't as torrid as the tabloids liked to report, but she liked having it confirmed.

"So what if, instead of entering likes and dislikes, we enter the fighters' specialties. What moves do they return to the most, how long do the matches last, that sort of thing. We create a profile based not just on their data, but on the big picture, and we figure out how to match fighters the same way we'd match a couple of single people. And we'd know when you were mismatched and needed to adjust your own strategies."

Bree grinned as the connections fired in Marcus's brain. This was the guy who kept her on her toes all through high school.

"What about the human element?" she asked. "There's no room in that plan for creativity, for a fighter who can think on his feet when his usual strategies don't work."

Marcus nodded, like he'd already considered her question. "We've done something similar for Hours. In most ways, people are predictable. The music fans want to see shows. The geeks want to go to movies and play games. The bookworms want to drink coffee and shop for books. But in every case, there's something more. No one is just the stereotype. We've had to figure out what that *more* is, because that's where the magic happens."

"How did you figure all this out?"

"When I realized that having a lot in common wasn't enough. There had to be a reason people wanted to be together."

Apparently, a thwarted blow job made Marcus passive-aggressive.

Niall busied himself punching keys. "So how does that *more* quality work here?"

Marcus brushed his knuckles against the stubble under his chin. His thinking pose, Bree remembered. She doubted he even knew he did it.

"There are daters like that, right?" she asked. "Ones who are a bit more erratic, who like adventure sports and dark cafes and knitting, all at the same time."

"Of course." The words came out slowly. He was already following her train of thought. "We don't so much link them by interest as category. So knitting and carpentry are in the same category. One makes clothes out of string. The other makes furniture out of wood. They share a similar drive. When people have enough categories in common, you're tapping into their needs on a basic level."

"That might work," Bree said. "We start by categorizing their movements."

Before she finished speaking, she'd opened a basic text editor. "Your computer is shit, Niall. I want five more lessons just for dealing with this operating system."

Marcus peered over her shoulder. "Damn. She's being generous. I'd have asked for ten more. And probably a hundred more for the work this project requires. How much RAM do you have?"

Niall squinted at them. "RAM?"

Bree answered for him. "Let's just say this computer would be amazing, if it was 1998. I left my laptop at home too."

"Mine's in the office. I was distracted earlier and forgot it." He didn't glance at her. Bree's cheeks heated.

"We can do a framework now. We only need to break

down what characteristics we need to track…" She trailed off, her mind spinning in a new direction.

"What is it?" Marcus waited, ready to follow her train of thought.

"The…person we're searching for. I've been trying to find their electronic trail, but it's been a struggle." Bree's mind spun ahead. "Can we create a simple version of Hours's algorithm to sort the employees into categories? I'm guessing we'll find lots of similarities, but maybe some people will pop out."

He understood immediately. "We analyze the people, not the actions."

"And we pull out the anomalies. The mismatches."

Marcus nodded, considering. "It's worth a shot, at least." He stood. "I'll come in tomorrow for a bit of punishment, Niall. We'll talk about this then."

Bree was already standing, excitement pulsing through her. It was a long shot, but at least it was something. After too many days of feeling helpless, she welcomed the opportunity to do something. Anything. "We shouldn't do this at the office. There are a few employees hanging around. Meet me at the cabin with your laptop." The words were out before she considered them. She couldn't remember the last time she invited someone to her house, but the invitation had been so easy.

"My apartment has better equipment," Marcus argued.

"Yes, but my home doesn't play 'I'm Too Sexy' when you walk into the closet."

"It doesn't…"

"It does now." She grinned. "Besides, this was my idea.

Get your butt over there, and show me you can still hold your own with a bit of code."

CHAPTER TWENTY

Five hours later, Marcus was buzzing from sugar and caffeine. Bree looked perfectly at ease.

He reached for another peanut butter cup. "Do you ever eat vitamins?"

"There's protein in peanut butter," she insisted. "Okay, I've run through everyone in the company. It's a pretty limited set of criteria, though."

"What data are you compiling?"

"Education, family background, social media behavior. I can add debt and spending habits, but you'd need to look the other way while I, ah, found the information."

"Getting arrested for hacking the employees' private data probably won't boost investor confidence," he said drily.

"Stick in the mud," she muttered, but he heard a smile in her voice. Since arriving at her house, she'd limited the conversation to work. He wasn't sure if they had called a temporary truce or were pretending their earlier interaction hadn't happened.

"Why include family?"

"Kids of divorce have different behavioral patterns. Same

with only children." She glanced at him for a second. "They tend to think the world revolves around them."

He rolled his eyes. "My parents couldn't afford another kid. I'm lucky they chose to have one."

Bree shook her head. "Try growing up with a strict father and overprotective big brother. It makes you long for independence."

"Is that why you were so determined to stay away? You still haven't told me why you changed your mind. You swore you were going to explore the world."

She didn't answer. He wasn't sure he expected her to.

Marcus leaned back against the sofa. They were seated on the floor. Bree was already there when he entered, and it was easier to join her than ask why. Besides, he thought he knew. The couch was too cozy, the dining room table too small. This was the only way they could maintain a bit of distance.

So he sat on the floor in his five-thousand-dollar suit and wondered why the hell he was wearing it. He should have stopped at home to change. Instead, he rolled up his sleeves and removed his shoes.

"I'm not sure those criteria will work," he said, remembering what they were supposed to be doing. Mentally, Marcus reviewed his employees. "I've tried hiring from a wide variety of backgrounds. It doesn't do me any good to have a bunch of people with similar experiences, for exactly that reason. They're more likely to think the same."

"And they all went to the best schools, so that pretty much takes education out of it." Bree took another long draw of soda, and Marcus examined the slim column of her throat as she raised her chin. If he could only run his fingers along that skin, feel her pulse jump beneath his fingers...

Then what? She'd explain what she meant about him not listening? Finally confess why she was in Lost Coast Harbor?

The question wouldn't stop gnawing at him. It felt like a vital piece of the puzzle. "Why won't you just tell me, Bree?"

"It doesn't matter." She punched a key and sat back. "It's compiling behavior now. We'll learn if there are any patterns when it's done, but I'm not optimistic. We don't have enough data to work with—and none of these criteria exactly relate to corporate espionage. We need more information before we can discover any anomalies."

"We'll think of more data to add later. *Legal* data," he added, before she could volunteer any suggestions. From the beginning, he'd known this was an unlikely way to weed out the employee, but he hadn't been able to turn down the chance to work closely with Bree.

It occurred to him that Bree would have also recognized how ineffective this program was—and she'd offered to work with him.

He didn't want to go home. "Can we order takeout? My stomach is threatening to leave my body and go hunt down actual food."

"You've been gone too long. We have pizza delivery, and they close at ten. So does the market. The convenience store attached to the nearest gas station is open."

Marcus groaned.

"Or you can forage in my fridge," she said.

She returned his suspicious look with a bland smile, and he went in search of whatever mold-covered food she kept in her kitchen.

Instead, he found a lasagna wrapped in foil. "You cook?" he asked in shock. "Like, actual food that doesn't come out of a plastic wrapper?" Marcus cut two slices and placed them in the microwave.

"Of course I cook," she said. "A big plate of something cheesy and carby soaks up the caffeine and sugar."

Marcus peered between the layers of pasta. "I hate to tell you this, but I think there are a few vegetables in here."

"Lies," Bree insisted. She didn't argue when he handed her a plate. They ate in silence for a few minutes. He studied her whenever he thought she wouldn't notice. Her expression was distant, as if she wasn't entirely in the room with him.

At last, Marcus set his plate aside and returned to the question Bree was determined to avoid. "It matters to me why you came back. I'm tired of secrets."

"I don't want to talk about it. Why is that so hard to accept?"

"Because the Bree I knew didn't run away from anything. You said what was on your mind, and you confronted life head-on. You didn't try to avoid problems."

She lifted her chin, defiant. "Did you really think I'd be that eighteen-year-old forever?"

Marcus shook his head. Sadness washed over him. "No. I thought you'd be a better version of yourself by now. Not some small-town girl who's wasting her talents in Lost Coast Harbor. One trip to Silicon Valley and you'd have investors lined up for your VR project, but you're not even trying. What happened to your ambition? Your determination to be more than just another coder?"

Her lips thinned, and she looked away from him. "Fuck

you, Marcus."

Marcus clenched his teeth in frustration. No matter how much progress they'd made since his return, there was this wall between them he couldn't scale. He wondered if he could smash it to pieces instead.

Maybe if he shared his own reasons, she would do the same. "I came back because I was homesick. For the last few years, it was all I could think of. Getting back. This is where I belong. Is that what happened for you, or was it something else? What kind of awful secret could you possibly be hiding?"

She averted her eyes and refused to answer. That was why he couldn't make it over the wall. Every time he made progress, she built it higher.

He sighed. "Well, fuck you too, Bree."

Marcus gathered the plates and took them to the kitchen. There were a few other dishes already soaking in the sink, and he washed them, as well. He knew he was delaying the moment he had to leave. The program was running. He had no reason to stay, except the desperate hope that something would shift between them.

Marcus wiped his hands on a towel and returned to the living room. "It's late. I'm going to—"

Something flew at his face, and Marcus barely got a hand up in time to catch it. He blinked in surprise. It was a prescription bottle. Bree's name was listed, along with a drug he didn't recognize.

She wasn't just mad. She was in a rage, every bit of anger she possessed vibrating out of her skin. "I have an anxiety disorder, you asshole. Not 'Oh, I get stressed on occasion.'

Sometimes, the world is too damn much for my stupid brain, which is why I haven't been able to see the world. Is that what you wanted to hear?"

He tried to find the words she needed. Comfort and reassurance. An apology, or a promise that this changed nothing. He hoped it was a promise he could keep.

Marcus didn't say anything, because Bree was still talking. "You want to know why I vanished? This is why. My anxiety showed up after the mugging, though there were signs before that. It stuck. You think I was supposed to be a better version of myself? Well, so do I, but this is what I got. And I may be screwed up, but I've also spent years learning how to cope with a brain that sometimes doesn't want to behave, and I've done a damn good job of it. So don't you dare stand there and tell me I'm less than I was. Don't you fucking dare."

Never in his life had it been so important to say the right thing. "Bree…" He took a step toward her, and she took two away.

"You don't get to act like this makes everything okay. Now that you know it was something beyond my control, you can forgive me. We can talk about it and move on. Because it's *not* okay, Marcus. This is private. I'm not ashamed of it, but I also don't tell people about it. They'll think I'm weak, and I want people to view me the way they always have. Not talking about it, that's a choice I made, and you couldn't leave it alone. Maybe I walked away from you because I needed a break, but I stayed away because my life was falling apart and I didn't know how to be with anyone. I still don't. That's the truth, but you decided I was a heartless bitch who left a great guy who only wanted to love her. Everything was my fault."

"I didn't mean…" he began.

"Yes, you did. Now get out."

She glowered at him. Her anger was edged, sharp enough to draw blood. When he didn't move, she crossed her arms and waited. Nothing in her face or body softened.

He'd done enough damage for one night. Marcus left before he could break anything else.

Chapter Twenty-one

B ree didn't go into the office the next day, or the day after that. She sent Marcus the results of the data compilation with a note that, without further information, the results were inconclusive. It was what they'd both expected, but it bothered her that she knew nothing about the person who almost took down Hours's network.

Then she installed the completed security system. The final product was gorgeous, if she said so herself. It contained so many encryption levels and various fail-safes that a strong hacker would need to devote a year just to access Hours's office supplies forms.

Even so, a sense of dissatisfaction nagged at her. She'd done what the company paid her to do and had already sent her final invoice to the accounting department, but the job didn't feel complete. Someone had tried to harm the company, and she didn't know if they planned on ransomware or publicly exposing user data. Either way, that kind of employee was poison—and they still worked for Hours.

And then there was the fire. It would be a few more weeks before the report was completed. Until it was confirmed, they couldn't be certain it was arson. Maybe the construction crew cut a few too many corners. Maybe the missing security footage was a bug in an already faulty system.

No. Her inner paranoiac couldn't believe that—but even if it was arson, it would be bizarre for a hacker to double as a pyromaniac. There was no clear connection.

A perverse part of her wished for another attack. It would provide another avenue to investigate...and it would provide a reason to keep working for Marcus.

He hadn't called since she threw him out of her house. Yes, she'd yelled at him, accused him of being an asshole, and told him she didn't know how to be in a relationship, but she hadn't expected him to simply walk away. He never had before.

Before, he hadn't known how limited she was. Marcus's life was amazing. He had money and power, and after the IPO he'd have more of both. If he woke up that morning and decided to spend a year in Barcelona or fly to Machu Picchu for lunch, he could make it happen. Could she blame him if he didn't want to date a woman who couldn't get on a plane without taking so many Xanax she stopped feeling her legs?

She wasn't an easy woman to date, for many reasons. Bree knew this, but somehow she hadn't thought Marcus would agree with her.

Now she just needed a plan to avoid him for the next decade or two while they lived in the same small town, because she couldn't handle being reminded on a daily basis that he didn't want her.

Or she could maybe, just maybe, learn to live somewhere else. For the first time in years, the idea didn't excite her.

The day before, she'd completed a rough VR version of the Venice video. It was ready for a test run.

Her hands shook as she put the helmet on. She adjusted the sound to its lowest setting, until the noises were little more than a distant hum. With time, she'd increase the volume, but the whole idea was to acclimate slowly to this new experience.

"You've got this," she assured herself, then launched the program.

She gasped in wonder as Venice unfolded before her. This was the first video, with very few people. She was positioned in the rear of the boat, with only a quiet couple and the driver sharing her space, and none of them made any sudden movements.

It wasn't perfect, but it didn't matter. It was Venice, and she was there. Grinning, she turned her head, eager to view the Grand Canal from all angles.

Dizziness hit her, and her stomach protested.

"Are you fucking kidding me?" She ripped off the headset and glared at it, as if it were personally responsible for her nausea.

She paced her living room. This was only a setback. She'd known all along this was a possibility—not just for her, but for thousands of others who might use the software. In theory, she could build up her tolerance by increasing the time she spent in the helmet each day, but she had no idea how long that would take, and she'd run out of patience years before. This program offered a solution, and she didn't want to wait any longer.

What she needed was a way to physically interact in a

space similar to what her eyes thought they saw.

Like, instead of sitting on a couch, she could be in a room.

She allowed herself three seconds to debate the wisdom of her idea, then packed everything up and headed for the second floor of Asgard.

Theoretically, Marcus was the only person with access to Prism, but it was easy enough to rewrite the system she'd designed to allow herself entry. What she hadn't expected was to find someone else already in the room.

Quentin Keller stood in the center of Prism, currently set to the moon program. He leaned hard on his crutches, like they barely offered enough support, but all his attention was focused on the surrounding room.

"What the hell is my son up to, Bree?"

She hesitated. Of course she knew Quentin, the way most of Lost Coast Harbor knew each other, but they'd had little interaction over the years. He seldom came into town, and on the rare occasions she'd run into him, she hadn't known what to say to the father of the man she'd deserted. She might have hidden her marriage to Marcus, but he and his father were close. Marcus would have told him.

The man's shrewd expression said as much. Quentin knew she wasn't just another employee.

That didn't mean she would share Marcus's secrets. "I don't know."

He snorted. "You wouldn't lie to a kindly old man, would you?"

Something about his wry delivery reminded her of Marcus. Before she knew what she was doing, Bree was teasing Quentin the same way she would his son. "I don't know. I'll let you know if I see one."

He gave a surprised laugh. "What are you doing here?"

She wasn't sure if he meant the room, the campus, or the town, so she turned the question around. "I'm wondering the same thing. You should only have clearance for the downstairs rooms."

Quentin moved toward the wall with the controls. His movements were slow, and he winced when he needed to support too much of his weight with his legs. He waited till he reached the edge of the room before answering, and he sounded a little breathless when he spoke.

"I rewrote my security clearance." At her shocked expression, he clarified. "A couple days ago, before you redid everything. I wouldn't touch your code. I'm not a fool."

"You know what I do?" Most people in town knew that Bree worked on computers, but the majority of them thought she fixed people's internet connections. At least, that explained the number of people who stopped her in the market to ask for tech support.

Quentin gave her an exasperated look. "I know more than you think, Bree. My son isn't a secretive man."

Bree hurried to change the subject. "I thought you didn't touch code anymore. Marcus said…"

"He said I refused to code because my pills turned my brain to mush?"

"He was a bit more circumspect than that."

Quentin snorted. "I'm sure. He's not wrong. I can't concentrate on much when I'm on the meds, which is why I haven't taken them the last few days. I wanted my brain in working order while I got situated in my new position." He nodded toward his legs. "It's also why I'm in a boatload of pain today, so I don't think it will last."

Her heart ached for him, but she instinctively knew he wouldn't want pity. "Pills or not, getting into this room wasn't an easy hack, even on the old system. You've got some skills."

"I used to be okay."

That was a serious understatement, if he was able to break into Prism after years of barely touching code. No wonder Marcus was so good. "I'd love to see some of your old work," she said.

"Most of it's gone. We didn't have cloud storage back then. All I have from that time is a busted computer and a handful of flash drives I haven't looked at in years." He adjusted the program to the Mars one. His expression turned calculating. "I'd be happy to send you the files...if you tell me what my son's doing."

"We're back to this?"

"Kindly old man, remember? I could die any minute. Humor me."

She snorted. "You're in your fifties. Besides, you know your son as well as anyone, and as you pointed out, he's not secretive. What do you think he's doing?"

Quentin touched a few more buttons on the panel, and the room returned to a simple white box. "I think he's sending a plea for help. He may not keep secrets from me, but we're all pretty good at keeping secrets from ourselves." Quentin pointed toward the floor and the downstairs labs. "This building is remarkable. It doesn't belong on this campus. It should be in a research facility, but I bet he's convinced himself he'll use it for his dating app. Am I far off?"

Bree said nothing. Quentin nodded, as if she'd provided the answer he expected. "The worst thing is, the investors might agree with him. They could try to set up virtual dates instead of understanding the full potential of this technology—and my son's too busy trying to prove a point to notice," he muttered. "Do me a favor. Convince Marcus that you don't care at all about the public offering."

She blinked. "My opinion doesn't matter."

His laugh was rueful. "Somehow, I doubt that." Quentin made an awkward turn and shuffled toward the hallway. When he reached the doorframe, he turned to face Bree. "You broke my son's heart. We both know it. Marcus has been trying to prove something ever since, and he thinks this IPO will do it. He has enough regrets already. I'm hoping to spare him any more."

Bree nodded at him, acknowledging the point, then he walked to the elevator. Once she was alone, she wandered around Prism and considered Quentin's words.

She remembered the way Marcus beamed with pride as he demonstrated the programs, the way he'd touched the controllers reverently. He felt about this room the way she felt about Wanderlust. Here, he was creating something. Challenging himself. How much of that would be lost if the company went public?

Too curious to resist the urge, she moved to the touchscreen monitor and studied the options. In addition to the moon, Mars, and Paris, she found a beach program. She set the time to sunset, then turned it on.

This wasn't the cold and rocky Lost Coast Harbor beach. The sky above her was streaked with orange and purple. Palm trees waved in the breeze, and the same wind ruffled her hair as it passed, thanks to the built-in fans. On the far wall, the tide danced toward her, then reluctantly withdrew. A gull cawed on her right side, and when she inhaled, she picked up the tang of salt and seaweed.

It wasn't as visually immersive as the virtual reality helmet, but this room was a prototype. There was room for improvement. It had plenty of other advantages, though. Being able to move made it feel more natural—and she didn't sense a hint of nausea.

This room was full of potential, and she wished she'd had more time to explore it before Marcus ran away.

Or before she pushed him away. She wasn't entirely sure which.

A voice in the doorway startled her from her thoughts. "What are you doing in here?"

Chapter Twenty-two

B ree spun to face Marcus. By his recent standards, he was dressed casually. He'd left off the tie, and his collar was unbuttoned. He carried a leather messenger bag across his body.

Marcus's eyes were sharp, missing nothing, but his tone was more curious than accusing.

She didn't want to admit that she was checking if the Prism technology could improve her own project, so she settled for a half-truth. "I wanted to see it again."

He nodded, thoughtful, and stepped inside. "I've been thinking about this room all morning. I came here to view the Paris program."

Bree inched toward the door, and he held up his hands. Not in surrender, but to calm her. Showing he had no weapons.

"I won't watch it with you here. I just wanted to re-experience it, knowing what I do. That's why you bolted last time, wasn't it? The program triggered your anxiety."

"Yes." There was no reason to deny it. "You're doing it."

"Doing what?"

"You've put on the kid gloves. Treating me like a delicate china doll who might break if you say the wrong thing. And you wonder why I don't like telling people."

"I'm sorry about that. I'm glad I know, but I shouldn't have said what I did."

"About being a better version of myself?"

He winced. "Yeah. It's not true, you know."

She wasn't certain about that, but she appreciated him saying it.

Marcus remained in the doorframe. "So no kid gloves. What should I do instead?"

Wrap your arms around me. Tell me none of this matters, because it's still me, and it's still you.

She wanted to go to him, use his hands and mouths and lips to end this conversation. They were good at that, using their bodies to forget.

The problem was, at some point they always remembered.

Bree moved to walk past him. "I'm sorry. I wouldn't be here if…"

"If you thought you might run into me?" His hand wrapped lightly around her upper arm, urging her to stay. "I know I was a jerk last night, but do I really deserve that? Don't push me away. Don't punish me because I didn't know you had anxiety, when you've done everything you can to hide it from me."

That sounded annoyingly reasonable. "I thought you might want to avoid me for a while."

His brows drew together. "Why?"

"I thought you'd need to figure stuff out."

"What's there to figure out?" He sounded confused. "I

mean, I have questions, if that's okay."

She supposed that was inevitable. Bree gestured for him to go on.

"How many people know?"

"Adam."

"That's it? Not your parents? Not even Maddie?"

"No."

He huffed out a small breath of air, and she thought he was biting his tongue. "You said this is why you stayed away from me. Have you been dealing with PTSD since freshman year?"

Bree crossed her arms. Prism had no furniture, and she felt exposed, standing in the middle of the empty room. "Not exactly. That's how it began. But then it…morphed, I guess you could say. It's like I've had this inside me my entire life, and it needed a trigger to come out."

"Were there other signs? Before the attack." She heard the subtext. *Should I have known this would happen?*

"Some. I drank too much at parties, because it made everything fuzzy. Less threatening. I didn't adjust to Boston as well as I expected, but I figured it was a matter of time. But those were small things. After the attack, it got worse, and it kept getting worse."

"Did you get help? Professional help, I mean."

"Eventually." After Adam dragged her cross-country and made the appointment for her.

"Why didn't you tell me?" His voice cracked at the end of the sentence.

She knew there was no answer she could give that would satisfy him. "It was a long time ago."

She thought he was going to argue with her, but instead he pulled a book from his bag and held it out to her.

"A dictionary of mental illness? Seriously?"

"This is where I started. I read about PTSD when I was in L.A., and last night I read about anxiety disorders. Well, I did as soon as I figured out which lights didn't play 'Mambo No. 5.'" He gave her the hint of a smile. She didn't know who was mad at who anymore, but she couldn't help returning it.

He tucked the book back in his bag. "After I read this, I hit the Mayo Clinic website. National Institute of Mental Health. WebMD. Wikipedia. Whatever I could find. There's tons of information out there."

"And a lot of it doesn't apply to me. I'm not a puzzle to be solved, Marcus."

The look he gave her was equal parts frustration and humor. "All I know how to do is solve puzzles. Let me at least try."

"Fine. What did you discover about my awful condition?"

A flicker of annoyance crossed his features. "That it can manifest in a lot of different ways, and you're the only one who can tell me what it's like for you. You know I want to hear about it, so if you want to tell me, I'll listen."

He was trying, and she couldn't ignore that. "For me, it's a moving target. Anxiety covers a lot of stuff. PTSD, phobias, generalized anxiety disorder. It's hard to narrow it down to just one thing. After the attack, I went to a counselor at school. He diagnosed it as PTSD, gave me some pills, and told me to come back in three months. I skipped the appointment. Six months after the attack, I wouldn't leave my house if I didn't have to. Classes, library, gym, errands, then home.

I didn't go out after dark. I doubled up on summer classes, because the days were longer and I could get more done, and it meant I could graduate sooner. The longer they went without catching the guys who did this to me, the more scared I was. They were out there, somewhere. My brain took that fear and distorted it into a lovely case of agoraphobia."

His eyebrows shot for the ceiling, and she laughed outright. "Agoraphobia isn't just people afraid to leave their houses. It's a spectrum. Some can't handle loud noises, or people surprising them in their peripheral vision, but they can go out in public. It's easier if they have someone with them as a kind of buffer. But yes, some can't leave the house at all. By the end of my time in Boston, I was pretty close to that. It's why I'm making the videos now. It's treatment. You can't drop an agoraphobe in the middle of a crowd, but you can slowly add one body after another, or use more high-pitched sounds. It's a safe way for some people to reenter the world. And if it's too hard for them to leave their homes, at least they got to play in the virtual world for a while."

He brushed his knuckles against his jaw, and Bree braced for whatever intrusive question was coming.

"Have you thought about connecting it to the wearer's vitals?"

Bree blinked. That was unexpected. "Like heart rate?"

"And temperature. I'm sure you could track breathing patterns, too. Is it possible for the machine to know an anxiety attack is coming before the person does?" The question was direct, with no hidden agenda.

"Maybe. It might work at an early stage, before it was a full-blown attack. And the device could turn itself off." She'd planned to put that power completely in the wearer's hands, but it was worth considering the option.

Marcus's brow was drawn tight. "Or it could go back to an earlier version of the software, one with fewer people or sounds. Or pipe in soothing music or scents."

Her excitement dimmed. "That's a lot of money, and I haven't even managed to get a bank loan for my current work. So far, I've been working on a single video of the Grand Canal."

"Screw the bank. We're standing in a room built for this. It's why you're here, isn't it? You saw the possibilities. Just order whatever equipment you need, and let me know if you prefer salary or contract."

Her mouth dropped in surprise, though she should have expected it. "This is *my* project. I'm not giving proprietary rights to Hours."

"That's not what I meant. I just wanted..."

"To help me, I know. But this is my baby. I've been working on it for years, and I don't want someone else to come along and turn it into something it's not. I'd rather do it on my own."

His jaw clenched. "Of course you would. That's what you always want, isn't it? But the project is too big to do on your own. You think I would have gotten where I am without help? Other people aren't the enemy, Bree." With a disgusted shake of his head, he left the room.

His back was stiff, his strides long. He walked like a man with no plans to return.

Of course Marcus had help, but he wasn't giving himself enough credit. Rae and Tommy had played key roles, but Marcus was the heart and brains behind Hours.

The more. That's what he'd called his secret. It was the connection that existed in the spaces between the answers on a questionnaire.

Once, she and Marcus believed they shared that connection. Back then, all their answers had been correct, but the spaces between had been silent. Those empty spaces, that was where they should have found trust, and faith in the other person.

She and Marcus hadn't been very good at that part.

Things were different now. Instead of assuming he knew what her life was like, he'd asked questions. Remembering the way Marcus responded with neither pity nor recrimination when he learned about her anxiety issues, she knew he deserved more trust than she was giving him.

"Wait."

He stilled.

Bree swallowed, and she stepped into one of those empty spaces. "I've never been to the ocean."

Marcus turned around. "We live on the coast."

"I mean one like this. Warm and comfortable. A tropical beach. I could handle a place like this, so long as it's not too crowded. It's the getting there that's a problem. Noisy airports and crowded planes. Everything would be strange and unfamiliar. I've barely left Lost Coast Harbor since I came back. I've traveled to nearby towns a few times, but I can't handle the traffic in the Bay Area. Planes feel impossible. My junior year, I flew to Virginia for a conference, and I felt like I was under attack the entire time. I'll need to create a simulation of a 747 before I can go anywhere. Either that or an entire bottle of antianxiety meds."

"This project isn't just meant for other people, is it? You're creating your own treatment."

She nodded. "I want Wanderlust to help others, but yes, I'm my ideal customer. I want out, Marcus. I'm fine in Lost Coast. I still struggle with anxiety—I suspect I always will—but the agoraphobia is much better...unless I think about traveling too far from home."

He took a single step forward. Returning to her.

"This is why you came back. Why you didn't live the life you wanted. God, Bree. You shouldn't..."

"Shouldn't what?" she pushed.

"Shouldn't have such a small life." The words were matter of fact, and she couldn't decide if she wanted to punch him for being so presumptuous or kiss him because he cared.

"I have a family that loves me, even if they are overbearing. A brother who cares so much I need to tell him to back off sometimes. I have friends I've known my whole life. I'm at the top of my field. That's more than a lot of people ever get, so you can keep your pity to yourself."

He shook his head. "This isn't pity. I'm pissed."

Bree's brows drew together. "You're pissed that I have anxiety?"

"Of course I am." His voice rose, and he paused to reign in his temper. "How much have you lost because of this damned illness?"

That time, there was no debate. Bree walked right up to Marcus, grabbed his lapels, and kissed him once, hard and fast.

She released him before he could respond, and stepped out of range.

Marcus stood frozen. "What was that for?"

"For calling it a illness."

He blinked in confusion. "That's what it is."

"You'd be amazed how many people don't think so. One of my professors—a PhD—told me it was all in my mind. He suggested I exercise more. When I missed my second appointment, the counselor told me to quit school until I got my shit together. I'm paraphrasing, barely. By my senior year, I rarely left my apartment, and I had to fight to work independently that final semester."

"Is that why you keep it to yourself now? Because people don't understand?"

"That's one reason. Maybe the biggest one. But also..." Bree took a deep breath. "I don't like talking about it, because it's not who I want to be."

Fuck. Tears prickled, and she hurried to finish. "I don't want to be scared. I don't want my stupid brain chemistry to keep me from living the life I wanted, even though that's exactly what happened. I don't want..."

"A small life," he repeated.

"It is not!" The words were heated. "My life is great, and I won't have anyone diminish that. But sometimes I wish it was a little bit..."

"More?"

She swallowed, and after a second that seemed to stretch for minutes, she nodded. "More."

"All those reasons you gave for wanting the divorce? Was that you hiding what was really going on?" He was concerned, but the words were also hopeful.

For the first time, she wished it were true. Wished she

could tell him she'd left because of her stupid brain chemistry.

No, it had been her stupid heart.

"I ended it because I was too young to be married. You know I filed for divorce before the attack, Marcus."

The flicker of hope faded. "Don't do that."

"Do what?"

"Make it about your age. People get married young all the time and manage to stay together. If you'd wanted it to work, you would have found a way. I've never known you to not get what you want."

She waved her hands in frustration. "Nice. I admit I want more and don't know how to get it, and that's how you respond?"

"Don't change the subject. I was the same age, and you were all I wanted." He sighed. "I'm an idiot. I guess I hoped if I knew everything, I'd finally understand what happened. And I'm glad I know, don't get me wrong. But in the end, it all comes back to the same thing, doesn't it? You didn't want to be married to me. The simple truth is you didn't want me."

"You don't get to tell me what I felt." A ribbon of anger threaded through her words. No matter how much she gave him, it kept coming back to this. She left him, and he couldn't understand why. "Of course I cared about you. I had to stay away *because* I wanted you. Seeing you would to be too confusing."

His mouth twisted. "That's the problem, isn't it? You cared about me. I fucking *loved* you."

The anger took over. She'd listened to Marcus tell her what she felt one too many times. She closed the distance between them with angry strides. "You think you were the only one? I fucking loved you too, you asshole."

They glared at each other, breathing hard. Only inches separated their lips—and then nothing did.

They kissed like they were starving, like they could erase years with just their lips. Tongues crashed together, the movement desperate.

Bree gripped his shoulders, pulling herself tight against Marcus's body. His hands cupped her ass and held her to him. He groaned, and she echoed the sound when his cock hardened between them.

His teeth grazed her jaw and ran down the column of her neck. He bit once, sharp enough to leave a bruise. Bree knew he was marking her, knew everyone would see it the next day, and she welcomed it. She ran her hands down his back, digging her nails into the fabric of his shirt, trying to mark him too. She wanted to cover him in scratches, so that every time he moved the next day he would be reminded of her touch.

But hands and teeth weren't enough, not when she wanted everything. "Fuck me." The words were breathless, dangerously close to begging. "I need you inside me."

Chapter Twenty-three

With a growl, Marcus fell to the floor, hauling Bree on top of him. He grabbed her shirt with both hands and tore it down the back. It gave way with a satisfying rip. He wanted to tear it into pieces.

Marcus wanted to destroy everything. He wanted to erase the years he'd spent without this woman because Bree hadn't believed loving him was reason enough to stay with him.

The top fell from her, and he tossed the ruined shirt to the side. Marcus inhaled sharply as her bare shoulders and arms appeared. She wore another black cotton bra. It was hard to believe so many men preferred lace when that bra was the sexiest thing he'd ever seen. It molded to her sweet curves, and when he cupped her breast, the fabric was warm from her skin.

She arched her back, pushing herself into his palm. With his other hand, he undid the clasp of her bra. Bree shrugged out of it, as eager to be rid of it as he was. He lifted his head and wrapped his lips around one taut nipple, sucking hard and drawing more of her soft flesh into his mouth, then he moved to the other side.

With no warning, he flipped her to her back and rose over her. His lips caught hers, the kiss deep and demanding. Marcus ran his finger between the valley of her breasts, then splayed his hand across her flat stomach. His thumb dipped under the waistband of her jeans. "Take these off. I want you naked."

"You too." Bree moved her hands to the buttons of his shirt.

He stopped her. "I've waited longer." Her expression turned mutinous, but he claimed her mouth once more, swallowing her protest.

When her eyes were glazed and her lids heavy, Marcus sat back on his heels. He grasped her jeans with both hands and tore the zipper open.

Bree still wore her boots. He was doing this all wrong, with no finesse, but finesse would take too long. He hurried to unlace them, then wrenched them off her feet. Marcus hooked his thumb under her panties and pulled them down with her jeans, catching her socks in the same movement.

For the first time in years, Bree was naked before him. He thought he might be dreaming, or maybe having a psychotic break. "You're perfect," he whispered.

She was. He ran his palms along the sides of her breasts, her waist, the rounded hips that led to strong thighs. Thighs he wanted clenched around his ears or his hips. He didn't care, so long as he was inside her somehow.

His cock strained against the zipper, impatient, but the damn thing could wait a few more minutes.

"I need to taste you." His voice was hoarse, strange to his own ears. He ran his lips and tongue over her neck and shoulders, over her full breasts and across her stomach, picking up the salt of her body. "Never wear perfume," he ordered. He craved her scent. It was a need that grew more demanding with every second.

He tried moving between her legs, but she locked her thighs together. "Take off your shirt."

His skin next to hers. God yes. Marcus reached for the neck of his shirt and pulled it off in a single movement, then returned to her.

Bree stopped him with a single hand on his chest. Her fingers outlined his pecs, and he gave a sharp inhale when she pinched his nipples.

"You've changed," she whispered. With her index finger, she traced the light hair that dusted his chest, following the thin line to his waistband.

"I grew up," he told her.

Bree stopped moving for a second too long.

"Don't you dare start thinking now," he ordered. Marcus moved between her legs and pressed his chest to hers. She sighed as their bare skin met.

He kissed her, slow and deep. Bree's thighs gripped his hips as she rose into him, taking all that he offered.

He wanted to give her everything.

She ground against him, pressing herself to his covered shaft.

"Can I make you come like this?" he asked. "Just rubbing against you?"

"Damn it, Marcus. You know what I want." Bree reached between them and unbuttoned his pants.

He lifted his hips away from her. "Or I could use my

hands." He groaned when he ran his fingers along the hot flesh of her pussy. She was so wet, her body ready for his. Marcus pinched her clit between his fingers, drawing a gasp.

He drew his fingers away, and Bree whimpered.

He inched down her body. "I could make you come with my fingers and tongue. Do you still like to be fucked that way? With three fingers deep inside you and my tongue flicking your hard little clit?"

"What about you?" She wound her fingers into his hair and gave a light tug. "Do you still like the way I cup your balls while I take you deep into my throat? We didn't get to finish what we started the other day."

His erection went from uncomfortable to painful. He moved to adjust, but her hands beat him to it. In a flash, she yanked his zipper down.

"I said I want you inside me, Keller."

The words were everything he wanted, but he wanted to hear them again. He wanted her to beg. Marcus pushed back, sitting on his heels.

"Spread your legs," he rasped. "Show me how wet you are."

She held his gaze, her own a challenge, as she widened her thighs. Dusky pink flesh glistened beneath dark curls.

He wanted to worship before her, but before he could bend to her, Bree's foot shot out. It landed on his sternum, holding him in place before he could bury his face in her gorgeous pussy.

"Show me how hard you are," she told him.

Marcus rose enough to remove the rest of his clothes. His erection bobbed against his stomach like he was a damned teenager.

Bree licked her lips at the sight of his cock. Marcus stroked the length, the movement languorous.

One side of Bree's mouth curled up, a tiny smile, and she grazed her fingers over her clit and down to her opening, then pushed two fingers inside.

With a groan, he pushed her hand out of the way, replacing it with his own. Two fingers eased inside. Her warm body stretched around him, and she was so wet she dripped onto his hand. He brushed his thumb over her clit. Bree raised her hips, pushing him to go faster.

Marcus increased the pressure and added a third finger, filling her. She clenched her muscles around his fingers, and his cock jerked in response.

Bree's cheeks grew flushed and her legs twitched. Her fast breaths turned into deep groans. She threw her head back, but Marcus caught it with his other hand and pulled her to him, swallowing her cries in a kiss.

He gave her a few moments to recover, then drew back enough to whisper against her mouth. "How should I make you come this time? Cock or tongue?"

Her lids were heavy with satisfaction, but she didn't hesitate. "Put your damn cock inside me, Marcus."

It only took a second to retrieve his wallet from his pants, but that was too long away from her.

He fumbled with the condom like he had the very first time they were together. Bree took it from him and ripped the foil open. He stilled as she unrolled the condom over his length, her hand caressing every inch of his shaft as she did so.

He moved into the frame of her body and positioned himself at her entrance. For a heartbeat, neither of them moved. Neither of them even breathed. Then Bree wrapped her arms around his shoulders and rose to whisper in his ear, and the single word damn near broke him.

"Please," she said.

With a single thrust, Marcus planted himself fully within her.

Surrounded by Bree's warmth, he struggled to find any control. His hips drew back slowly, his body reluctant to leave hers.

Bree lifted her knees and wrapped her arms tight around his back, her fingernails digging into the skin. "Damn it, Marcus. Fuck me."

Whatever restraint he had snapped. Marcus drove into her hard. Bree rocked with him, meeting every thrust. The sound of bare skin meeting filled the room, the slap of flesh.

She was there with him, completely there, and that thought alone was almost enough to send him over. Marcus gripped her ass and moved faster, no longer sure if he was entering her or she was claiming him.

It was both. It had always been both with her.

She reared back with a cry, and Marcus leaned into her neck. He ran his tongue across the skin, tasting her sweat. "Come for me," he growled. "I want to feel you clench around me."

Her fingernails dug into his shoulders. Bree's nipples tightened until they were small dark buds. Her legs twitched, and she went over the edge with a low moan.

Marcus didn't let up, riding her hard as she came. His

balls and the base of his cock were completely covered in her juices, and that was what pushed him over.

With a shout, he spilled inside her. He came in a rush, shaking with the force of his release.

Marcus rested his cheek next to hers while he waited for his breath to return to normal. The smell of clean sweat mingled with the scent of their arousal.

Bree's arms were wrapped tight across his back. In that moment, it felt like he was precious to her. Like she didn't want to let him go.

At last he pulled back. He kissed her once on the lips, soft and tender, then withdrew. Marcus turned away as he removed the condom, hiding his expression.

Because if he wasn't mistaken, he'd fallen in love with Bree Rogers all over again.

CHAPTER TWENTY-FOUR

Though the room was as warm as a tropical island, Bree felt cold without Marcus's skin on hers.

"You owe me a shirt." She willed him to face her.

It took him too long, and in those seconds before he turned, her heart dropped. Moments before, it felt like everything between them had changed, but now there was distance, a yawning chasm she didn't have the words to cross.

He could barely meet her eyes. "Use mine." He handed her his wrinkled shirt, and she hurried to put it on. She felt too exposed, sitting naked on the floor. Bree hurried to do up the buttons. The shirt smelled of Marcus. Hell, *she* smelled of him. It felt like he surrounded her, even as he put distance between them.

"What are you thinking?" she asked, her voice level.

He tugged on his pants. "Nothing."

"Don't give me that. You're always thinking about something."

He shook his head. "That's not the right word. Chaotic jumble of thoughts, sure. Thinking? Not so much."

Bree didn't push. She reached for her pile of clothes.

Though she tried not to rush, her fingers shook a little as she picked up her underwear.

She had to get out of here. Now. She needed to get home, to her couch and her computer and her books, to a quiet spot on the floor where she could light a candle and focus on her breathing for several minutes.

And if that didn't work, she could lock the door, pour a drink, and tell the rest of the world to fuck off until she felt ready to face them. Because at the moment, she felt exposed. Raw. As if anyone who looked at her could see past her skin and muscles and bone to a soul that was breaking.

This was Marcus. He wasn't supposed to do the asshole-guy thing.

"Bree…" He was hesitant in a way she hadn't heard since he was nineteen. She knew the tone, though usually she was the one using it. It was the prelude to *we need to talk*.

A loud beep came from her backpack, and she jumped in surprise. Glad of the interruption, she withdrew her cell and read the notification.

"What is it?"

Her fingers closed over the device, covering the screen. "Don't ask. It's better for you to have plausible deniability."

"Plausible… Bree, give me the phone." He stalked toward her. It wasn't fair, the way her body lit up at his approach.

It definitely wasn't fair how quickly he spun her around, pressing her back to his chest and twisting her wrist at the same time. She recognized one of the disarming moves Niall taught. Marcus lunged for the fallen phone.

He read the message, and a muscle jumped in his jaw. "Financial results? What is this?"

Bree wrenched the phone back from him. "Not legal, that's what it is. I couldn't do anything with the information we had, so I searched for more data."

"Elaborate."

She grimaced, but she drew her laptop from her bag. Whatever it was, he would want to know. "You won't be able to use this information. Not legally. And maybe it's nothing."

She sat on the floor with the computer. Marcus took a spot at her side, where he could also read the screen. He was still bare-chested. She swallowed and reminded herself that this was what she did. She worked on complicated programs with laser focus. A half-naked Marcus Keller shouldn't change that.

Marcus bent his head to read the screen. His hair dropped into his face, a few thick strands. It took more control than she would have imagined not to tuck them back into place.

It hurt, not touching him, especially when she didn't know why he was pulling away.

"Bank transactions," he said.

"I, um, hacked a few of your employees' accounts."

He pressed his fingers to his forehead. "A few?"

"You know. One, two, a dozen. Something like that."

"That is so illegal."

"I warned you."

Marcus gave a heavy exhale. "Well, if the damage is already done…"

"I couldn't access past information," Bree explained, "but I set up real-time notifications for any big transactions. Anything over a thousand dollars."

"You're following the money."

"Yeah." She clicked on the results, and a name appeared at the top of a bank document.

Marcus was wrong. The damage was just beginning.

Bree's heart ached for him as he read the screen. "There could be a dozen explanations for this," she said.

Marcus's jaw locked. His expression was closer to a statue's than a man's.

She wanted to run her fingers across that face, bring it back to life with her touch. "Numbers don't tell the full story," she reminded him.

"Maybe not, but they don't lie, either." Marcus pointed to a column on the screen. "Two transactions for the same amount. One hundred thousand in, and one hundred thousand back out five minutes later. What the hell's she doing?"

"It could be a lot of things. Account transfers, or preparing for a large purchase. She could be moving her money to another bank." Bree didn't believe any of that, but for Marcus, she would try.

"Like an offshore account?" Marcus expressed her unspoken thought. "Where is Rae getting this money?"

It wasn't difficult to backwards trace the routing numbers. "Oh. Fuck."

"Gotham Investments." He stood and paced, long angry strides that ate up the room. "Why the hell are they paying her? They've committed to investing, and she doesn't even want the IPO."

"Unless…" Bree didn't want to articulate her thought. "Maybe they wanted her to sabotage it so the company was undervalued. The initial price would be a lot cheaper."

Marcus pressed his palms flat to the floor. "They're paying

her to ruin Hours."

"The stock prices will stabilize eventually. She'll still make millions."

"Not anymore she won't," he snarled. "I'm firing her."

She snapped her fingers in front of his face. "Hey. Come back to me. What did I just say? You can't use this information, not publicly."

He inhaled sharply. "I can privately fire her."

"And if she goes to the press?"

He ground his teeth so hard she could hear it. "I have to do something." Marcus's expression was as lost as it was angry.

He damn near broke her heart. He looked like a man betrayed—and he didn't even seem surprised. She moved to his side and rested her hand on his arm. "I'll help. Send her away on some bullshit trip to buy us time. Between the two of us, you know we'll figure something out."

He studied her hand as if it were a dangerous animal, one that could poison him with ease.

Slowly, deliberately, he took a step back, and Bree's hand fell to her side.

She wanted to run to him, cover his mouth with her palm, do whatever it took to stop him from saying the words that spilled out.

"I think we need to put the brakes on this. Just for now."

Bree considered throwing something at him. She finally told him everything, and he decided to call a halt? "Is that really what you want?"

"No." It was a simple statement of fact. "I want this. I think I always have. But trying again requires a big leap of faith—and I don't have a lot of faith to spare right now."

Before he left, he pulled her in for a short, hard hug, as if he couldn't help himself. He kissed her on the forehead once, then walked away.

MARCUS CAUGHT THE BALL, THEN CHUCKED IT AT HIS office wall. He'd been doing that for five minutes. It wasn't relieving any stress.

Bree stomped into his office. "If you don't stop it, you're going to find that ball in an uncomfortable place."

He threw it harder. "What are you working on now?" She'd promised to help him find undeniable proof that Rae was doing something illegal. That was eight hours ago. He'd expected something by now.

"You know. Evil plans. World domination. That sort of thing."

Once more, he slammed the ball and reached up to catch it. Another hand shot in front of him, snatching it out of the air.

"What are you doing, Marcus?"

"Thinking."

"Uh-huh. Your version of thinking looks a lot like a toddler in a sulk."

He scowled. He'd been in a foul mood all day, and he couldn't chalk it all up to Rae's suspicious money transfers.

From the moment he'd walked away from Bree, maybe twenty percent of his brain was worried about his vice president. The other eighty percent was trying to find reasons not to stride into Bree's office, throw her across her desk, and fuck her until he forgot why he'd decided to slow things down.

He loved her. Somehow, he'd once again managed to give Bree Rogers power over his heart. Marcus wasn't fool enough to think he'd get over it, but maybe, with a bit of time, he could at least find some measure of control. Enough that if everything went wrong for the second time, he wouldn't break into pieces.

Marcus tried to remember what they were talking about. Rae. The first woman he'd trusted after Bree. He was beginning to notice a pattern in his life.

"I've been thinking about the night of the fire," he said. "She was in pretty bad shape. Tommy had to save her. Why would she do that to herself?"

"To make herself appear innocent? Or maybe the fire really was an accident, or we have a town arsonist." Bree perched on his desk, so close. She wore a ripped-up pair of jeans that revealed several inches of white thigh. If he hadn't hit pause, he could have his mouth on that warm flesh this very moment. Bree tapped his chin with her knuckles, silently asking him to look up at her. "Or maybe she's innocent. We don't know."

"I want to talk to her."

"Give me another day. Let me find something concrete."

He nodded.

"And open your mouth."

His cock stirred. "What?" he said stupidly.

A small smile played on her lips. "You're locking your jaw. You keep grinding your teeth like that, you'll be in dentures by the time you're forty."

His laugh was quiet, but it was the first time he'd felt

lighter all day. "That sounds sexy."

"Don't worry. I'll remind you to open your mouth on a regular basis." Bree stroked his jaw, and his dick skipped right past semi-hard to painful. He shifted in his chair, adjusting himself.

"What are you doing, Bree?"

Her casual shrug was studied. "Putting the brakes on." She placed one leg on either side of him, then sank into his lap.

He swallowed hard. "You and I have very different definitions of what that means."

She ran her lips across his forehead and down the ridge of his nose. "Do you want me to stop?" She punctuated the question with a small twist of her hips, grinding into his erection.

"Yes."

Bree began to rise. Marcus grabbed her hips to keep her in place.

"No," he said. "God no. But this isn't putting the brakes on. We should stop, at least until things settle down."

"When is that? After you know what Rae's doing? After the IPO? After the campus is up and running?

All those things sounded too far in the future, especially with Bree on his lap, pressed against his erection. Marcus bit back a groan.

She leaned forward and caught his earlobe between her teeth. "People also use brakes to slow down," she whispered in his ear, her breath hot. "For instance, we don't need to have sex."

That sounded like a terrible solution. "It's not about sex."

The words sounded strangled. "It's…" He couldn't finish. It was about his heart, and how terrifying it would be to expose it to her all over again.

He feared she heard every unspoken word, but she only said, "You know, we didn't make out in high school."

Marcus snorted. Considering he spent four years fantasizing about doing just that, he didn't need the reminder. "I recall."

Bree ran her fingers through his hair and tugged his head back. "We didn't date. We didn't mess around. We went straight to married drama. So this *is* us putting the brakes on. You could even say we're in reverse." Bree pressed her forehead to his. The tips of their noses met. "Date me, Marcus."

His heart cracked open. It didn't care that he was trying to protect it. The foolish thing had only ever wanted one thing, and she was sitting on his lap. "Yes," he said.

Bree smiled. He had just enough time to see her expression of pure happiness, and then she kissed him.

Bree kissed *him*. In that moment, she'd chosen him, and he dared hope there would be hundreds of those moments. Thousands. A lifetime. Because the pleasure he'd seen on her face made him think, just maybe, he wasn't in this alone.

Marcus returned the kiss. He cupped her cheeks, loving the feel of her skin beneath the rough pads of his fingers, and he lost himself in the taste and scent and feel of Bree Rogers.

For one perfect minute, the only sound was their breath and the quiet sounds of their lips meeting and parting. The buzz of his intercom jolted them apart.

Levi's voice crackled through the speaker. "You told me to let you know when Helen Barker called. She's on line one."

The words might as well have been ice water. Bree disengaged and stood. "I'll leave you alone." She picked up her laptop and headed for the door.

"Sunday."

She turned around. "Is that when you have plans with Helen?" Her voice was politeness covered in poison, and he laughed. He shouldn't be so entertained by her jealousy, but it felt damn good.

"She's one of the investors. Even if Gotham are evil bastards, I need them on board."

She glared daggers at the phone, but the tension in her shoulders eased.

"Sunday is when we'll have our first date. I'll pick you up at seven." Before she could argue, he grabbed the phone. "This is Keller."

Bree's expression was calculating and a little suspicious. He gave her a cheerful smile, then spun the chair until his back was to her. When she left, she closed the door harder than necessary.

But she didn't tell him no.

CHAPTER TWENTY-FIVE

B ree didn't go on first dates. She didn't go on any dates, really. Most of the time, she met someone for a drink or two, decided if they were going to have sex or not, then moved on to happy naked time. As soon as she scratched the itch, she returned to her quiet home and got back to work.

She was twenty-eight years old and about to have the first date of her life with the first man she ever loved. She had no idea what one wore on a date with a millionaire ex-husband. He'd probably take her to The Vine, the new restaurant in town that was supposed to put Lost Coast Harbor on the culinary map. She hoped he didn't expect her to wear a dress. She'd already met her dress-wearing quota for the year.

Instead, she pulled on a clean pair of dark blue jeans with no holes and a sheer forest green sweater over a black camisole. She wore a simple pair of ankle boots.

That was one nice thing about living in a small town in Northern California. No one cared if you wore jeans to the fanciest restaurant in town.

Two minutes after seven, Marcus knocked on her front door.

He wore jeans, too. Wore them really well, especially paired with a close-fitting black top. His designer suits were nowhere in sight, and she didn't miss them one bit.

If this whole dating thing hadn't been her idea, she would have grabbed that shirt, pulled him inside, and bolted the door behind them. Another week trapped in a cabin with Marcus, completely separated from the outside world, sounded like the best choice she could possibly make.

Instead, she stepped outside and closed the door behind her.

The Aston Martin was the nicest car she'd ever sat in, all plush leather and sophisticated lines. Once she fastened her seatbelt, she found herself oddly without words. It wasn't awkward, the silence between them, but it was strange. She and Marcus never had problems talking before. Their ability to talk for hours had led to their marriage, and their willingness to fight until the truth came out led to them making up years later.

But now they were in an unfamiliar space. Not quite together, but no longer apart.

Bree glanced at the trees rushing past. "Where are we going?" Not only were they headed in the opposite direction of the restaurant, they were driving back to the campus.

"What, you don't want cafeteria food?" He rolled his eyes in mock exasperation. "Now she tells me."

"If your plan for the night is dinner and a movie in your private theater, I'm not impressed, Keller."

The grin he sent her way was half playful and half smug—and completely devastating. "I've got a little more planned. What's the fun in being filthy rich if you can't impress your date?"

The car came to a stop outside Olympus, and she had her door open before Marcus reached the passenger side. Immediately, she put her fingers in her ears to block the noise.

A helicopter waited on the roof, blades spinning.

She winced at the sound, and Marcus's smile slipped. He tugged her inside the building, and she sighed in relief as the noise faded.

"God, I'm an asshole. I didn't think to ask if this would be a problem."

They moved farther into the building, and Bree took a deep, calming breath as the noise faded. "Sounds and crowds. Those are my triggers."

Marcus tucked a strand of hair behind her ear. On her good days, her hair could best be described as a wild mess, so it felt like he only wanted to touch her.

"The other day, you said you couldn't fly because of noisy airports and crowded planes." He indicated the roof. "No airports. No crowds. Just you, me, and the pilot."

Marcus made her wait outside his office while he retrieved something. He emerged with a victorious grin. "Next-gen noise-canceling headphones."

"You have the best toys."

"Damn right." He paused. "Oh, you meant the tech gear?"

"These things will silence you too, right?" She put them on and was immediately enveloped in silence. Marcus's lips moved, and she mimed confusion at him.

Marcus lifted one headphone off her ear. "Are you okay with flying?"

"I love flying." Joy bloomed as she spoke the words. It was

true. Beyond the noise and the people, she used to relish the moment a plane took off and the world below grew smaller. It felt like a gift, the result of humankind's determination to use technology to do the impossible.

That was before flying became more about crowds and long security lines and being stuck in the middle row between strangers. She wouldn't need to worry about any of that this time.

The helicopter could fly in a large circle around Lost Coast Harbor, and this would be an amazing date.

"These will get you to the helicopter. If you want to talk when we're in the air, you'll need to change to another pair. Can you handle a few seconds of noise while you switch?"

"Maybe. If not, just save all your important thoughts for when we land, okay?" She couldn't stop grinning. She was going to fly.

Marcus smiled with her. "Come on."

"Wait." She pulled off the headphones and dropped them around her neck. "Where are we going?"

His expression turned more serious. "I want to surprise you, but you're not a fan of surprises, are you?"

"Not really." She could tell he was trying to hide his disappointment. "You're not taking me to a Giants game or a concert, right?"

He shook his head. "Nothing like that, but we're getting out of Lost Coast Harbor. You said that the anxiety was better if you were with someone else. Can I be that someone?"

Marcus was so sincere and hopeful. She almost felt her heart grow larger. "Yes. But if I say turn around—"

"I won't even ask why. I promise."

In answer, she placed the headphones over her ears. Marcus took her hand and led her to the roof. She picked out the faint drone of the helicopter, but it wasn't loud enough to bother her.

Marcus helped her in, then claimed the back seat. She peered through the window. Excitement unfurled in her chest. Who needed dinner and a movie when she had a helicopter with a view?

She waved off the pilot's offer of another set of headphones. She could handle the few seconds of noise she'd be exposed to, but she was enjoying herself too much for even that brief moment of discomfort. Besides, she planned to stare silently out the window the entire time.

For most of the trip, she did exactly that. As they flew, the sun sank below the ocean. The twilight provided enough illumination to watch the ocean churn, and once whales broke the surface. When that happened, she tugged on Marcus's sleeve, and he leaned forward to share her window, a matching look of wonder on his face.

It was good to know the jaded millionaire could still wear that expression. He wrapped his hand around hers and didn't let go.

Soon, electric lights appeared in the distance—lights that multiplied with alarming speed, until Bree had no choice but to exchange her fancy headphones for ones with a microphone.

"This might be a good time to clue me in to your plans."

Marcus hesitated for a second. She didn't think he was trying to keep the surprise. Rather, she sensed only concern, the worry that he'd been reckless when planning their date.

"The helicopter will land on the roof of Hours's Mountain View building. We'll go straight to the fourth floor, which should be empty. We don't even need to visit the third floor, if you don't want to."

"Is your idea of a date showing a girl your big building?"

"Not even close. This place has nothing on Olympus. Can you do it?"

Bree inhaled, long and slow, as the buildings appeared. From here, they were nothing but light and concrete. "I can do it."

When they landed, the pilot cut the propeller, so she was able to walk across the roof without the noise of the helicopter stealing her capacity for thought. There were other sounds, though. Traffic. It wasn't late enough for the city to shut down, even on a Sunday. There were probably more cars on the street below than in the entire town center of Lost Coast Harbor. Tires squealed and horns blared. Bree spun around, seeking the exit.

Marcus's fingers threaded through hers, and his touch was an anchor. "The door's right there."

He tugged her, and she stumbled after him.

As soon as the heavy door shut behind them, the noises of the street vanished. Bree sighed in relief and sagged against the wall.

"How are you?"

"Okay." When he looked skeptical, she elaborated. "Really. It wasn't fun, but it was over quickly. And you were there." She squeezed his hand.

He grimaced. "I feel like an asshole. I wanted…"

"You wanted to help me live a bigger life. I know."

They were in Hours's building. She spun around, taking it all in. The Silicon Valley headquarters was nothing like the campus in Lost Coast. That place was created to reflect and enhance its surroundings, and every piece of it felt like Marcus. This office was stylish and well-decorated, and she got the feeling he hadn't picked out a single cream couch or gold light fixture.

"I hired a designer," he confirmed. "She made it classy and a little romantic, which fits the company. Back then, I probably would have just hung movie posters on the walls."

Bree brushed her fingers across a capiz-shell lampshade. "It's pretty, but this could be anyone's company. Not yours."

He glanced around the office like he was seeing it for the first time. "Sometimes that's how I feel. This company built me, but it's been a while since it felt like mine."

It was an odd phrase. Most people would say they built the company. "How did you land on a dating app of all things?"

"You'll laugh."

"Probably."

He snorted, then tugged her farther down the hall. "I'll tell you over dinner."

Marcus pushed open the door of a huge office. At her raised eyebrow, he shrugged. "Once, I thought it was important to have this kind of office. It went well with all the magazine profiles and talk shows."

She wandered around the room. The shelves were bare, as was the desk. It felt like the office was waiting for the next person to move in. "You don't plan on coming back here, do you? Not even to commute between the two towns."

"No. Lost Coast Harbor is home."

She wished she could say that with the same certainty. "What's for dinner?"

He grinned like he'd been waiting for that question. "Levi, can you come in here?"

Marcus's assistant seemed to appear out of nowhere. He pushed a large, two-tiered cart covered in dishes into the room.

"You had your assistant fly down ahead of us? On a Sunday night?"

"Of course. I wouldn't trust anyone else to get this right."

"It's okay," Levi assured her. "He paid me a lot of money."

"See?" Marcus gave her a smug smile.

"You really like being rich, don't you?"

"It makes life easier. It's not much help with the things that truly matter, though." His tone was matter of fact, but there was a weight behind the words.

"I don't know. The helicopter is a pretty good start."

"This part's not bad, either." Marcus lifted one of the plate-cover domes with a flourish. "Pho." He pulled off the second dome. "Or perhaps *misir wot*?"

Bree's mouth watered at the sight of the soup and the spiced lentils on *injera*. She hadn't had Vietnamese or Ethiopian food since her freshman year at MIT.

His smile widened, and he pulled off the third and fourth covers. "Kebabs, in case you wanted Persian. Finally, sushi, because it's always a good time for sushi."

"The packaged stuff at Hastings Market never really hits the spot." Her stomach growled. "Were you feeling indecisive?"

"I've been home three weeks, and I'm already craving this

food. I can only imagine how much you missed it."

"You were right. But what are you going to eat?"

He chuckled, the sound low and relaxed. God, this was so easy. So natural. Bree tried not to think of all the time that had passed. What would life have been like if she'd phoned him years ago and told him the truth?

Bree was glad she had no issues about eating delicately on the first date. She filled her plate with huge portions, then grabbed a bowl of pho.

There was a small meeting table in the corner. It held an open bottle of wine and two glasses, but it felt too formal. Instead, Bree took the love seat on the other side of the room. She kicked off her boots, then curled up on the leather. Marcus joined her, moving the wine to the coffee table.

He poured, then raised his glass. His brow furrowed. "I'm trying to think of something profound to say."

Bree gave a surprised laugh. "To new beginnings?"

"Too cheesy."

"To first dates?"

"Too predictable."

"I'm trying, man. Work with me here."

He grinned, but the playful smile soon turned soft. He lifted the glass. "To more."

She could drink to that.

They were halfway through the meal before he returned to her question. "You asked why I created a dating app. Try not to laugh at me, okay?"

Bree gave what she hoped was a sincere nod.

"Right. Well, I was trying to replace you."

She stopped with her glass halfway to her mouth. "What?"

"For a long time, I convinced myself I only loved you because we checked so many of the same boxes. We loved computers and comics. We liked the same TV shows. Politics, religion, everything. On paper, we were totally in sync. After the divorce was finalized, I decided the best way to fall in love again was to find someone with those same interests. I figured if Mark Zuckerberg could create Facebook in his dorm, I could manage a basic dating app. Rae and Tommy helped, and the rest is history."

A shadow crossed his face at the mention of Rae, and she nudged Marcus with her foot until he smiled. "Did it work?" She almost didn't want to hear the answer. "Did you find a replacement?"

"Come on. We both know that's impossible."

"But you were at Berkeley, in a computer science program, and you looked like...well, you. Don't tell me you weren't surrounded by interested girl geeks who checked all the same boxes and weren't all broken and uncommunicative like me."

He shrugged. "There were a few. But they weren't right. All the qualities, none of the spark. Maybe I wanted a repeat of Tahoe, and nothing could ever live up to that."

"I know." He appeared surprised that she admitted it. "Did you really think you were alone in that? I'm impulsive, not stupid. I married you because, that week, I was absolutely certain I'd love you forever."

Silence descended, filled with years of unsaid words.

Bree downed the rest of her wine and rose. She crossed the room to the large window that overlooked several other buildings. "Your view from Olympus is much nicer."

"I don't know. I rather like the view now."

She peered over her shoulder to find him watching her ass intently. She tilted her hips backwards, taunting him.

Marcus prowled toward her. He only stopped when he was close enough to whisper in her ear. "So, do you put out on the first date?"

Her skin flushed, and need pooled between her legs. Just his words, his low voice, that was all it took. "I might be convinced."

"Good." He tapped the window in front of her. "One-way glass. No one else gets to see this." Marcus trailed a finger down her spine and across the seam of her ass. He slid his hand between her legs and cupped her.

Her breathing grew shallow, and she pressed herself into his touch. "See what?"

He grazed his lips over the shell of her ear, the caress a delicate contrast to the hand squeezing her pussy through the denim. "Take off your pants, Bree."

CHAPTER TWENTY-SIX

She couldn't think of a single reason to say no.

Bree slid her right hand up her thighs. She threaded her fingers through his and ground their clasped hands to her core.

Marcus nuzzled her neck, his breath warm against her skin. "I forget. Is this second or third base?"

She tilted her head to give him better access. "I think third base requires nudity."

"Good idea." He pulled his hand free and unzipped her pants. Marcus knelt behind her, grasped the jeans on either side, and yanked them down. He helped her step out of them, removing her socks at the same time.

There was enough light in the room that their reflection overlapped with the view. The mostly empty building across the street fell away, all her attention drawn to the image of Marcus kneeling at her feet. His hands slid up her calves, over the curve of her knees and onto the strong muscles of her thighs.

Marcus ran the long fingers of both hands under the leg band and stroked her from her ass to her hips and across the other side. When he reached her curls, he lightly rubbed the skin of her mound, kneading the soft flesh.

"Touch me." She tried making it an order, but a pleading note crept in. "Rub my clit."

Marcus brushed two fingers across the swollen nub. She exhaled in relief, but that was all he gave her. He pulled back and tugged her panties to the floor.

His hands moved to her pussy, spreading her wide. "Look at yourself," he commanded.

She groaned at the sight of Marcus stroking her. Everywhere he touched, nerves shot to attention. Keeping her open with one hand, he eased a single finger inside, then added a second. It was a hypnotizing sight, his hand moving in and out of her body, and her hips rocked in time to his movements.

"Do you want more?" Her answer was a soft moan, and Marcus slid a third finger inside her.

She whimpered as her body became nothing but sensation. She felt overcome, completely filled, and she couldn't tear her gaze away from his hand moving in and out of her pussy, his fingers covered in her arousal.

Marcus changed position, blocking her view with his head. Her protest twisted into a cry as his tongue circled her clit in a long, relaxed stroke. He licked up and down her flesh, tasting every fold. The entire time, his fingers fucked her with slow, lazy thrusts.

She was filled, complete, and she wanted more. "Please, Marcus."

He stiffened his tongue and ran it over her clit. Her knees weakened, and she braced her palm against the window to support herself.

Marcus made a low sound that was half satisfaction, half hunger as he buried his face between her legs. He flicked her clit with his tongue, picking up speed as her legs grew more unsteady.

Bree pressed his dark head to her body as she ground her hips into him, loving the image reflected back at her, their mutual need on display.

Marcus pushed his fingers deep inside her at the same moment he closed his lips to suck her clit. Her release came instantly, her muscles spasming around him. He held her upright and licked her gently through the final tremors.

He withdrew his hand and rose, standing behind her. He wrapped his arm across her shoulders, then licked clean the fingers that had been inside her. "I could spend hours tasting you." His free hand dropped between her legs and caressed the delicate flesh.

"I'm sure I could make time in my schedule." Her satisfied smile turned to a gasp as he pinched her clit. "God, Marcus."

"What do you want?"

She tilted her hips, fitting the outline of his erection between her cheeks. "You."

With a groan, he unbuckled his pants and pushed them down his hips. A condom appeared in his hand, and a second later he unrolled it down the length. Marcus bent his knees and placed himself at her opening, then thrust upward, impaling himself in a single movement.

They both exhaled as they were joined, a sigh of relief as they came together, and then he began to move. Marcus wrapped an arm across her chest, holding her tight. His hand cupped her breast, the thumb brushing her taut nipple. The other hand braced against the window, holding them steady as he drove into her with a fierce hunger.

Their reflections locked eyes as he bucked into her, moving faster with each stroke. His control cracked as his breathing grew ragged and his skin flushed, and she knew her expression mirrored his.

"Rub your clit," he ordered in her ear, the words rough.

Bree reached between her legs. It only took a couple of quick brushes of her fingers across the swollen nub. Her groan was loud, guttural. Marcus joined her, the sounds of their pleasure filling the room as he came, his hips jerking against hers.

Bree collapsed into the glass, and he fell with her, his body pinning her in place.

She didn't have words yet. Hell, she could barely breathe. But she stretched her arms back until she found both his hands, and she intertwined her fingers with his. Marcus squeezed. It felt like a silent question, and she gripped his hand tighter. *Yes. Yes, we are together.*

It was remarkable. It was a gift. And it was the most beautiful and terrifying feeling she could imagine.

THEY CURLED UP ON THE LOVE SEAT, WITH BREE'S BARE legs across Marcus's lap. Though they were in his empty office in the middle of a Silicon Valley industrial park, it was an unexpectedly domestic moment.

"There's something I've been dying to know."

"Mmmm?"

A surge of satisfaction rushed through him at her satisfied

sound. He caught her right foot in his hand and massaged the heel. Bree's eyes drifted shut in pleasure.

"Opera?"

Her lips curled into a smile. "It's wonderful."

"I don't remember you listening to anything without a backbeat. When did you decide to expand your horizons?"

She stretched her other leg toward him, wordlessly asking him to switch feet. "When I was at my worst, any sound got to me. Sirens were awful, but street traffic was bad too. Horns. Squealing brakes. My apartment was on the second floor, and the windows had poor insulation. I started playing music loud enough to cover the noise."

"An overly dramatic soprano was able to soothe you?"

Bree cracked one eye open. "I'll convert you. Just you wait. I like some of the big voices, but my favorites are the choral ones. Monteverdi especially. It's the exact opposite of what I was fighting. Nothing electronic or modern. The voices are pure. Heavenly. It was a nice contrast to people shouting drunkenly across the street. I'd put on my headphones, lie down, and let the music unwind the knot in my chest. Sometimes it would calm me enough that I could leave the house for an hour or two."

"What changed between then and now? Other than moving back to Lost Coast?" He moved his thumb to the ball of her foot and kneaded.

"I graduated early because of the summer classes, but I made no plans to come home. The idea of such a huge move was overwhelming. But my brother figured out something was wrong, and he came to get me. I had a panic attack when it was time to leave. Adam carried every box to the U-Haul, and when I hesitated, he carried me too. After I arrived home, he helped me find a decent psychiatrist outside of town, and he drove me to the appointments. She was a hell of a lot better than the school counselor I visited once. I swear, that guy just photocopied Prozac prescriptions and handed them out. She put me on beta blockers, which had fewer side effects, and some antianxiety meds I take as needed."

"The ones you threw at me."

"Yep. After that, it was just a matter of time. I did some talk therapy, though I wasn't a fan. Stopped that as soon as I could."

His eyes widened in feigned shock. "No way. You didn't like talking about your emotions?"

She gave him a playful kick. "I'm a lot better, but anxiety's a weird thing. There's treatment, but not a cure."

He stopped rubbing her foot, but he didn't let it go. "Why did Adam need to figure it out? Why couldn't you just tell him, or Maddie?" The unspoken *or me* hung in the air. As much as he wanted to let it go and appreciate what they'd found after all this time, he kept circling back to that one thought. So many years wasted, all because she wouldn't admit to a weakness.

She shot him an annoyed glance. "You never met my dad. He's old school. Adam and I were raised to believe we were responsible for our own lives. We made our own money, did our assigned chores, paid for our own mistakes."

"Having anxiety isn't a mistake."

"It felt like it at the time. It felt like a character defect." The words were strained, like she was forcing herself to say them. "It still does sometimes. I don't know how to be with another person. I haven't tried."

"Since our divorce, you never...?"

"Dated anyone seriously. No."

He squeezed her foot. "Me neither. I told myself it was because I was too busy, but I didn't want to date anyone. Not really."

"Hard to settle for hamburger when you've had prime rib," she said with a sad smile. He didn't know if she was talking about herself or him.

"Is this why you didn't make contact? You didn't think you could date anyone?"

"It was one reason. You deserved better than what I was then. I wasn't in any state to be in a relationship."

Marcus lifted her foot high enough to kiss the tip of her big toe. "I wish you'd let me make that decision."

She curled her toes away from him. "It wasn't your decision to make."

They fell quiet. He thought they both needed to revisit the past for a few moments. It might be a long time before they left it entirely. Perhaps it would always be part of their story, inextricably linked to who they were now.

Bree broke the silence. She studied his fingers, which were still wrapped around the arch of her foot. "What did you do with your ring?"

He held out his left hand, the fingers splayed. "Ah. That."

"You threw it down a drain, didn't you? Chucked it into the ocean?" She kept her voice light, but he thought a hint of pain threaded through the words.

He took a deep breath. It's not like he had much pride left where Bree was concerned. "It's in a box under my bed."

"Oh." She smiled. "Mine's in the drawer of my night-stand."

"Oh."

Bree shifted position and crawled to him. With her knees on either side of his thighs, she leaned in for a long kiss. It was a drug, an addiction he couldn't kick. She opened his pants and wrapped her hands around his hardening cock. Marcus groaned as she stroked him, the gentle touches balanced by the light scratch of her nails. He gasped when she pinched his tip, and pre-come beaded on the head.

"Got another condom?" she whispered.

He dug one out of his pocket and handed it to her. Bree unrolled it down his length. She covered him slowly, letting the anticipation build.

Bree guided him to her wet center and sank down, feeding his cock into her body one inch at a time. This had none of the frenzy of their previous couplings. Even when they were fully joined, their movements were small and unhurried.

He cupped her face, running his thumb across the soft skin of her cheek. Marcus saw the exact moment she lost herself to pleasure. As she came around him, he held her hips steady while he thrust up, finding his own release.

Bree collapsed across his chest, and Marcus wrapped his arms tight around her. They couldn't stay like that long. When he began to soften, he reluctantly left the warmth of her body to dispose of the condom.

Grumbling, she rose with him and pulled on her underwear and jeans. "I suppose we should head home."

"I suppose we should."

"Maybe you could stay with me tonight." For a second,

she glanced away, and his already full heart expanded.

"My apartment's nicer."

"Your apartment is shiny and new. It's not nicer."

"Fair point."

"Also, no light switches in my house trigger *The Brady Bunch* theme song."

"You really are evil."

"Never forget it."

When they were presentable, he opened the door, then paused, laughing. "I completely forgot why I brought you here."

Her brows drew together. "Not pho and window sex?"

"Well, yes, but I have a surprise for you too. Come on."

Before she could ask any questions, Marcus grabbed her hand and pulled her down the hall. He stopped before a set of double doors. "You ready?"

"What are you up to?" She sounded suspicious, but also intrigued.

He flung the doors open. The ceiling lights automatically flickered to life. He faced Bree, beaming.

Chapter Twenty-seven

It was a conference room. That was all. It was a nice conference room, complete with a range of projectors and screens, and the chairs looked quite comfortable, but she found nothing to elicit Marcus's level of enthusiasm.

"You have some sort of conference table fetish?" She tapped her fist on the solid wood. "I mean, it doesn't do much for me, but I'm willing to give it a try."

"Maybe later. The table isn't always here. Sometimes we remove it and lay out the chairs for presentations. We do that a lot, actually, whenever we have a new product we want to show the press or possible investors."

A warning rang in the back of her mind. "Why are you showing me this, Marcus?"

He walked to one of the projectors and turned it on. It was already connected to a laptop. Once Marcus typed in his password, his personal desktop was displayed on the screen. A few more taps and an email appeared, four feet high.

"I haven't sent it yet. I wanted to make sure you could handle the trip first."

She read the first paragraph, her stomach tightening with

every word. By the time she reached the end, it felt like a ball of iron. "What is this, Marcus?" It was a stupid question. She knew what it was.

She just couldn't believe he would do this.

He was still smiling. "It's an invitation. There's a lot of money in this area, and everyone wants to find the next big thing. They already want me to contact them whenever I have a new product. They want first dibs, and they're going to want in on Wanderlust. What you've done on your own is incredible. As soon as you have a bit of support backing you, you'll take over the damn world."

"I didn't ask for this. I like doing it on my own. I told you that." Her voice was flat. Lifeless.

For the first time, Marcus noticed she didn't share his enthusiasm. "I know, but you need help. How long have you been working on one part of Venice? You haven't even touched the airport software that will allow people to get to Italy. With just a few investors, you could hire people. Increase your equipment. Imagine it."

"I *have* imagined it." Her voice rose, and she struggled to control her temper. "I've imagined meetings with investors who interrupt my work, and demands to travel to places I can't handle yet. I'd have to deal with people on days when I only want to hide."

"It doesn't have to be like that."

"No? Have you looked at your life recently? From what I can tell, all you want to do is play with Prism, and instead you're stuck behind your desk. When you're not reviewing yet another budget, you're flying to L.A. to preen on talk shows and kiss investors' asses."

"Is this about Helen? I told you…"

"Screw Helen. I know nothing happened. So far as I can tell, you don't even like your job anymore, but you keep doing it because you've backed yourself into a corner. I won't do that to myself. You back me into a corner, and I lash out. You know this."

Marcus smacked his fist against a switch. The projector turned off, the damning words on the screen vanishing. She couldn't forget them, though. They were seared into her brain, the proof of everything she'd forgotten in the last few days. For a brief moment, she'd thought he learned to ask questions about her concerns and fears. To let her speak for herself, and believe her. She'd been a fool. They'd both changed so much, and they hadn't changed at all.

"So what's the plan?" Marcus flicked on the overhead lights, filling the room with a harsh, artificial glare. "Are you going to spend years programming one city and hope a bank loans you hundreds of thousands of dollars? You'll still need to hire people and go to meetings."

"Condescending much? I know that, but if it's my money, I can do it on my terms. That—" She waved at the now-dark screen. "Those are *your* terms. Your choices, and you expect me to make them, even though I explicitly told you that I don't want investors."

"I thought—"

"You thought you knew what I needed better than I did. Like when you flew out to Boston, because you knew better than I did that we should be married. When you refused to sign the divorce papers, because I couldn't possibly have a good reason to end things. You hear what you want to hear."

Marcus scowled so hard his face twisted into unfamiliar lines. "Maybe, if you told me what was going on, I wouldn't need to read between the lines. Maybe, if you ever asked for help, none of this would have happened. You think I would have ignored your wishes if I knew why?"

"That's my fucking point. You shouldn't have to know why. If I tell you something matters to me, that should be good enough."

He threw his hands up in frustration. "So if I think you're hurting yourself, I don't get to say anything?"

"Of course you can say something, but you also have to listen—and you don't get to make all the decisions on your own."

"And if it hurts me? I'm supposed to just take it, no questions asked?"

"Yes! Because I wouldn't hurt you if I didn't have to." She shouted the words, then winced as the sound echoed through the room.

His laugh was ugly. "But you keep doing it. All you need to do is ask for help, and you're not capable of it, are you? You're so damn determined to do it on your own that you're willing to delay or even lose your dream project. I've been through this, Bree. A project of this size, it isn't something you can do on your own. For once in your goddamn life, let someone help you. You say you want a bigger life? Then go after it, and let me help you."

"You don't want more. You want everything." Her voice cracked. "Marcus, you don't get to decide what everyone else needs."

"That's not fair."

"You sure about that? You moved Tommy back here, even though he hates it. You created a job for your father. He didn't ask you to do that, but you're convinced, as soon as he's back in a lab, his mind will magically be as sharp as it used to be. And now this. If you can't see the pattern, you aren't looking."

"I could say the same for you." His voice rose. "You didn't tell Adam. He had to figure it out and come get you. You haven't told Maddie and Erin, though you admitted anxiety is easier to manage with people at your side. You'd rather struggle on your own than admit to a single weakness. Even your parents don't know."

She dug her nails into her palms until half moons formed. She needed the pain. Otherwise she might cry. "Don't turn this around on me."

"Why not? Someone needs to give you a mirror and make you fucking look at yourself. God, Bree. Every time I turn around, you have a new excuse not to be with me. It's like you don't want to be happy."

She shook her head, suddenly tired of the fight. "You know so much, don't you? So busy deciding what everyone else wants, but you don't ask yourself the same question. You say you want the company to go public, but you don't talk about what that will mean for your future. You claim you're thrilled to be home, but you keep wearing the designer suits that made you Marcus Keller, tabloid star. Worry about yourself for a while, and leave the rest of us alone."

He opened his mouth to respond. He would keep arguing all night, until she agreed with him. That was the problem.

Bree spoke before he could. "Take me home, Marcus.

We're done."

She wore the noise-canceling headphones the entire trip back.

CHAPTER TWENTY-EIGHT

The next day sucked. It sucked a lot.

Bree spent most of it on her sofa, trying to lose herself in another country. She suffered through the nausea of the VR helmet, because virtual reality was a far more pleasant place than the current one.

The video was different today. The water was murkier, the buildings a dull beige. The fairytale city she'd dreamed of for years was nowhere in sight.

She yanked the helmet off and chucked it to the other end of the couch. She took several long gulps of oxygen. Her stomach settled, but she didn't feel better.

It wasn't the file. It was her. Sleep had eluded her the night before. For a brief moment, she'd thought they found their way back to each other, but it had been a mirage. Even as he rubbed her feet and listened to her stories, there were warnings.

I wasn't in any state to be in a relationship, she'd told him.

I wish you'd let me make that decision, he'd replied.

In that moment, she should have known.

The two of them had plenty of problems. Bree was stubborn and yeah, she could probably ask for help more than she did. Marcus got an idea in his head and wouldn't let it go. But they should be able to accept that about each other. Talk things out, and when that didn't work, remember that they had their own way of doing things.

Marcus wasn't capable of that. Nothing had changed. He still thought he should make the important decisions.

Even now, he believed he should have been allowed to judge if she was mentally ready to be in a relationship. The night before, he ignored her plainly stated desire to be the sole owner of Wanderlust, because he decided the project should have investors.

He'd ruined it. Marcus crashed back into her life and made her hope things could be different when it was just more of the same. They were great together...until they weren't.

She'd been fine before he returned. She worked hard, she had great friends, and she had hope for a better future.

Now, when she tried recalling her life before Marcus reentered it, it was as dull and murky as the video, and her future appeared equally grim.

Once, she'd been certain she would love him forever. Years later, she knew she'd been right. Bree would always love Marcus, but she couldn't spend her life with a man who steamrolled over her. It would break her heart, even more than living without him.

Every time I turn around, you have a new excuse not to be with me.

The words slithered into her mind, insidious and disturbing. There was truth to them, she knew. If she looked at their past, she found many times a single phone call would have changed her future.

Except there was a difference between an excuse and a valid reason, and Marcus couldn't see that.

Excuses were born out of shame, or fear, or laziness. They were created from the worst parts of a person.

Like the fear that a friend she'd known since second grade would believe Bree was weak because she occasionally had panic attacks.

"You're an idiot," she informed herself.

Everything else might suck right now, but there was one thing she could fix.

The call went to Maddie's voicemail. Bree grumbled and hung up, then hit redial.

"Hey, Mads. So, you should probably know that I've had occasionally debilitating anxiety since college. Sorry I didn't mention it before. I know you have a hundred questions and will need to yell at me for a good long time, so let's get together next week. How's Tuesday? Let me know."

She hung up and waited for the sense of dread to settle around her shoulders, but it didn't appear. Instead, a weight she'd carried for years lifted.

Bree hit redial for the second time. "Oh, and Maddie? I love you."

Yeah, life sucked, but that made it a little better.

An email notification flashed on her laptop. Her heart jumped at the sender's name, until she realized it was the wrong Keller. Quentin was emailing her, not his son.

The message was short and to the point. He'd attached the code she'd requested. It was eight years old, so she expected it to be outdated, but she was curious what he'd once been capable of doing.

Bree's heart picked up speed as she scanned the text. It was a freaking gorgeous piece of programming, elegant in its simplicity. Genius, really.

And familiar.

"Are you fucking kidding me?" she muttered. She stood, holding the laptop and reading as she walked to the door. She put down the computer just long enough to pull on her boots, then she was running toward her truck.

Tommy had a lot of explaining to do.

MARCUS SLAMMED HIS DOOR. THE PHONE RANG AS SOON as he entered. It had been ringing all day, and each time he let it go to voicemail. He didn't want to answer another damn reporter's question or put out another fire someone else could handle. That was why he paid them.

The IPO was tomorrow. He just had to get through one more day, then Hours was in the clear. Following Bree's suggestion, he'd arranged for Rae to attend a tech conference in Mexico City. As soon as she left, he'd revoked her access to the user data network. She could receive email, but at the moment she had as much control over the systems as a marketing intern.

The public offering was going to happen. It was a snowball, picking up speed. A runaway train. Some other cliché about an event out of his control.

That was stupid. Of course he was in control. It was his company. Nothing would change—and that was the problem.

There would be budget meetings. Business plans.

Schmoozing. More schmoozing. So much fucking schmoozing, when all he wanted was to spend more time working on
Prism.

It had happened so slowly he'd barely noticed it, but at
some point he stopped caring about Hours. It probably
began years ago, once he realized no amount of programming could replace Bree. It was a great app, and it had lots of
potential, but Marcus no longer gave a fuck about setting up
dates for other people.

He didn't want dates. He wanted a wife, and she didn't
want him.

The phone rang. Tommy should be dealing with this
last-minute stuff. His phone should be ringing nonstop, not
Marcus's.

He flung his door open, then froze when he found Bree
in the hallway, peering through the window of his vice president's office.

"What are you doing here?" he grated out.

She blinked at him, and he could only guess what sort of
image he presented. Unshaven, with dark circles under his
eyes. He'd grabbed the first clothes he found that morning,
and he couldn't remember what he wore without looking
down.

Bree set her shoulders and lifted her chin. "Is Tommy
around?"

For the first time that day, he noticed that Tommy's
office was dark and his computer was off. All morning, he'd
assumed Tommy was back at work. Marcus tried to recall
when he'd last talked to his friend. For that matter, when was
the last time he'd really thought about what was happening

in the company? Days. Maybe a week. Hell, one of his VPs was taking bribes from an investment firm, and all he'd been able to think about that morning was Bree's face when she told him they were done.

"Bree…" he began.

"No." The words were firm. Her shields were back in place. "I said everything I had to say last night."

"I didn't."

She threw up her hands in exasperation. "Exactly. You want to keep talking, even though I told you I was done. Your needs. Your desires. Until you figure that out, keep your damn mouth shut, Marcus."

He longed to close the distance between them and wrap her in his arms, kiss her until they were both breathless and begging for each other.

Bree crossed her arms and stood straighter, as rigid as a brick wall—and as impenetrable.

Somehow, he'd ruined everything, and he didn't know how to fix it.

His attention was drawn to the sound of approaching footsteps. Rae appeared at the top of the stairs, looking completely relaxed. She waved to them, then stepped into her office at the other end of the hall.

"What is she doing here?" Marcus lurched forward, and Bree fingers wrapped around his wrist. He stilled at her touch.

"Wait. I'm working on something. The network is safe, and she wasn't carrying any gas cans." Her smile was weak, but she was trying. "Please."

Even now, he couldn't deny her anything she wanted. Instead of running down the hall, Marcus strode back into his office and slammed the door.

Another twenty emails had arrived while he stood in the hall. He sent twelve of them straight to the trash folder and hit the snooze button on seven others. Maybe he'd want to deal with them next week.

He cursed when he read the sender's name on the final email. Like today wasn't bad enough.

Grimacing, he opened the message from Oliver Hastings. Might as well get it over with. Whatever the investigator's report said, it didn't really matter. It was too late to change the past.

IF TOMMY WASN'T IN HIS OFFICE, HE WAS PROBABLY IN town. Bree hit the usual places first, but he wasn't at Donnelly's or the local diner. It was a sunny enough day to draw people to the park in the middle of the town square, but he wasn't one of them. Bree peeked through the windows of the local shops, though she couldn't imagine Tommy would spend money in town when all of San Francisco was a helicopter ride away.

Maybe that's where he was, doing some last-minute IPO…things. She had no idea what that would entail. The only thing she understood about the IPO was it would make Marcus miserable.

Based on his appearance that morning, he was already there. Her heart broke all over again as she remembered how he looked, bleary-eyed and unkempt, with an untucked shirt over black pants. No suit or tie in sight.

Marcus's words echoed in the back of her mind. *It's like you don't want to be happy.*

Her chest tightened, and she began clenching her hands over and over. Not now. Not fucking now, in the middle of town.

She needed to sit. Someplace quiet.

Bree darted across the street and through the front door of the ancient Capital Hotel. The place had been shabby a decade ago, and no one had improved it since. It went up for sale not long ago, but no one in town had much hope the place would be renovated. They weren't even sure they wanted it cleaned up. It was a rundown mess, but it was their rundown mess.

It also had a bar, one that wasn't crowded on weekdays. Bree snuck in and found a corner table. A couple of figures sat at the bar, but the place was quiet. That was all she needed, just a few minutes to find her center.

What the hell had triggered it? Town was a safe zone. It had been for years. Yes, she was a little high-strung because of the search for Tommy, but she hadn't been thinking about that.

She'd been thinking about happiness—and whether she was walking away from the best thing that ever happened to her.

No. She was identifying a problem and excising it from her life. That was exactly what she was supposed to do. It was the healthy choice.

Except the healthy choice shouldn't lead to her hiding in the corner of the Capital's bar, struggling to breathe.

She inhaled, long and slow. She unclenched her hands and placed them on her thighs.

What if she'd given up too soon? Marcus could be an overbearing asshole, but she was no one's doormat. If he pushed too hard, she would push back.

It would stress her out. It wouldn't be easy. She'd always wish he tried harder to see things from her perspective. But in between those hard times, there would be moments of happiness. She could be with the man she loved.

And they would still have problems. Marcus wanted to fix things. Bree hated asking for help. She didn't want to talk about her problems, and he didn't know how to listen. Where was the line between sacrifice and incompatibility?

She inhaled, and this time it was easier. A few more minutes, and the attack passed. The adrenaline spike wore her out, but that was normal.

Bree rose, then immediately sat back down. Across the room, Tommy was pulling on Stewart's arm, trying to convince the man to leave.

Damn it. She'd found Tommy, but she couldn't confront him while he was dealing with his drunk father.

Stewart's voice rose, the words slurred. "You don't get to tell me what to do."

Tommy replied, his voice low and pleading, though Bree couldn't make out the words.

She wanted to know what Tommy was saying. Partly because she was pissed at him for stealing Quentin's code and partly because she was nosy.

She peered over the bar. Both men had their backs turned, so she crept to a closer table. At the same moment she took a seat, Tommy got his arm around his father and swung him toward the door, putting her right in their line of vision.

"Hi," Bree said, swinging her boots onto an empty chair

like she'd just been waiting for him to notice her. "I want to talk to you."

Stewart glared at her and wrenched himself free.

Tommy glanced between them, undecided. "Can this wait, Bree?"

Stewart stumbled to the bar and indicated that he wanted another shot.

"I guess it *could*, though I was hoping to get an answer today." It was true. Despite the problems with Stewart, she wouldn't delay this conversation. Marcus deserved to know. "I'll just ask Marcus. I'm sure he already knows how you came up with the idea for Hours's original security protocols."

Bree had heard the cliché dozens of times, but she'd never actually seen someone turn white. The blood rushed from Tommy's cheeks, and his lips grew slack. "We'll talk now," he mumbled. "Just let me get my dad home."

Tommy called to the bartender, asking him to phone Lost Coast Harbor's only cab company, then Tommy hauled his father toward the door. The men argued in low voices. Stewart was belligerent, and Tommy was determined—and exhausted. She wondered how many times he'd done this.

It almost made her feel sorry for the thieving bastard.

Once Stewart was placed in the taxi, Tommy returned. He took the seat across from her.

"Talk," she ordered.

Too much time passed while he considered his words. "I'm a terrible programmer," he said at last. "I had no idea. By high school standards, I was a genius, so I figured it was the right major for me. When I got a scholarship to Berkeley, my dad insisted I go into computer programming or business. He wanted me to be financially secure in a way he never could be. Finance sounded boring, so I chose computers. Ironic, huh?"

"I don't need the color commentary."

He gave a nervous head bob. "I squeaked through the first three years, but it was ugly. Senior year, I had to complete an independent project to prove I'd earned my diploma. I had nothing." Tommy glanced at the empty glass on a nearby table and licked his lips like he wouldn't mind a drink.

"So you stole Quentin's."

He didn't deny it.

"How did you even get it? Why doesn't Marcus know?"

"Marcus was a sophomore when I was a senior, but we were on the same floor. We were working in his room one afternoon. When I left, I grabbed my USB disk off his desk. This was before large email attachments and cloud storage, remember. Turned out I grabbed the wrong disk. Marcus never even saw it."

Lines formed between her brows as she sorted through the story. "But Quentin had already been in the accident. He hadn't programmed in a year."

Tommy looked physically ill. "I didn't ask questions. I didn't want to think too hard about what I was doing. The code was so solid. I used it as the base for a new security framework, and that's why I graduated."

"And then you gave it back to Marcus? Are you an asshole, or did you want to get caught?"

His mouth contorted into an ugly smile. "Both, maybe. I told myself Quentin wouldn't see the program. Marcus said he couldn't get his dad to even talk about computers. I thought it was the right thing to do. It should have been his to begin with."

"Why didn't you tell him where you got it? He wouldn't have turned you in."

Tommy rubbed his palms on his jeans. "Because I was twenty-two, proud, and stupid. The program got me a lot of praise. Marcus thought it meant I was smart enough to handle the finances of Hours. After a while, the lie didn't seem to matter."

Bree shook her head, disgusted. "Until Quentin came to work for the company, and you were afraid he might finally see the code."

Tommy nodded, miserable. "I had to convince Marcus the security was flawed enough that he'd build a new system. I crashed the network."

Tommy was weak, and he was a liar. He'd betrayed Marcus in an unforgivable way. He was also so pathetic that Bree struggled to hold on to her anger.

"What about the fire?"

The head shake was vehement, unhesitating. "I didn't do that. I wouldn't risk hurting someone."

"Not physically, at least." Bree sighed. "Do you want to tell him, or should I?"

He said nothing, but his eyes pleaded with her to understand.

"If you'd told him you were having trouble with your project, Marcus would have been there." Bree rose. "You should have just asked for help."

CHAPTER TWENTY-NINE

Marcus finished reading the report for the second time. He gripped the edge of his desk until his knuckles turned white. Of course it said Hastings Fishing wasn't at fault. He'd been a fool to believe Oliver might be different than his father. That family would always protect its own.

The phone rang. Marcus grabbed it and launched it across the room. It hit the wall and splintered. Jagged pieces of plastic fell to the floor.

Rae didn't bother to knock. She opened the door and glared at him, and he glared right back. "What is wrong with you?" she asked. "The company is messed up. I can't get into the network, and you're ignoring every email. Now you're breaking shit? Pull it together."

Marcus rose until he towered over her, then braced his palms on the desk. "You. Are. Fired." He over-enunciated each word.

Her jaw dropped. "Have you lost your mind?"

"I'll buy you out. You'll get nothing from the IPO."

"Like hell you will. You have no grounds to cut me out of the company."

"No grounds? Working for Gotham isn't enough?" Bree said to wait for proof, but he'd waited long enough. He was done being silent in the face of disloyalty.

Rae gaped at him. "What are you talking about?"

He wasn't the one who needed to explain himself. "Why did you really argue against the IPO?"

"The reasons I gave you weren't enough? Fine. Try this on. It's a stupid-ass plan, Marcus. What kind of fool moves an app-based tech company to the middle of nowhere, then asks the public to take a chance on him?" Though she had to tilt her head to look up at him, she glowered with such ferocity she might have been seven feet tall. "The whole thing is ridiculous, but I'm sticking around because I love Hours."

He gave a disgusted snort. "You love it so much you're willing to destroy it?"

She opened and closed her mouth twice, completely lost for words. "What?" she managed at last. Her shock was almost palpable.

"Stop pretending. I saw the transactions from Gotham. One hundred thousand dollars."

"You hacked my bank account?" Rae stalked around the desk. "What gave you the right…?"

"A network breach that could have taken down my company and a damned fire. That's what gave me the right. You were good too. Pointing out the security leak so no one would think you caused it. Getting caught in the fire. It never occurred to me you were the one sabotaging us."

She spoke with such precision the words felt like blades. "Gotham Investments has handled my money for years, long before you began the IPO process. As soon as you decided to go public, I've been selling off stock and other investments because I wanted to put as much money as I could into Hours. I plan to buy all the shares I can get my hands on. The more I own, the more power I have, and the more likely you'll finally let me try development. I could have used the money for my own startup, but I want to stay here. That's how much I believe in this company, Marcus."

Marcus swallowed. Everything she'd just said made far more sense than sabotage—which meant he'd acted like a world-class idiot.

An uncomfortable feeling bloomed in his chest. It felt a lot like shame. Marcus exhaled. "I'm sorry. I didn't know."

"Well, you should have."

She was right. Over the years, Rae had told him in a hundred different ways how much Hours meant to her. She was the company's guinea pig, going on the very first date, and she hadn't stopped being fearless. Every new idea, every expansion, every quarterly profit, she'd been a part of it. Rae didn't want a bigger role for the money or prestige, but for the improvements she could make.

He hadn't listened.

Marcus collapsed in his chair and indicated the one on the other side of the desk. "Please. Sit." When she didn't move, he tried again. "I am truly sorry. I'm an asshole."

"You are," she agreed, but she took the seat. "Really, Marcus? After so many years, all it took was a few bank transactions you had no business seeing?"

He winced. He would need to buy her a lot of Jimmy Choos to begin making this right.

"I haven't been thinking clearly lately," he confessed.

"That's obvious. I don't know where your heart is, but it sure isn't here."

She was wrong. His heart was here. Completely, irrevocably here. His heart belonged to Lost Coast Harbor, a pioneering piece of tech, and a snarky blonde capable of changing his life forever.

"Give me a sec," he asked Rae.

She leaned back in her chair and waited while Marcus sorted through the jumble of thoughts racing through his head. He let everything that wasn't a piece of his heart fall away.

As soon as he did that, the answer was painfully obvious.

"I'm canceling the IPO," he announced. "I'll make the phone call right now. Once that's done, we're splitting the company. You're right. An isolated app company won't work out here. Hours needs the kind of community found in other tech centers—but a holographic imaging company will do just fine on its own."

"What are you saying?" The words were cautious, like she was afraid to believe him.

"I'm saying pack your bags. You're going back to Mountain View tonight. Take Tommy with you, but let him know you're in charge. Hours will keep its old building, but it has a new president."

Her expression was suspicious. "Don't you dare mess with me. If you do this, that's it. I'm not giving it back."

"I don't want it back. I never will. You can use the money you've been hoarding to buy me out, at least enough to give you fifty-one percent. If it's not enough, we'll figure something out." Each word he spoke felt more right, like he was simply putting things back the way they were meant to be. Marcus's smile faltered. "I mean, is this what you want? I shouldn't make the decision for you."

"Is this what I want?" Rae's laugh filled the room. "I don't think I've ever gone from wanting to kick a man's ass to wanting to kiss him quite so fast."

His own laugh was rueful. "You're not the first woman to feel that way. This is how it should have been all along, Rae. Hours is yours. It has been for years. We're just making it official. I get to keep the campus, and I'll choose a new name. How does that sound?"

She rose and held out her hand. "It sounds like you finally came to your senses. But you better let Hours have first dibs when Prism is ready for dates. It was my idea, you know."

He shook his head. "I can't do that. Someone else is first in line, if she wants it."

Rae shrugged. "I had to try. Second dibs, then?"

"Deal." As his hand clasped hers, his entire body lightened. Marcus felt like he could stand straighter, breathe easier, take longer steps.

He moved to the window. This was his now. His campus. His home.

In the distance a red pickup truck puttered up the driveway.

Everything he loved was here.

FOR THE FIRST TIME IN HER ADULT LIFE, BREE CURSED AT her truck. She might love the beat-up red monster, but its insistence on going at a speed a sloth might consider dull was slowly driving her mad—emphasis on slow.

All she wanted was to get to Marcus. She needed to tell him that, while he was totally wrong, she might be a little wrong too.

She was Bree Rogers. She was awesome. That didn't mean there wasn't room for improvement.

Ten minutes longer than it should have taken, she finally pulled into the Hours covered parking lot. The Aston Martin was in its usual place. She grabbed the first spot. Three hundred feet to the door. Two flights of stairs. One hallway. That was all that stood between them. Yes, she had to tell him about Tommy, but maybe that could wait until she told him she loved him.

Bree peered into her bag as she hurried around the rear of the truck, checking for her electronic keycard.

Already counting the steps to Marcus, Bree did something she rarely did.

She forgot to check her surroundings.

Later, her mind would play and replay everything that followed. It would study each second and move them around like a puzzle until she constructed a series of linear events.

But in the moment, it happened in pieces. Her peripheral vision sent panicked messages too fast for her brain to process them. All she understood was a sense of not-right. Something unknown. Dangerous.

Adrenaline sliced through her, her body preparing while her mind struggled to catch up.

Awareness came slowly, fragments of knowledge. The tailgate was down, though she hadn't unlatched it. There was a shadow in the empty bed, a presence. It was moving. Fast.

Bree lurched forward, away from the threat, but she was

too late. Too slow.

A hard forearm wrapped around her neck, cutting off her air. She was yanked back against a body a few inches taller than her. Though he wasn't large, his arm muscles were wiry, his chest solid.

Panic bloomed as the arm tightened.

Alcohol fumes assailed her nostrils, the foul breath of the man who had appeared out of nowhere.

Not nowhere. He'd hitched a ride in her truck.

"Why didn't you leave it alone?" The man's voice was little more than a rasp, but she recognized it. An hour ago, the same voice had argued with his son.

Tommy put his father in a taxi, but Stewart hadn't stayed there.

He'd come back for her.

Fear crawled through her, locking her muscles even as her nerves went into overdrive. He'd pursued her. Hunted her.

"It was going to be okay." Stewart tightened his grip. "It was over."

Terror threatened to consume her. Helplessness mixed with horror, an emotional stew she remembered far too well.

Bree clawed at the forearm trapping her. It was immobile, locked tight around her windpipe. Black spots danced in her vision. She dug her nails into the rough skin until she drew blood, and the grip loosened enough for her to draw in a ragged breath.

"I don't want to do this." The words sounded heavy. "Just a little money. That's all I ever needed. A son who could pay for his old man so I didn't have to work that crappy job till I'm seventy."

Bree grew lightheaded. A distant part of her brain knew Stewart's words were important, but she was incapable of thinking about anything but her next breath.

A proper chokehold would have hit her carotid artery, not her trachea. That meant it would take her longer to pass out. It also meant she was more likely to suffer permanent damage or die. It was the risk of a sloppy technique.

She gritted her teeth. Of course he was sloppy. Stewart was unexpectedly strong, but he was also drunk, and he didn't pay regular visits to Niall Donnelly's studio. She did.

She might be terrified, but she wasn't helpless. Not this time.

Baring her teeth, Bree flung her hips to the left, exposing his groin. She slammed her right arm up hard, using the rigid edge of her ulna as a weapon. Stewart staggered back, releasing her.

Bree dashed out of the parking lot into the bright sun. She heard no sound of pursuit. Eyes wide, she checked over her shoulder, half-certain he'd be right behind her.

Stewart hadn't moved. He swayed in place, confused and broken.

She longed to keep running, as fast and as far as she could, but the terrified part of her brain was ceding a small measure of control to the rational side, and that side insisted on hearing whatever Stewart planned to say.

"I don't want to kill you." He took a step forward. Bree braced to run, but the man's aggression had vanished as quickly as it appeared. "I just need you to be quiet. I need it to stop."

He moved closer, and she took another step back, maintaining the distance between them. Her heart beat too fast and her muscles remained tense and ready. If he lunged, she could flee.

Stewart kept talking. "I didn't want to hurt Quentin, either. But he showed me that drive. He said he'd be able to work with his son. The two of them might make millions. He couldn't stop smiling, because it meant he'd get off the docks. No more fish."

Dread unfurled in her stomach as she began to comprehend.

He took another step closer. "He thought I wouldn't know what to do with it. He never thought I'd…" His voice faded. Even drunk, he couldn't speak the words aloud.

Bree kept her face blank, hiding her horror. "Tommy didn't find the flash drive. You stole it from Quentin, and you gave it to your son."

Stewart shook his head, though he wasn't saying no. "It was going to waste. Quentin was done with programming, and he never talked about the drive. I thought he forgot about it. The doctors said the accident could cause short-term memory loss. I figured that was what happened."

Her mind raced, doing the math. Tommy didn't use the code until his senior year, more than twelve months after the accident. Months spent waiting to learn if Quentin even remembered the code he'd been so excited about, let alone gave it to Marcus.

When he thought it was safe, Stewart gave it to Tommy instead.

It was shameful, but she knew it wasn't his worst sin. Stewart had choked her, almost killed her. A violent man lived inside this pathetic shell.

She clenched her hands into fists to control the shaking.

"It wasn't an accident, was it?" She couldn't hide her revulsion. "You tried to murder him. You thought you and Tommy could make those millions instead of Quentin and Marcus. You were willing to kill your friend for a fucking program."

"Not a program. Freedom. A new start." His eyes were sad as he held up the stump of his right hand. "I changed my mind. I tried to save him, but it was too late." Stewart studied a spot over her shoulder. "I never meant for..." He blinked, tears forming in his bloodshot eyes. In that moment, he seemed like nothing but an sad, drunk old man.

An arm wrapped around her waist, pulling her to Marcus's side. She didn't know how long he'd been there. He held her to him as if she could become part of his body if he just held tight enough.

Tension poured through her, and she couldn't relax against him.

"You're not sorry." Marcus's voice held no pity. "You tried to kill him again to protect yourself. You stalked him at the party, then set the building on fire. Everyone would think it was an attack on Hours, not my dad. Did Tommy tell you to do that?"

Stewart's tears dried in the face of Marcus's anger. "Tommy's innocent."

Marcus sneered. "That's debatable. He removed the security footage before I could discover who was responsible."

Stewart didn't argue. He didn't say anything. He stood there and waited to learn his fate.

Then he wasn't standing anymore. Stewart's eyes rolled up into his head, and he crumpled to the ground.

Quentin stood over Stewart's prone body. He leaned on one crutch, and the other pointed outward, ready to smack Stewart's skull a second time.

He glared at his one-time friend. His expression held both anger and sadness, and more than a hint of betrayal. "I could never believe it was him," he said. "Who could do that to another person?"

Marcus's arm tightened around Bree's waist. "Not everyone's as strong as we are."

He pulled out his phone. With steady fingers, he dialed 911. Bree had no idea how his hands weren't shaking. A man had attacked her and tried to kill his father, and he was perfectly calm.

She began to shiver, unable to match his calm exterior, and he drew her closer.

"By the way, Dad, it sounds like Hours was partly built on your code. You have millions coming to you. You earned it, so you don't get to argue."

Quentin opened his mouth, but someone picked up on the other end. Marcus began giving orders.

Her entire body felt cold, and her muscles forgot how to function. With no warning, her legs gave out. Her knees scraped the ground, and then the pain stopped.

She blinked. She should have gravel under her cheek, not linen. She ought to be lying on the hard pavement instead of hard thighs.

Marcus had caught her. She wasn't alone.

Fuck. She was going to cry. "Cops?"

The words were a little hoarse, but it was her voice. No permanent damage to the windpipe.

He brushed a strand of hair off her forehead. "They'll be here soon, and they'll have a few questions. Can you handle it?"

She gave a weak nod. "I can write down my answers if I need to."

"Not your voice. Can *you* handle it? If you need some time, I'll tell them that."

"I can handle it," she confirmed. She was only seventy percent certain that was true, but she would try. For Marcus.

Screw that. She would try for herself.

He looked uncertain, but he didn't second-guess her. Marcus nodded and helped her to a seated position.

The cops had more than a few questions. She, Marcus, and Quentin were driven to the station and quizzed for hours—not just about the attack, but about the fire and the industrial accident from years before. Oliver Hastings was summoned, as well, and he brought the report that proved the accident was caused by a man, not a machine. At one point in the evening, Marcus held out his hand to Oliver. The other man took it.

Marcus had nothing to say to Tommy when he was marched through the station on his way to a cell. In the morning, he'd be charged with accessory to attempted murder.

By midnight, Bree was exhausted, but she'd made it. One question at a time, she relived her attack, and one answer at a time, she felt a little stronger.

Marcus was still explaining the long history of Hours and

how a few lines of code had destroyed lives.

Valerie Childs, one of the local detectives, drove her home. Bree crawled into bed, but sleep eluded her. She waited for PTSD to kick in, the same terrifying out-of-control feeling that ruled her life for so long. She was prepared this time. If it came, she had people willing to help.

It didn't come. She was sad that Marcus and his father had suffered so much betrayal, and she was angry that two weak men had hurt them all. She was shaken, and she left the lights on all night, but that seemed like a reasonable reaction.

And if she found herself struggling tomorrow, it would be okay. If she didn't want to leave the house, people would understand.

If she fell, she thought maybe Marcus would catch her again, and she would let him.

CHAPTER THIRTY

The campus was deserted.

Marcus's cars were in the lot, both the SUV and the Aston Martin, but he wasn't in Olympus. No one was. She checked each room and didn't find another soul. The offices were empty. The cafeteria was closed. Even the reception desk had been abandoned.

It made no sense for a company that was supposed to be having its IPO today. Marcus had texted her, asking her to meet him on campus, but he hadn't been specific about where. She could reply and demand more information, but she knew it wasn't an oversight on his part. He wanted her to search for him, and she was too curious to resist the game.

Bree checked Oz. She'd spent little time in that building, as it was intended to hold the company's marketing, sales, and accounting departments. It should be hopping today. Instead, it was a ghost town.

The first floor of Narnia contained the human resources and IT offices. Nothing. As much as Bree appreciated silence, it was unnerving. She was beginning to fear the apocalypse came while she slept, and it began with the employees of

Hours.

She climbed to the second floor. She hadn't been in Marcus's apartment yet, though she knew its schematics by heart. Bree withdrew her phone and pulled up his home's electronic grid. It would be easy enough to let herself inside, but that probably crossed a few boundaries. Still, she made a small tweak. The next time Marcus crossed the threshold of his apartment, he'd be greeted with a Rick Astley song. Sometimes you couldn't beat the classics.

Cleveland was a ruin, so there was only one other place Marcus might be.

The holographic imaging lab on the ground floor was locked. The last time she saw Quentin, he'd been leaving the station, leaning on his wife's arm as she led him to the car. The entire time he'd answered the cops' questions, his expression hadn't deviated from uncomprehending shock. Bree suspected it would take time before he was ready to return to work.

One last spot, then. Her smile grew and her heart beat faster as she approached the door to Prism. Marcus was on the other side. She didn't know how much she would need to give up if they chose to be together, but she owed it to herself to find out.

She swung the door open and forgot how to speak.

Marcus sat in a boat in the middle of the room. Except it wasn't just a boat—it was a gondola. And it wasn't a room.

It was the Grand Canal in Venice.

From his seated position, he performed a respectable bow. "*Benvenuti in Italia.*" Welcome to Italy. He wore a faded pair of jeans and a dark blue T-shirt. With a broad smile on his face, he looked more like the eighteen-year-old she'd fallen in love with than he ever had before.

A hotter, more complex version of that man.

"What have you done?" she managed.

A smug grin appeared on his face. "I stole your files. You can give me shit about it when you return my apartment to my control."

"That'll never happen," she murmured absently. Bree took a hesitant step into the room and spun in a slow circle. It was her footage blown up. Once, she'd needed to pan up to see the sky. Now, she only needed to tilt her head. It arced above her, blue and cloudless. Three hundred sixty degrees of Venice.

Marcus stretched his legs. "I'm sure you want to explore, but we're kind of on a clock." He tapped his watch. "I only plan hour-long dates, if you recall."

Buildings lined the wall, and images of water were projected on the floor. While she could walk across the water to reach him, Bree chose to use the dock. Marcus rose as she approached. He held out his arms and wobbled, like he was fighting to keep his balance. She laughed and took his hand, stepping into the boat.

She took her seat next to him, both of them facing forward. "You just happened to have a gondola lying around?"

"I ordered it yesterday morning. It's amazing what you can achieve with the right amount of money. In case you hadn't heard, I'm very rich." He gave her a sly grin.

"I'm pretty sure I noticed that by now. Speaking of..." She waved at their surroundings. "This isn't the New York Stock Exchange."

Marcus shuddered. "Yep. I canceled the IPO yesterday and decided to sell Hours to Rae. Someone made me remember what I truly love doing, and it's not being Marcus Keller, TM."

"That sounds like a very wise person. You should remember that person is often right."

Marcus punched a button on his watch, and the surrounding images began moving, creating the effect that they were gliding through the canals of Venice. Though Bree had reviewed the footage so many times she'd memorized it, it took her breath away to view it life-sized before her. The details were mesmerizing: the red flowers strung from second-story windows, the tiny alleys that appeared out of nowhere, where people could hop out of their boats and wander the city. The soft rush of water reached her ears along with the cries of gulls and, perhaps best of all, very few voices.

"I used your first version, without many people," he said. "I thought it was the best choice."

"It was the only one you could access, wasn't it?"

"There was that, yes."

Bree couldn't stop staring at her surroundings. "It's amazing."

"Of course it is. You made this."

Another couple in a gondola passed them, heading in the other direction. Their hands were locked together, like they never wanted to let go of the other. The woman waved, and Bree waved back before she could stop herself.

"Not this," she murmured. "I made a world that existed in a helmet."

"All I did was change the scale. A few adjustments, all of

which you'll improve once you have a look at it."

Just like that, her joy dimmed. "You're doing it. Making plans for me. Deciding what I should do."

"That's not what I—"

"This is *my* project, Marcus. My baby. You don't get to take years of work and rewrite it without asking me." Her anger flared, hotter than usual, and she inched away, putting more space between them. She didn't want to argue, not in the middle of the most beautiful city in the world. She was in Venice with the man she loved, and they still found a way to fight.

Marcus leaned forward. "Bree...this *is* me asking. I'm sorry if I'm doing it wrong, but I've always been wrong, at least in this way. I get an idea in my head and I can't let it go. It's why Hours is the success it is, and it's why I stuck with it years after I should have moved on to a different project. It's why I knew we needed to be married after one night together, and why I didn't sign the divorce papers. It's my best and my worst quality, just like your pigheaded determination is yours."

"Please. Keep sweet-talking me like that." The words were caustic, but the edges of her temper dulled.

"I did this because I wanted to show you everything your work could be. *Your* work. Take my help if you want it. Reject it. It's your choice. Bree, I want you to have the biggest life you possibly can. Every option should be available to you. Take the path that works for you. All I ask is that you let me walk at your side."

"And when there are boulders on the path that you know how to clear?"

His grimace was comical. "I'll wait for you to ask me for my opinion."

She laughed. She couldn't help it. "No, you won't. You'll offer advice. You know you will."

He reached for her hand and wrapped it loosely in his own. "But if you tell me to be quiet, I will be. Then I'll hold out my hand to help you over those boulders."

His hand was awfully solid, but she wasn't ready to thread her fingers through his yet. "Marcus, if you're just saying what you think I want to hear..."

He shook his head. "That same wise person pointed out this was a pattern in my life, and she was right. I love you too much for this to be the thing that keeps us apart. Though you may need to tell me to shut up on occasion."

"I've never had a problem doing that," she agreed. Her smile was small, but it felt like her heart expanded with every passing second.

"Just remember that it will be easier for me to listen if you talk to me." He stroked her hair, pushing one strand behind her ear. The single touch warmed her entire body.

Bree withdrew her hand from his and rose. She stepped out of the boat, directly into the water.

Marcus leaned back in the gondola. "You know, when we get to Venice, you won't be able to walk away from me like that." The words were playful, but he wasn't teasing. When, not if.

"Well, I do have a very rich boyfriend. Those private jets mean I can avoid airports." She couldn't resist a coy glance over her shoulder. All playfulness had left his expression. His gaze was hungry as she moved around the room. Her skin prickled in awareness.

She made herself focus on the world surrounding them. She studied each image—what it contained, how it interacted with the other projections, what additional senses could be added to make it a more complete experience. Some of it could be translated to a headset version, and some would work better in a larger space. Bree placed her fingers tentatively against the wall.

"You're not the only one who feels at home in Lost Coast Harbor. I may have returned out of necessity, but now I have a lot of reasons to stay." She glanced back at him. "The man I love lives here, after all."

Marcus's hands gripped the edges of the gondola, and she knew he was fighting the urge to go to her. She hurried to finish.

"But this town can't be my prison. I need the option to leave, which is why I built Wanderlust. And yes, the private jets will help, but most people don't have rich boyfriends. They have a right to a bigger life too. I've been so fixed on my own needs, I've forgotten that."

Marcus didn't say anything. He was listening.

"They'll need additional support. We can't ask them to travel to Lost Coast Harbor when they may not want to leave their own town. We'll need to build more of these. A lot more. At least one per state. Mobile versions too, to reach those who are housebound. We'll need to build traditional headsets, of course. More software, for basic activities. Shopping. Flying. Going to the DMV, though that might be the worst program in the history of the world."

He remained quiet.

The words sat on her tongue. They felt as foreign as another language. "I can't do it on my own. We need to create hundreds of different programs. That will require employees. Lots of them." She swallowed the nerves that threatened. "Maybe investors."

Bree walked toward him, took a deep breath, and spoke the words she should have said long ago. "Will you help me?"

Marcus held out his hand. "Get in the boat." As soon as she was settled, he reset the program. "I put in a rush order. It only arrived an hour ago, and it's pretty basic." A static image appeared, more a photograph than a piece of virtual reality. Even so, it was stunning. Orange and purple streaked across the sky—a sky that was partly obscured by the bridge above their heads.

"The Bridge of Sighs," she said in wonder. "I've read about this one. There's a legend that…" Her heart needed a moment before she could finish the sentence. "If lovers kiss beneath this bridge at sunset, they'll be granted eternal love."

His mouth curled. "That sounds pretty nice. What do you say, Rogers? Want to kiss me?"

Her answer was easy, like she'd waited years to speak the words. "For the rest of my life, Keller."

Before she could lean forward, his hands were already in her hair, dragging her in for the longest, sweetest kiss of her life. Their lips spoke of promises not broken, but delayed, and a new beginning for an old love.

And when they finally broke apart, they remembered that virtual Venice had one significant advantage over real Venice.

In virtual Venice, if two people chose to remove each other's clothes with shaking hands, and kiss and taste every inch of skin revealed, no one saw. If Marcus moved Bree onto his lap and thrust deep into her wet heat, digging his fingers into her hips while their bodies met again and again, there were no witnesses to their joining.

They only visited Venice for an hour, but that hour was enough to change their lives forever.

THEY BEGAN MAKING PLANS FOR THEIR OWN HOUSE IN THE trees right away, though it would be months before construction was completed—construction that would happen so far away Bree wouldn't hear a single hammer pound a single nail.

In the meantime, Marcus suggested they move into his more luxurious apartment. Bree disabled half the light switches in his house, then played "The Twelve Days of Christmas" on a loop until he saw the error of his ways.

She really was his evil ex-wife, though the ex part would soon be remedied. At the moment, they didn't have time to manage a weekend in Tahoe, let alone a proper ceremony.

Plus, there was the matter of logistics.

"You know," Bree informed him, "if you insist on having the church wedding my parents want, I'll wear combat boots under my dress."

He expected no less. "So long as you say the words, I don't care if you wear purple platforms with bells on the laces."

A week later, a large package from an internet shoe vendor arrived on their doorstep.

Most nights, she was too busy developing Wanderlust to think about wedding plans. Her first executive decision had been to hire a woman Rae recommended, who would handle all the meetings and travel.

After walking away from Hours, Marcus took a week to clean up the mess he'd made with the IPO, then spent another week binging on Netflix. By that point, he was going stir-crazy, so he started building a new company.

It was a good thing he still had loyal investors, because the business plan was a mess. Some of the company was dedicated to expanding Prism's capabilities. Another branch focused on wearable tech for people with anxiety disorders, wristwatches that could monitor vitals and provide a small dose of antianxiety meds as needed. A third department was in talks with Hastings Enterprises about creating better systems to prevent user errors.

All the new company needed was a name. "What do you think of Keller Research?" he asked. After several weeks of working side-by-side, It was becoming second nature to ask her opinions.

Bree blinked at him, all innocence. "I thought you were taking my name when we get married."

In the end, they agreed to keep their own last names, and Marcus officially registered the new Lost Coast Harbor research and development center as the Avenging Bat Corporation.

Bree responded with an eye roll and a six-hour Marvel/DC movie marathon. Well, four hours, followed by two naked hours when they couldn't be bothered to hit the pause button.

Her cabin wasn't as luxurious as his apartment, but it was warm and cozy, especially after she agreed to let a cleaner visit once a week. Being there with her was almost perfect.

No, that wasn't true.

Each night, when they finished their work, the two of them curled up on the couch. Marcus would place his left hand atop hers, because he loved seeing their old wedding rings back where they belonged, regardless of their current legal status. His gaze would fall on a souvenir snow globe bought nine years ago in Lake Tahoe, now sitting proudly on the mantel. In those moments, it was more than perfect.

It was everything.

Acknowledgments

I've been eager to write Bree's story since she first appeared in *Kiss of a Stranger*, but of course, being Bree, she didn't make it easy on me. Many, many thanks to those who helped this book find its way into the world.

I'm trying to think of a more subtle way to describe Sasha Knight than "rock star editor," but that pretty much sums it up. Her notes and insight were invaluable.

Thanks as well to Kerri Nelson to giving the book its final polish.

The women of Chatzy were always there when I needed a boost or a kick in the butt, and their enthusiasm for the dirty bits made those scenes extra fun to write.

As always, much love to my co-conspirator Eve Kincaid, who listened with a straight face when I said, "I don't know, something about an IPO and corporate espionage. That's sexy, right?" Your patience knows no bounds.

About the Author

Lily Danes is a native Californian who loves cold weather, snow, and rain. A recovering city girl, she now lives in the Sierra Nevadas, where she gardens, knits, herds cats, and plans DIY projects she's too lazy to complete. She has few practical skills and would be absolutely useless in the zombie apocalypse.

Learn more and sign up for the newsletter at lilydanes.com.